Over The Fence

The diary of two women, how they view and judge
life, and how one discovers a secret so well hidden,
it could tear both their worlds apart.

Karen Haase &
Julie Martin-Jones

Fisher King Publishing

Over The Fence

Published by

Fisher King Publishing
fisherkingpublishing.co.uk

This book is dedicated to husbands,
Garrey and Stuart.
Where would wives be without them!

Thank you to our children, families and
friends for being there and urging us on.

To Rick and Rich for putting their
faith and trust in us.

And a special thank you to Jackie
Kirkman for her support and for
encouraging us to write together.

There are two sides to a fence

The rough and the smooth

Painted and varnished

One situation, two views

Two sets of lives

Two different outlooks

Julie Martin Jones

Karen Haase

Tuesday 1/1/2002 - Happy birthday to me

Happy New Year!

I can't believe where the last twelve months have gone, my birthday seems to come around quicker and quicker. I'll be thirty before I know it.

I still count my blessings that I am married to a handsome, dashing doctor and have two beautiful boys. I love my perfect life.

I have a gut feeling that things are going to be different this year. Not that the last few years have been bad, quite the opposite. I can't quite put my finger on it. But I'm very excited to see what the future holds. You never know what's around the corner in life.

We had a fantastic New Year's Eve party, as always I might add.

The music rocking until 4.30am!

Played quite a few unusual party games with a piece of string and a spoon. Could not stop laughing, my sides are still aching today.

We are so lucky to have fabulous friends and amazing neighbours.

I have discovered a new drink - Cosmopolitan.

Beth had brought a huge jug of this delicious cocktail, absolutely loved it! Although I think I loved it a bit too much as feeling a bit delicate today.

The house was an absolute bomb site! But it didn't take us too long to clean up. There are advantages to living with someone who has OCD.

I cannot believe how much alcohol was consumed.

Bobby was on a mission, then I just started giggling as I had a silly image pop into my head of wanting to line up all the bottles and beer cans to see how far they would go down the street. Obviously not a sensible thing to do but could be an indication of how good a party is.

Bobby just gave me one of his looks. Sometimes I think we are on different wave lengths.

Good job Robbie Jnr and Frank were with Bobby's parents last night, Helen and Peter are good to us.

Mum and dad rang to wish me happy birthday and happy New Year.

They are having an amazing time on their travels. So jealous. They are on a spiritual journey around India, not sure where they are planning to go next, but I do know Australia is going to be part of their journey. One day when the boys are older Bobby and I said Australia is on our to do list. (Although I think we may miss out the spiritual bit, it's not Bobby's cup of tea). I do miss mum and dad.

Helen and Peter, bless them, had gotten me a green caterpillar birthday cake, when we arrived to pick up the boys this afternoon, although I did notice a few fingerprints on the top of the icing. Little monkeys they were giggling away. Helen even put candles on the cake, which gave the boys great delight to blow them out six or seven times. I was surprised they managed to relight the candles with all the spit.

Note to self, never eat the icing on the top of a birthday cake.

Thank you for a lovely birthday and the amazing tickets to see Les Misérables from my Bobby, and of course thank you for my wonderful family.

Tuesday 1st January 2002

So here we are, another year. How they drift past.

This year Michael and I will be celebrating our 27th wedding anniversary.

The years have flown since our marriage was planned and executed in its minimal, least disruptive haste. At the time it seemed like such a whirlwind, and I was terribly unsure I could meet his expectations; I was so young and had such unrealistic dreams but here we still are. He soon managed to set me on the right path.

I've learnt to be the perfect wife and hostess.

I move in exclusive circles and always remember that first and foremost I have an important position as Michael's wife and an appearance to maintain. I should be so grateful to have been given such a role in my life. I should not complain in the least.

Michael was quite unimpressed when I mentioned our anniversary. Just grunted and continued reading The Times. I suppose it is different for him. I was never his first choice. Yet here I am, I hardly remember when I wasn't the woman I am today.

As a younger person I never dreamed my life would be like this. It is so important to keep those kinds of memories at bay. Best foot forward, as Seb says.

Lots of couples don't celebrate these occasions. Michael and I certainly never did so, won't be starting any time soon, I wouldn't imagine!

But sometimes I do struggle not to look back which is most ungrateful! Enough reminiscing...

I was looking at next door today, the for-sale sign is up. That's a positive start to the year.

Old lady, Mrs Argar-Jones, has died, probably just as well as the place really was beyond her and lowering the tone of the neighbourhood, we didn't like to complain as she had lived there so long before we moved in. It appeared that like us, she had no children, so there was no one for Michael and I to approach.

I do hope the house won't be priced too low; we don't want just anybody as our neighbours.

The drive up to the house looks quite dark and overgrown, very foreboding, I just hope the new owners will soon put the garden to rights, it's quite depressing to look out onto it from our house and heavens knows what our visitors must think. There was a time her plants were quite lovely, rare exotic types, that made you wonder if she hadn't been inspired by more formal gardens such as Kew.

Let's hope the buyers look at our house and realise there is a standard to be met on this street and strive to maintain it. After all, we are all quite established here, and I like to think my friends are a little envious of how select this area is.

Michael and Seb were chatting about their beloved golf. It sounds as though there is a strong possibility, they may make captain. That will be jolly exciting. A nice chance to show my organisational skills and be the great woman behind the powerful men! It's such a shame, in ways, that Seb never married. It would have been wonderful to have a friend, a real friend not just an acquaintance. But then I suppose I wouldn't get the chance to be the hostess for both Michael and Seb.

His friendship with Michael has been established for so many years that it is quite an accepted fact among both our circles that I am as indispensable to Seb as I am to Michael.

Friday 1/02/2002 - Bobby's Birthday

Made breakfast for Bobby to have in bed as a birthday treat. Well tea and toast. All a bit rushed as he had a busy early morning clinic. He said he wanted to open his cards and presents with the boys this evening.

Got the boys to school and nursery. Finally had time to meet my best friend for coffee. I always feel so grown up ordering a latte. It was so nice getting a little bit of quality time. Although I did feel very under dressed and plain compared to Beth. She wore a fabulous blue and red stripy pleated dress that made her look even taller and slimmer. Wherever she goes she turns heads but seems to be oblivious. She always looks so in control and glamorous.

I'd slapped some lipstick on and managed to squeeze into my jeans. Then I noticed I had Ready Brek dribbled down my black jumper from dashing to get the boys out of the house.

Bless Beth, when she saw me looking at it, she discreetly passed me a tissue so I could wipe myself. She's like my big sister who's always there to help and never judges me. The sign of a true friend.

Picked the boys up, had a lovely walk home, a beautiful sunny day for this time of year so we stopped off and I treated the boys to some sweets and to get a Spiderman birthday cake for Bobby.

It was a bit of a mistake allowing the boys to have as many sweets as they had, they were so hyper!

Bobby was going to take us all out for dinner but when

he saw the state of the house and the boys running riot, he decided to get a takeaway and a bottle of wine instead.

Finally managed to get the boys to settle down and sing happy birthday so Bobby could open his gifts.

My mum and dad had sent him a book on The Bodies Politics. Disease, Death and Doctors in Britain 1650-1900 by Roy Porter. Not my type of read, but he was really excited about it.

A new Marks and Spencer's jumper from Helen and Peter and I got him tickets for the local comedy club. I think he was pleased.

Bobby then put the boys to bed, which was a real treat for them and read a bedtime story. He's usually at some meeting or tennis match.

We then sat and had a few drinks. I do love him so much. He's my world and to add to it he told me he got his dream job of partnership in one of the top GP practices in the U.K.!

I'm so proud of him. Bobby then produced a bottle of champagne to celebrate!

What an amazing day and a perfect way to celebrate Bobby's birthday.

Thank you for a lovely catch up with Beth and thank you for Bobby's fabulous opportunity.

Note to self, avoid feeding the boys too many sweets on the way home.

Friday 1st February 2002

How wonderful! I am going to be hosting the annual garden party this year.

I will have to work on something quite stunning to make a statement that reflects our good taste.

Roll on September, so exciting.

It will be so marvellous to be able to show off my garden and home.

I strolled down to the end of the garden to look at doing some work down there and noticed the tree between us and next door is very sparse at the moment, so I squeezed through to next doors garden. Just checking there are no problems of course, as any good neighbour would do. My it's a mess but I remembered that there used to be some very unusual plants growing up towards the house. I felt very wicked, but it was terribly exciting snooping around a little!

I think I have found a few I could dig up and put in my garden that will be stunning for the garden party.

I'm sure it will be ok, as the house is still empty and no sign of a potential buyer so I may as well salvage what I can before it comes to the point where it is too overgrown, and the plants are lost.

I couldn't resist having a little look through the windows. My it looks outdated and an absolute disaster; it will take some money to bring it up to standard... But that's a good thing it means only the right type of person can afford to buy it.

I didn't tell Michael I had found a way to get into the garden, he might not approve. It will be my secret until I have rescued the plants I want.

Saturday 2/2/2002

Oh my word! My head after that Champagne. Good job I'm married to a GP who had some anti-sickie tablets and a cup of tea waiting for me on my bedside table. I'm sure the NHS won't mind it was for medicinal purposes.

Had to have a little longer to sleep and finally got up about ten o'clock. It's such a treat having a lie in.

Bobby had tidied downstairs and was out in our garden kicking a football with the boys. He's so good with them and I love it when he wears his jeans. Honestly, his arse just looks amazing! Brains and a nice arse, I'm so lucky, definitely living the dream!

Bobby had managed to wear the boys out so we put Thomas the Tank Engine film on, so we could sit down and talk. I did need another cup of tea; I can't believe how rubbish I am at drinking these days.

Note to self don't have more than one bottle.

So, it looks like we are having to move. Bobby's new partnership is in the north, he said it's mainly private patients, but he can still do NHS work. He's finally got his dream job. I'm so proud of him and super excited to start a new life, although I will miss our little terrace and fabulous neighbours. We have a couple of months before Bobby needs to be in Yorkshire.

I rang Beth to tell her the news, as I was so excited, she has offered to help us find a new home as she quite often works in Yorkshire and knows the area well where Bobby's new practice is.

Thank you for giving us the chance to start a new challenge and Bobby this wonderful career opportunity.

Saturday 2nd February 2002

I hardly slept last night, planning what could be salvaged from next door's garden. I mean really, I may as well help myself or the plants will just go to waste or be trampled by builders.

It is not like they will be missed. After all there is no one to miss them.

It's so exciting and very daring, although in a way I am merely being a good neighbour keeping an eye on the old place.

No harm in that!

I waited for Michael to leave for golf then had a long look to see how I can make the opening more accessible. I have trimmed the lower branches on my side so it's not too bad, but not too obvious.

I spent most of the morning digging up bits and pieces while keeping an ear out for cars as one really wouldn't want to get caught if anyone came to view because of course one would not like to have new neighbours first meet you in gardening clothes!

It did occur to me that I could create a whole feature area in my garden, purely from the bits I plan to salvage from there.

I have stored the plants in the greenhouse for now.

It is a shame I can't go and rummage in the front garden but that is too exposed to prying eyes on the street. It would look odd if anyone spotted me.

Michael and Seb arrived back while I was there and were calling for me, I had to pretend I was in the shed and didn't hear them. I feel terribly wicked. It's so daring, sneaking in and out of next door's garden. Much more fun than going to the local garden centre.

I feel quite elated by my secret trips.

Sunday 3/2/2002

Woke up to a cup of tea, I think I need to start drinking Yorkshire tea if I want to fit in 'up north' as they say. Bobby had taken the boys out to the park, so I sat down with his laptop. I'd forgotten how to google; it's been so long since I looked at a computer screen. I do think that having children takes away your common sense. I am sure I read somewhere that each time the placenta comes out you lose 25% of braincells. Well, that means I only have 50%.brain left!

Finally managed to google Yorkshire and it looks beautiful but miles away. I messaged Beth and she said stop panicking they do actually have electricity in Yorkshire, and it is a really lovely area where Bobby's new practice is.

Bobby came back with the boys, had some lunch and then we all went to visit his parents. I love having Sunday tea with them, Helen always makes me Marmite sandwiches. Can't believe Bobby banned Marmite from our home just because he hates it and has never forgiven me for adding it into some of my cooking. I will miss Helen and Peter dearly as we are always popping into see them. Helen said that Bobby's godparents live in the area close to the new practice and assured me they would be on hand for us as they would love to see our boys. I'd forgotten Hannah and John lived in Yorkshire; it's been a good few years since we saw them.

I will just have to get a house big enough for everyone to stay with us, especially when my parents come back to the U.K. I do miss mum, she would have me organised, packed and ready to go.

Thank you for today. I've had a lovely family day.

Sunday 3rd February 2002

Today I popped next door and while wandering in the garden I accidentally took a fall into what must once have been the pond. I felt such a fool and swore quite loudly, something I never do, as Michael would not tolerate such uncouth behaviour.

The act of swearing made me laugh out loud. It felt so good.

I had to go home to change as it is so cold my clothes were beginning to freeze.

I had only just got in and my shoes off when Michael and Seb arrived back from golf. Michael wondered out loud how on earth I had got in such a state.

I was actually stuck for how to reply when he just shrugged and walked off. Seb at least asked me if I was injured as clearly, I had taken a tumble. Before I could respond Michael said he was ready to leave and off they went to meet some friends.

What a relief!!!

I love these secret excursions.

I have found so many rare and unusual plants, my garden will be amazing.

I didn't manage to get back there today as I had forgotten I was due at the golf club to discuss the captain's dinner arrangements. Very mundane but quite thrilling to be potentially organising such a prestigious event, Mrs Fitzgerald was most helpful and gave me some good pointers that I will discuss with Seb when he formally invites me to begin making the arrangements.

Friday 29/3/2002

Oh, my word. Beth is the best! She has organised a day of viewing properties for next week.

Helen and Peter said they would pick up the boys from nursery and school and keep them over night. Beth has booked us into a delightful hotel. We are going to do the viewings then have a spa! Her treat.

Looking forward to having an amazing pamper, then more viewings the next day. Perfect!

Bobby has had a couple of trips to his new practice. He said everyone is really nice and as long as I find a home I like; he will be happy. He doesn't care where we live as long as we are together. I'm so lucky!

So far, I've managed to pack 3 boxes, all wrapped up with newspaper. Bobby came home from work and asked if I had been working down a mine. I wasn't sure at first what he meant, then I looked in the mirror. The problem is when using newspaper, the print gets everywhere. Then I realised I'd been to the local shops with print all over my face, not a good look!

Note to self don't use newspaper for wrapping. Although who would have thought my teenage years of working in a fish and chip shop would pay off for quick wrapping!

I am panicking with the amount I have to tidy, as we have a couple of viewings for our house tomorrow morning. The estate agent said that houses are selling super quick at the moment. I had better not get the wine out tonight, as we don't want to have the house smelling of drink. I must remember to put the fresh coffee on to give a homely smell.

Thank you for a productive day.

Friday 29th March 2002

I took Seb and Michael to the station today; they are going on a business trip to London, so I have the whole weekend and most of next week to spend amusing myself.

I was rummaging through next doors' potting shed, really the things people collect. It is full of all sorts of odds and ends that have just been abandoned. Some of which one wonders why you would have even owned! I did find a very nice planter, which I have rescued and inside were some keys.

Tomorrow I will have to try them and see if they open the house. I would have done it today, but I had to get ready to go to the tea club. Didn't want to miss it as Mrs Smythe was hosting it and it was, as expected a very nice do. She is such an important figure in our community, everyone who is anyone is in her circle.

It was lovely to be dressed up and chatting to very well-connected ladies knowing that secretly I have been doing things they would never dream of!

I don't even feel guilty I'm not really stealing the plants just re-homing them. Better than leaving them to perish.

Monday 1/4/2002

I actually managed to get to nursery and school on time this morning.

Even though I didn't get much sleep last night, excited about going to see where our new life will take us, despite been shattered. I was up four times with Frank and to top it off, all Bobby did was snore! Potty training isn't as easy as the health visitor said. Honestly if anyone who does not have children, ever mentioned to me about being tired I will just jump down their throat and tell them you have no idea what tired is!!

Beth has got the details from the estate agents. I think she's excited too.

We got to Yorkshire around mid-day. I'm so glad Beth offered to drive. As I slept most of the journey. Despite trying to keep my eyes open.

We arrived at the first property and met a very smiley estate agent; it was a new build on this very new estate. We looked around the show home first, beautiful, all very tasteful, cream and white everywhere, bi-folding doors from the dining room to the garden. She then took us to the plot of land where the house would be built, provided we pay a huge deposit to guarantee the plot. Unfortunately, they had only dug the foundations and the house would not be ready for quite a few months. Obviously, April fool's day has extended times zones here. So that was a definite no. Shame as it would be quite nice just to move straight in and not have to do any decorating.

The next house was old with lots of character, absolutely beautiful but it was on the side of a dual carriageway.

There was no way we could live there; I'd be having nightmares about the kids escaping and running into the middle of the road or the number of footballs being kicked over the fence and causing an accident. The house itself was actually fabulous, but not for us.

We then drove to a big family house in the middle of nowhere. It ticked all the boxes in size and garden, but the nearest shop was a 40-minute drive. The views were amazing. Just a bit too isolated.

We got back to the hotel. I called Bobby and then had a

lovely chat with Robbie and Frank. Bobby said he's excited and trusts me and Beth to find us a fabulous home.

I'm really feeling the pressure now as today didn't go too well.

Beth then produced a bottle of wine. That went down far too easily so we have decided to go to the bar, cancel our spa treatments and have something to eat.

Monday 1st April 2002

Oh, my what fun today.

I cancelled my nail appointment and slipped next door. I was desperate to check to see if these keys fit any of the locks.

One of them fit the beautiful old summer house so naturally I had to go in. I completely lost track of time going through the boxes of books, photos and junk. I found an art set; it was so beautiful in its wooden box and reminded me of days I try to forget, for some reason I was unable to leave it to the rubbish that the new owners would obviously feel was stored here. I have brought it home and hidden it in the back of my wardrobe. It seems a better fate for it than a skip.

The place has obviously at some time been used as an art studio, the smell of the oils and texture of the brushes reignited an old flame, long subdued, as Michael was extremely disapproving of my love of art and candidly told me I had no talent and needed to concentrate on the demands of being a wife so I had to give it up and any foolish ideas I had about becoming an artist.

So many years have passed that I am surprised at the sudden sense of loss that overcame me.

Quite ridiculous.

There were some pictures, but they were very amateurish except for one of the gardens in its original glory. I have rescued that too so that I can plan where to plant the rescued plants.

I spent so long in the summer house I did not have time to try the other keys.

It would make a lovely studio except for the leaking roof and the fact that I no longer paint. Of course, the roof could be mended, after all the new owners will need to see to it, they will probably be thrilled if I mend it for them.

Tomorrow after the library I will try the other keys, then go back and finish looking at the other boxes.

Tuesday 2/4/2002

Woke up this morning in a right state. We had ordered another bottle last night and ended up having shots bought for us by some guy at the bar! Took me back to our student days. Great night! (I think).

I could not face breakfast, at least three cups of tea before I could get into the car. I really had to make the effort for our next viewing.

Why is it I look like I have been dragged through a hedge backwards and Beth still looks amazing! I'm blaming the boys; they have given me a natural beer belly and constant bags under my eyes, actually suitcases, but I wouldn't be without them.

I have to be honest I was feeling a little bit disillusioned about Yorkshire. It all felt very overwhelming.

Then Bobby texted me to say he's accepted an offer on

our house, even more pressure to find a new home for us.

Beth, bless her kept my spirits up. Always chirpy and positive. She knows me so well. She didn't have to say anything. She pulled over and put the roof of her car down. The fresh air definitely helped me feel a little better. We were like girls on tour! Music blasting the wind in our hair. It was like the old days. Sometimes you just forget who you are when you are busy looking after everyone. It's good to have time out. Although not sure the image was right as I still felt a bit sick, had to sit with a carrier bag on my lap.

The next house, I was a little unsure about after reading the details. It did say it needed modernisation. Whatever that means, and there were only two images, unlike the other properties. I think estate agents wear rose tinted glasses.

We drove towards a little town and pulled on to Willow Road. None of the houses had numbers they all had names. Beautiful Victorian detached family houses. You could imagine in their day having horses, carriages and servants. A historians dream I should imagine. We then took a couple more turns onto Willow Lane.

We were looking for number 57. The houses were still amazing but not quite as grand as Willow Road. Good job, could you imagine how long it would take to tidy up. I'd never get the boys out to anything; I'd be too busy cleaning (well trying).

The road was wide and very quiet. I noticed the other houses had names, so we slowly drove and then spotted the number on a black wooden gatepost. Surrounded by huge pine trees. We couldn't see the house; it was so far back down a long dark drive. But there was a lovely feel about it. A feeling of it needed looking after, revitalising. The house next door was immaculate. Beautiful, manicured gardens. I bet whoever lived there was desperate for number 57 to be sold and have some TLC and a few thousand pounds spent on it.

We spotted an old man sitting in a little white Fiesta on the drive. The car had big stickers on advertising the company he worked for or could he even be the owner. Whoever he was, he was certainly looking ready to retire.

Beth got out first, then I opened the door. My sick bag blew down the street and as I turned, I got my leg caught in my jumper that was by my feet and somehow opening the door I managed to fall out of the car. Knees and hands on the floor. Beth burst out laughing. I looked up to see the old man having a bit of a panic attack. Honestly, I felt so embarrassed. Big hole in my jeans and I scraped my hands and knees like a three-year-old who had just fallen off their bike. Glad I was still a bit drunk otherwise I think it would have really hurt.

Why can't I ever be as graceful as Beth? I do try.

Anyway, it was quite funny as the estate agent totally ignored me and just spoke to Beth all the way round giving her advice and ideas on the potential of all rooms.

I trotted off by myself. Left them to it. The house was fabulous. An old Victorian family home, with a basement and an attic room. You could feel it was longing for new life to be put back into it. There is a lot of work to be done. But I'm sure it will definitely be worth it.

I walked out to a sunny very overgrown large garden. It has so much potential! I could see the boys loving this. A perfect football pitch.

You read the blurb on all these houses and actually the reality is nothing like what is in the print. I walked back into the house and said to the estate agent. "It's perfect, we will have it". He turned to Beth just checking it was alright with her. I think he may have thought we were a couple.

Beth just pointed at me and told him to deal with me.

Poor bloke wasn't sure at all what was going on.

Some people may buy an expensive pair of shoes or a designer handbag under the influence of drink. OMG not me I've just bought a massive family house, that needs so much work doing to it! How do I explain this one to Bobby?

Decided no point seeing any more houses and besides that I really needed a cup of tea and more sleep. Beth drove us back home. I couldn't keep my eyes open again, but Beth said it was ok to have a sleep she was quite happy driving as she is used to it with her job. I didn't argue with her.

A great night away but I was ready to see my boys.

Note to self never EVER drinking again!

Thank you Beth for helping me find our perfect family home.

Tuesday 2nd April 2002

Oh, my what a drama

I had made it as far as the second bedroom, exploring the grand old house next door, which has more original character than ours. It smells terribly and will need fumigating.

I was in the front bedroom when the little white car turned up outside turning onto the drive.

The estate agent.

What a dreadfully exciting dash to get back down the stairs and out of the back door. Luckily, I had the keys in my hand because I did not have time to lock the door behind me.

I made it back to my garden before anyone could see me

and had a good look at the potential viewer with the estate agent.

From what I could see, without being too indiscreet, the woman was very tall and refined looking. I'm sure she was wearing a designer jacket and the car she was driving appeared to be an expensive looking convertible, perhaps a little too flashy for this street, but at least it shows she clearly has money.

I'm sure the other rather scruffy, dishevelled woman with her must be her cleaner. How very organised to have brought her along to see the extent of the work to be done.

Unfortunately, Mrs Warbottom called to see me from the gardening club I didn't even notice her coming down my driveway, annoyingly interrupting my perusal and making me feel somewhat like a peeping Tom.

In a very suspicious tone of voice, she asked me if I was alright, saying I looked very flushed.

I caught sight of myself in the mirror as I led her into the house, and almost giggled childishly I did indeed look flushed and my eyes over bright. Oh, she has no idea of the goings on!

This whole thing is so exciting.

Mrs Warbottom has suggested a suitable date for the garden party, my birthday. Absolutely wonderful.

Friday 12/4/2002

We had a trip to Yorkshire with Helen, Peter and the boys.

All very excited, I couldn't wait to show them where our new home will be.

I think Bobby had a bit of a fit when he saw the state of

the house from the outside. Helen and Peter just kept saying it's got potential. I must admit I am a little concerned we may have bitten off far more than we can chew. I keep telling myself it will be wonderful. The boys will have so much space to run around.

Bobby had a meeting with his new partners in the afternoon.

Helen, Peter, the boys and I met Hannah and John. They showed us round the beautiful Victorian town centre. It felt so clean, and a slower pace of life and I have to say it is very green in Yorkshire. They then took us to a wonderful park for Robbie and Frank to have a kick around with their football and play on the swings.

Then Bobby and I went for dinner to meet all the partners and their other halves.

With the help of my Bridget Jones pants I managed to squeeze into my red Ralf Lauren dress.

Helen put my hair up for me. It's been so long since I last got really dressed up.

Bobby's parents stayed in the hotel with the boys, while Bobby drove us to a fabulous restaurant. I cannot remember the name, must look it up for the next time we come. It was beautiful, so tastefully decorated, with its original features, and little areas, that made you feel quite exclusive.

Although there was a man on the far table who was just staring in our direction. It felt a little bit creepy, maybe he knew one of the doctors. Anyway, the food was amazing! I got chatting to one of Bobby's new partners, Chris. He seemed very nice.

I'm not quite sure why Bobby got a little annoyed with me. It was an honest mistake and if Chris didn't talk with a plum in his mouth, I'm sure the mistake wouldn't have happened. I just thought Chris said he went to Manchester College not Winchester. Bobby said his parents would have spent an arm and a leg sending him to Winchester and it was an insult. I still can't see what the big deal was all about. The irony is, today is the American Day of Silence. Perhaps I should have kept quiet.

Had far too much to drink but had a good night with everyone, they made us feel so welcome and they drank more than me!

Looking forward to our new life.

Thank you for Bobby not being too cross with the amount of work will probably have to do in our new home, and Helen and Peter for being so supportive.

Friday 12th April 2002

It was so lovely to dress up and go out to the new restaurant this evening. Seb is so kind at times, to encourage Michael and I to visit these wonderful places. He does seem to bring out the best of Michael's personality and he knows all the best people and places. This was a marvellous treat and surprise.

We are lucky to have such a friend.

While they were chatting, I noticed that at a nearby table, our doctor and partners were also enjoying a meal.

I had heard that a new GP was replacing Dr Stratton when he finally retired.

I imagine the very smart younger man must be him. It was difficult to get a good look without being too obvious. I couldn't see his companion as her back was to me, but she was wearing the most elegant red dress.

I think I will try and get an appointment with him so I can check if he is a suitable replacement as he does look terribly young in comparison to the others.

Michael clearly had the best view and on more than one occasion I caught him quite fascinated by the occupants of the table. Seb also seemed to be distracted by them, most unlike him to be so inattentive to his own guests.

Honestly, I was quite embarrassed by the attention they suddenly seemed to be giving the other table, I mean honestly it's not as if they associate with the Doctors. Our friends are much more elite.

I half expected Seb to go and speak to them, but he merely continued to observe. It was quite irritating as he clearly was not interested in my plans for the captain's dinner at the golf club and was very difficult to engage in conversation.

As for Michael I think he was rather put out that Seb was so obviously preoccupied so was also quite bullish.

It thoroughly tainted the whole evening.

Thankfully, the food and excellent service made up for it.

Saturday 13/4/2002

I must stop drinking! My head was throbbing. Bobby had no sympathy for me. Luckily, Helen loves me and sorted the boys before we all went out for breakfast, to an old cafe/restaurant that was recommended to us last night.

It was like going back in time, with beautiful mahogany wooden features, high ceilings with ornate lighting and windows that seem to curve round the building. The waitresses wore little white mop caps, a black uniform with little white aprons and the waiters wore black waistcoats with white shirts and bow ties.

They brought us tea in a silver tea pot with a separate pot of hot water. I was impressed, I got five cups from my little pots I really do love Yorkshire tea.

Bobby, Peter and the boys had a posh full English Breakfast and Helen, and I ate Eggs Benedict. It was delicious.

The whole area is so beautiful, so much green grass around the little town centre. I can imagine having a picnic with the boys in the summer.

I'm really looking forward to our next journey of life.

We then drove past the house again. Bobby went very quiet; I could see him thinking but not reacting in front of his parents. I'm sure Helen was having a bit of a heart attack. (Just as well her son is a doctor).

To me it looked like the house was waiting for us to arrive and put life and soul back into it.

I am sure I will get inspiration from the beautiful house next door. Maybe they are such lovely neighbours who love children that they may even want to babysit for us. I know that's wishful thinking! But you never know, it's such a lovely area, I'm sure only lovely people live here.

Thank you for a fabulous weekend in a beautiful town, I am so excited to have this opportunity for our family to move here.

Saturday 13th April 2002

Michael was so very pleased to tell me today, that finally he has discovered who has bought next door. Seb has shared with him they are called Williams, Doctor Robert Williams, so very appropriate as neighbours. I am delighted it will be a doctor and his wife and not just anybody.

Possibly the couple from last night! I must make enquiries.

They will be perfect for this area, and just the type of neighbour I can introduce to our friends, respectable, quiet upstanding pillars of the community. I will watch with pleasure as the sold sign goes up!

I think I may have seen the wife when she came to look round with her cleaner.

I told Michael about her fancy sports car and added I'm sure it wasn't suitable for a woman who is supposed to be setting an example to the community and representing her husband. Much to extrovert, surely something small and inconspicuous would have been more appropriate.

Anyway, when I get the chance I will mention it to her, and I might mention that wearing jeans is perhaps not acceptable for the role of doctors' wife in this area.

No, I'm sure something a little more conservative will be far more becoming, and after all I have lived here and know the area, long enough and well enough to be able to offer her this kind of help.

I'll point out she obviously doesn't want to look like the terrible cleaner she had in tow. I think I might also mention to her that I can recommend my cleaner to her.

She is a far more professional looking cleaner than the woman she had with her. She didn't look fit to even be in such a wonderful car as the passenger where everyone could see the state she was in.

Anyway, it will be wonderful to be a guiding hand to her, soon have her up to standard and Michael says he may even ask the Doctor to join him and Seb at the Golf club, that will give him a good standing in our little social circle.

Get him in touch with the kind of people he will benefit from knowing.

It's so terribly exciting, the house has been empty for so long it is beginning to look beyond neglected which somewhat lowers the tone of the street and really is quite unacceptable, so it is to be hoped they soon restore it or at least get the front garden landscaped as a matter of urgency.

Of course, I will need to finish salvaging the plants I want from the back quite urgently now.

Thursday 6/6/2002

A new start and the end of an era for the Williams De Lacy family.

Weeks of planning and packing. I excitedly watched the last of the boxes being loaded into the removal van.

Moving house is extremely stressful, I'm so glad my Bobby has dealt with most of the hassle.

I did feel a twinge of sadness as I walked around our empty home, checking every room in case we had missed something and saying goodbye each time I closed a door.

Memories came flooding back from the day Bobby and I moved in, when we got married and he carried me over the threshold, bringing our baby boys home, Robbie Jnr and then Frank. Parties, amazing parties, we definitely knew how to party! With great neighbours and friends always turning up.

So many lovely memories, like sitting in our dining room and watching the blue tits in the garden as the blossom blooms, busily building their nest, then before you know it watching the babies take their first flight and leave. It's the little things that make a home a home.

It was really hard turning the key for the last time. I hope the new family moving in here will be as happy as we have been. I think our house liked us living there.

Bobby and I took a child each and our cars stacked to the brim. We followed the removal van to Yorkshire. It was a long journey and we had to make quite a few stops. Especially for the toilet!!!

I drove straight to the house while Bobby went to collect the keys.

It turns out our house has got a name like the others, it's just the old lady who lived there preferred to use a number.

Ardenstur House - What a fabulous name to go with our fabulous house.

It was so exciting opening the big oak door together. The boys ran in screaming and shouting. So much space. I could only dream of ever having a house like this. We are so lucky.

I think I saw a few curtains twitching especially when the removal men dropped a very large box that had the dinner service in. A bit of a mess outside! Never mind it can always be replaced.

After running around every room, we went to inspect the massive garden. The boys were so excited. They've got plenty of space to play football and charge around. It was wonderful hearing their shrieking laughter. Children make such magical noises.

I know we are going to be so happy here, this will be the most wonderful family home.

I spotted the next-door neighbour looking out of her bedroom window as we were coming in from the garden. I gave her a big wave, but I don't think she saw me. Once we've got some of the unpacking done, I'll go and introduce myself. You never know she may be a lovely friend.

We managed to get beds set up for us all and the kettle on for a cup of tea, had Yorkshire fish and chips for dinner, although I did find it a bit odd, they eat out of newspaper 'up north', but brilliant as saved on washing up.

All very tired but a good tired.

Thank you for our new family home and amazing new life.

Thursday 6th June 2002

What a terrible day, an absolute nightmare.

Michael had heard it was the doctor and his wife moving in, it appears this is not the case.

Clearly the Doctors wife, when she visited must have been showing their potential tenant around the house as these people cannot possibly be a doctors family.

Our peace is shattered they are the most horrendous looking family.

I watched them from the bedroom window this afternoon as they arrived with cars and disgusting vans full of boxes and awful noisy brats.

The nosey young woman who I thought was the cleaner, with her wild, unkempt strawberry blonde hair and that ridiculous wide-open smile, had the audacity to wave to me, she actually didn't even have the grace to lower her eyes and walk away in shame at being caught looking up at my bedroom window.

There is something about her that makes me shudder and my hackles rise. She is so, so, forward I think is the term. Behaving as though she is expecting me to be pleased to have her and her dreadful children as neighbours.

She is definitely no doctor's wife, far too loose looking, not at all what we want in this street. Michael and I do not want a young family as neighbours, that is why we chose this area.

I am determined they won't be living there for long with their noisy young brats.

No this is a respectable street. I intend to find out why the doctor decided to rent it out and advise him it's not that kind of area, so they will need to go as clearly, they do not fit in. I will find out how to contact him and write a very strong letter. If I can resolve this quickly Michael may not be quite so furious about it and life will be much better all around.

He was absolutely appalled by the carrying on and went off to the golf club in disgust.

I continued to watch the disorganised chaos, after all who knows what kind of damage they may do while moving in the endless boxes etc. There was a terrible crash that sounded like smashing glass, typical of that type and I have a feeling there is something vaguely familiar about the entire family.

I have probably seen them at the homeless hostel when I have had to take a turn there volunteering.

The brats all have ridiculous red hair, not a very flattering look, except on the right kind of person. Michael would say, usually, hair that red leads to trouble, so I will need to be extra vigilant and make sure they stay away from our property.

We don't want trespassers!

This really is not the kind of area to have young children living in. They will ruin the peace and quiet.

This really will not do!

Friday 7/6/2002

Not a very good night's sleep, despite being totally exhausted from yesterday. You forget that each house has its own character, moans and groans, noises you don't recognise at first but then become normal. Just part of your home.

The boys both ended up in our bed, it was all a little too strange for them. Best thing we ever did was get a Super King size bed, but it was still a squash. I ended up with Frank's bottom in my face. Not pleasant.

The house needs so much work doing to it. It was a little over whelming. I wish mum and dad were here. Mum is brilliant at sorting and organising. A decluttered home is a decluttered life, or something like that she would say. Mum would have gone around with white sage and put crystals on every windowsill for positive energy.

We opened all the windows to try and get rid of the smell. I told the boys they needed to keep their shoes on while in the house. We had no idea what we were walking in. The old brown and beige swirly carpet definitely had cultures growing in it. It made me feel a bit sick. I don't remember any of this from the viewing. Thank goodness for Bobby's NHS rubber gloves.

One of the first jobs was to disconnect the Stannah stair lift. The boys found it incredibly amusing to be going up and down, then jump on it from the top to see if it would go faster.

There are parts of the house that really haven't been touched in years which means lots of the beautiful old features have been left.

We got some Eminem blasting out, a bit of rapping to help our scrubbing!

There is one minor thing. The cooker doesn't work.

Bobby went to the local electrical store to buy a new one. Unfortunately, you cannot just walk out of the shop with a cooker. He's had to order one to be delivered but they couldn't give us a date. So, Bobby in his wisdom went to buy a BBQ, at least we can have sausages and burgers.

DIY really isn't Bobby's strong point but at least he tries. BBQ half put together. I'm not actually sure if Bobby has ever used one before. Well, we will find out as Bobby's best friend from School is playing football for Leeds United now, and Bobby has invited him for a BBQ this Sunday afternoon. It will be lovely to see Paul, we've not met up in years but have followed his progress. The boys think he's amazing.

Indian take away for dinner and a few well-deserved beers.

Thank you for a very productive day and a slightly cleaner home.

Friday 7th June 2002

My head is pounding. All day such an infernal racket coming from next door.

Heavens knows what's going on. I think they are deliberately trying to annoy me.

For Heaven's sake!

How much more of this am I expected to put up with.

I haven't been able to get into the garden next door for days and now to make matters worse I have had to put up with an infernal racket that one can only assume was supposed to resemble singing of some kind.

It was so awful Michael decided to go to the golf club. I asked if I could accompany him but he reminded me he was in for tea later so I would need to cook and could not be expected to do both.

Of course, he is right, and I should have known better than to ask.

Already they are causing a problem by making me forget my place and cause Michael to scowl at me as if I should not have needed to be told.

It's so tiresome and frustrating not being able to go to next door.

I sat in the front room watching out of the window hoping they would go out, but they just carried on wailing like cats and so eventually I gave up and wandered upstairs to take another look at the picture and art set I had rescued.

The box is quite lovely with a very intricate design.

I wonder where it had come from. I know Mrs Argur-Jones had been quite well travelled.

When we first moved in as her new neighbours she was quite spritely and Michael considered her respectable company for me, it was only when she began to need help he decided we should step back and not become involved in that kind of thing. He felt that she should employ carers.

I was quite sad that he was so adamant as I enjoyed her company. But there, he always knows best.

It didn't matter, as Mrs Wade from across the road, often spent time with her after I stopped going in, so much more in keeping than us running her errands and she is clearly not bothered by how she appears to our other neighbours on the street. Nor does she have to keep up appearances as she has no husband.

I may have missed our afternoon tea but couldn't expect them to continue when she had clearly become so frail and needy.

It was very tempting this afternoon, to see if I could still draw but really those days are so far behind me, I managed to quell the idea as ridiculous. Besides, it would not do for Michael to think I was slipping back into my so-called wild ways, as he has worked so hard to make me a decent upstanding member of his community.

I really should be happy as I am, and not harbouring such ideas.

Such an unproductive unsettling day.

Saturday 8/6/2002

Woke up to sunshine streaming through our bedroom window. What a wonderful way to start the day, apart from little Frank. He was a bit upset and said he'd been in the garden and seen an old lady at the bottom of it. Bless him, it must all be very strange for him. Then I panicked did we forget to lock the back door? Or can he reach the handle now? We need to be more careful; we could have lost our little Frank. I feel quite sick at that thought and told him never to go out by himself again.

I then had a mad thought that the house maybe haunted. I dare not mention that to Bobby. Anyway, I've enough going on without dealing with ghosts.

Frank was very reluctant to go out at first. But he soon came round when Robbie said he could play football with him.

I decided as the weather was so nice, we would do some

33

work in the garden. The garden appears to be so much larger than I remembered, and that's just the top half, there's even more garden at the other side of a fence with an old summer house and what looks like a little potting shed further down. We have a lot more work to do than I realised. But I can visualise growing our own vegetables, even have chickens so we can have fresh eggs for breakfast.

Got stuck in with the strimmer and managed to clear enough to make a BBQ area. A perfect spot in a little sun trapped area against the hedge.

The boys had a great time running around and hiding in the long grass. We discovered a pond by chance as Robbie ran straight into it and was covered from head to toe with green algae. He didn't seem too bothered so we got a bucket of water to wash him down outside. If there were any fish, I'm sure they would have died of shock from the commotion.

Must add chicken wire to my shopping list to cover the pond, we can't be having any more accidents.

Went round to the neighbours, thought it would be really nice to introduce ourselves and invite them for a drink as it was such a lovely evening. I carried Frank round with me. He was so sweet with his face covered in chocolate snuggling into my chest. He just makes my heart melt.

I was a little bit shocked when I made my acquaintance with next door. She was quite sharp with me and just said 'sorry we don't do that type of thing' and shut the door in my face.

A little odd. Maybe she's having a difficult day. I'll ask her for coffee next time.

Microwave ready meal for tea. Got the boys to bed and fixed the old baby monitor outside so we could hear the boys and Bobby and I could enjoy the summers evening in our garden with a of bottle of wine.

Thank you for today. Hard work but rewarding.

Saturday 8th June 2002

I got up very early this morning and went through the hedge to rescue a few more plants.

I simply could not leave them.

I was quite alarmed that as I straightened up, I met the bright blue eyes of one of the brats, standing there with his mouth open gawping at me through the small fence that was clearly to divide the two parts of the garden, he just stood staring, looking quite terrified, as if I was some kind of apparition. I couldn't resist crouching back down, then straightening up and saying Boo.

It had the desired effect, he fled in terrified tears.

I felt I had to grab my things and head home in case the stupid woman came out.

Honestly, a waste of my effort to start the morning early and salvage some more plants. But at least I may have stopped the brat spying on me and the effect was most amusing.

It's just to inconvenient having them live here.

Most of the day an infernal racket coming from next door, then a terrible commotion, when I got to the window the stupid woman was pouring a bucket of water over one of the children who appeared to look like a swamp monster.

They were all laughing... loudly, piercing shrieking, awful racket... I had to cover my ears.

It's absolutely terrible. I suppose she thinks drowning them in a bucket of water is cheaper than running them a bath!

As if that wasn't bad enough, she then had the audacity to turn up at my door with her filthy child hanging onto her. I thought it was going to recognise me, but she just wanted to say hello and invite me round for some sort of do.

I didn't even bother to listen just quickly shut the door, after all who knows what germs or fleas the filthy children carry!!!

I went straight for a shower.

I can't bear the sight of them. We are not supposed to have people like that here.

Thank heavens I didn't have visitors and that earlier I had dropped Michael off at golf. He isn't coming home tonight as he and Seb have an engagement. I doubt I'll see him before three tomorrow. It's as well I'm home alone!

I really can't tolerate that terrible family. They are always laughing and the children running wild. This is not the right area for a family with children.

I suppose she thinks she is some kind of wonderful mother; well, I will make certain she realises she is not! There is no such thing as a wonderful mother, and she will soon see children only break your heart.

I dislike them so much, there must be some way to discourage them from settling here.

Perhaps I will start a notebook and see if I can report her to the authorities.

Sunday 9/6/2002 - Frank's Birthday

Woke up to a very excited little boy. Frank is three today. I love him so much. He just gives the best hugs ever!

We have bought him a rabbit. It's so cute! Beautiful black fluffy fur.

Yesterday Bobby slipped out to the pet shop and hid the cage in one of the empty removal boxes. Frank was over the moon and called it Paul after Bobby's best friend. The rabbit even has a blue, white and yellow interior cage to match his favourite team.

We let Paul run around in his new pen. The boys thought it would be really nice for Paul to play with their football. It definitely looks like it's a male rabbit. I changed the subject when the boys asked me what he was doing with the ball.

Unpacked a few more boxes, then helped Bobby finish putting the BBQ together, although it didn't really look like the picture on the box. Maybe it was boxed wrongly.

The real Paul turned up just after mid-day. Frank and Robbie were all over him. Just wanting to kick a ball with their idol.

Any excuse to start drinking! Although he doesn't drink these days. I have to admire him for that. But that didn't stop Bobby and me.

Bless him, Paul (the real Paul) had bought us a slow cooker as a housewarming present. Perfect! How did he know we have no cooker? He said, 'they are really easy to use, just put your uncooked food in, leave for a few hours and sorted!' His exact words. Looking forward to trying it.

Salad ready, sausages and burgers ready to cook, but the BBQ wasn't quite as we expected.

Bobby was struggling to get it going so he added more lighter fuel and gel to the coals.

He also added some bits of wood in desperate measure to get it all going. Bobby said that's how he was taught to light fires in the boy scouts. Not sure he was right as all that did was create more smoke.

Honestly, it was bellowing. We could have communicated with the next town with our smoke signals.

The next thing we hear are sirens, and then three fire fighters came running down our drive. Then more sirens and two policemen came charging into our garden.

It was a little surreal.

We explained it was our first time we had done a BBQ, and we really weren't doing any damage anywhere.

Luckily, they recognised Paul (not the rabbit) and that seemed to take way any tension.

I made them all a cup of tea for their troubles. I would have offered them a beer, but it was unfair as they were on duty.

One of the firemen, went to help Bobby get the BBQ going properly.

As everyone was feeling very hungry, they joined us for sausages and burgers while asking Paul questions about his footballing career, getting autographs and photos.

We had a lovely afternoon and they apologised profusely for any inconvenience they caused.

What lovely friendly professional people in Yorkshire.

I did ask them if it's normal to patrol the area for smoke.

I was told we had been reported for arson, and it was life threatening, that's why they had to come.

I think it's really sad that someone has reported our BBQ.

Who would do that?

Although the boys got to sit in the fire engine. Frank said he had the best birthday ever!

Note to self - need to practice lighting fires before we invite more friends round for a BBQ.

Thank you for the services making it an extra special day.

Saturday 9th June 2002

As Michael and I were leaving for the golf club this morning for brunch, we passed a rather important looking car turning up our street. Michael was sure he recognised the driver as a football player from a top team, but as we were running late for his round, he wouldn't go back and check if they were visiting us.

I can't think who else on our street would know anyone with such a prestigious car. I just hope to goodness they don't run into the low life's next door!

Michael pointed out, as I was getting out of the car after a fabulous brunch, that the red in my hair is coming through. He reminded me it's unbecoming and suggested it resembled the colour of the brats hair next door. He can be quite unkind at times. He made the morning feel quite a let down, he really does know how to make me feel inadequate.

I will complain to the hairdresser as I really do not want to resemble such a terrible woman's brats in any way and it is most important I maintain my image to please both Michael and Seb!

He went back out to the golf course complaining he couldn't stand the row coming from next door.

After that the day just got worse as it wore on.

Next door was very noisy, clearly something was happening there. Lots of raised voices and laughter.

Then smoke was billowing up from the hedge and fence and swirling like a black cloud into my garden.

I opened the patio doors, and it choked me as it came into the house.

I was so horrified that those dreadful trouble causers were burning down the hedge I rang for Michael, the fire brigade and the police.

I was very upset that the operator kept insisting I calm down. I was quite cross by her attitude. I mean really, I am not one to overreact, but she was awful.

How would she have felt with all that choking smoke in her house. Everywhere smelt so awful.

It took the police a few minutes to arrive, and I was furious they had their sirens blaring then had the audacity to park in my drive.

For heaven's sake the whole street knew they were at my house! Whatever would the other neighbours think!

The police officer suggested I was overreacting, for heaven's sake what did he know! I told him he looked too young for the job, and I wanted to file a complaint.

He was ridiculous saying he was sure nothing intentional was happening next door then he had the cheek to suggest I was being dramatic, perhaps not his exact words. Things got completely out of hand, and he said if I continued, he would caution me.

At least he directed the fire brigade to next door, the thought of all those men trailing through my house was just too much.

As if that wasn't bad enough Michael arrived back with Seb and was furious at being interrupted during his game and demanding to know what was going on. I tried to explain that the officer was a young idiot and the low life's next door were burning the place down.

The officer said if we didn't all calm down, he would caution us both.

Seb stepped in and calmed Michael down suggesting that we let the officer do his job.

When the officer returned from next door, he suggested I had indeed misunderstood what was actually happening next door and tried to reassure me there was nothing to be concerned about. It was a genuine false alarm; all smoke no fire.

In no uncertain terms I told him he was wrong, that they are the wrong type of people for this area. He suggested I was overwrought.

Seb very kindly poured me a brandy and suggested I should drink it then go for a lie down.

Michael said the house smelt too smoky so collected more clothes saying he would stay at Sebs and left with Seb saying I would be fine after a rest.

He will come back tomorrow when the air has cleared as I can't possibly expect him to stay in such a smoky atmosphere, poor Seb did seem a little concerned for me and said I should go and rest.

Those terrible people really have to go!

I will find a way to get rid of them.

They are quite unbearable.

Saturday 29/6/2002

Hannah and John came to visit, it turns out that Bobby's

godparents only live five minutes away on Willow Road.

We took them for a tour of our house. I felt at first they were looking at us as if we were mad, but they were so positive, telling us about the amazing potential the house has. Potential seems to be the word of the month for us at the moment.

Bless them, they then suggested we all went back to their house and have tea so we could have a break from all our work.

The Boys were impressed with their big black Range Rover, so they went with them, and Bobby and I followed.

Hannah and John's house is amazing! A beautiful double fronted house even bigger than ours.

How does Hannah keep a tidy house, that looks like it's been featured in a magazine, and still looks so immaculate herself. They are both so kind and generous.

John took the boys and Bobby into the garden to play tennis on their own private court. They were happy for hours while I chatted to Hannah and made tea.

We then opened a bottle of wine and that was it. We were settled for the rest of the evening.

The boys crashed in their movie room while us adults had quite a few more drinks. (Not sure how many to be honest as I felt like I had a magic glass, it never seemed to empty). Bobby then went onto the whiskey!

It got quite late, but it was still a lovely warm evening, so we decided to walk home.

Frank was on Bobby's shoulders and Robbie held me up.

We had such a lovely time, and it was so good to see them. They have always been good to us and the boys. They've never forgotten a birthday or anniversary.

Thank you for a perfect afternoon and evening with Hannah and John, it really was so good to see them.

Saturday 29th June 2002

I was just coming back from town at lunch time when I passed what appeared to be Jo-Hannah Smythes Range Rover pulling off our street.

Most strange if it were as I am sure Michael and I are the only people here who they would associate with. Perhaps I should ring and apologise for missing them. How lovely that they appear to have visited. It just shows that Michael and I are very high up the social ladder.

I tried to ring Michael to tell him we had missed a visit, but his phone just went to voice mail.

I was so distracted by the Smythes I almost missed the rabble from next door disappearing off in their car, how fortunate they were not seen by the Smythes, I would have been so embarrassed if their paths had crossed!

I took the chance to pop round to their garden as soon as I was sure they had gone. Oh my, it appears they are not bothering with the half of the garden with the potting shed and summer house. How lucky for me!

I have had a look at the little gate between the two ends and to keep them out have managed to padlock it from my side.

I had another rummage through the potting shed and moved some of the better stuff to the summerhouse. It's such a lovely space. I will make it my own seeing as they clearly cannot cope with so much garden.

Sadly, I couldn't stay too long because in the middle of the day who knows when they might interrupt me by coming back.

Wednesday 24/7/2002

Can't believe we have been living here over a month.

We have done so much work to this house, it really is beginning to feel like our home.

Had a message from mum and dad. They are hoping to be back in the U.K. for Christmas and have promised to stay with us. A little bit of extra pressure to get the spare bedroom ready, but it will be worth it.

I've been feeling a little tired lately. Just not quite myself. I put it down to all the work we have been doing. Bobby insisted I have a check-up and blood tests. As the weather was nice I decided to walk up to the surgery with the boys and meet Bobby. The were being little angels until I caught Frank pulling his trousers down in the waiting area, getting his willy out for everyone to see because he needed a wee. Robbie thought it was hysterical, he laughed so loud it made everyone look in our direction.

I was absolutely mortified.

Bobby came out into the waiting area to see what all the noise was, then stood there shaking his head in disbelief. He really was not impressed with our children. He quickly rushed me and Robbie into the nurses room making out he didn't know us. Then took Frank to the staff toilets. I felt quite put out. I know he has to be professional, but they are his children too. Luckily, the nurse, Sarah, was lovely and totally understood as she had three boys of her own.

After giving the boys a dressing down about their behaviour, we took a slow walk home. As we were almost there, I met our neighbours. Fred and Jean who live next door and another lady, Christine, who lives over the road. I introduced myself and the boys, as they were chatting across the top of their drive.

They have said if we need anything then just pop over. Fred and Jean must be in their late 80's, both very hard of hearing, probably not a bad thing living next door to us. I got the impression Christine was a widow, not sure how old she is but there was something really lovely and familiar about her.

We were having a delightful chat, until Robbie and Frank climbed up their very nice garden wall and jump onto their well-manicured lawn. Then proceed to do roly poly's and squashed some of their beautiful white flowers. I felt very awkward and embarrassed. All I could do was apologise. (I dare not tell Bobby, especially after our earlier incident). Bless them, Fred and Jean said it was ok, boys will be boys and it was lovely to see children playing again. They continued the conversation about our other neighbours and said they were called Clarissa and Michael. It was a bit strange as I noticed all three of them sort of roll their eyeballs when they said the neighbours names.

Maybe just my imagination. I'm sure they are very nice.

Obviously, I hadn't exercised the boys enough today!

Still waiting for our new cooker to arrive.

Note to self - fish fingers do not work in a slow cooker!

Wednesday 24th July 2002

This morning, I had an appointment with the nurse at the surgery. Just my routine bloods. I was rather hoping to meet the new GP, Dr Robert Williams, but apparently, he was completely booked up.

While I was waiting that awful new neighbour arrived in absolute chaos with her two unruly brats.

I took refuge in a magazine and attempted not to notice when one of the brats exposed himself for all to see. Really it was disgusting. What kind of animals are they going to grow into!

I expect she had them there for some kind of behaviour therapy and as for her, well, clearly, she can't cope.

It looked like she had managed to get an appointment with the very smart, intelligent looking new GP as he took her and the brats down to a consulting room. I must say he does look very well turned out and quite capable, he wears very nice-looking designer glasses that give him an air of capability.

I will have a word with the secretary about my next appointment as I'm sure I should have had priority to meet him over that awful woman. What ever will he think, joining our practise and then having her as a patient. He will have entirely the wrong idea of the type of patients who come here.

I've made a note in my notebook about their lewd behaviour. I am getting quite a compilation. It won't be long before I sort them out.

I hadn't been back long when from Michael's bedroom window, I watched that awful woman and her terrible children talking to the Wrights and Mrs Wade. I am surprised they were standing so close to the brats, who knows what germs they are carrying, and older people really should take more care of themselves.

She was all smiles and friendly, taking them in with her

apparent good humour. She looked terribly haggard, clearly unable to take care of her appearance, fancy going out looking so frayed. I expect those hellions keep her up all night.

Ha, the bright smile soon faded, and her front didn't last when those terrible creatures started to wreck the Wrights Garden. Climbing up and jumping off the wall, no that really won't have gone down well.

Next time I catch them I will suggest they don't fraternise with her, especially Mrs. Wade, she must be so desperate for company. It's such a shame she is so mousy and scurries away every time she sees me.

I really couldn't befriend her but still it's my duty to be a good neighbour. I will make it clear they are not the type for this street.

Michael and Seb disappeared to lunch at the golf club and Michael called to say he doubted he would be home tonight as a few of them were going to Sebs for a game of cards. Such a good job he keeps toiletries and spare clothes there for occasions like this. It's so considerate of him not to want to disturb me by coming home late and dear Seb assures me it is no inconvenience to have Michael to stay over.

I am going to Gardening club early in the morning, then to lunch with the ladies' circle so at least he won't be holding me up and I won't need to worry about cooking him his breakfast.

I slipped next door at dusk and scouted out some more plants for my display. I do wish there were some way I could stop having to share the garden with her and the brats.

I did look for the blue-eyed brat, but I suppose he must have stayed in his bed as he wasn't at the window, such a shame I do like scaring him, it is almost as enjoyable as rescuing the plants.

Wednesday 31/7/2002

Frank is still acting very strange about our house, especially the garden. He keeps telling me there's an old lady who keeps going into the old potting shed. It's so overgrown at the bottom end, I was unable to get through the gate as it was padlocked the other side, so I can't see how an old lady can walk down there.

Bobby was getting a bit cross with me and Frank, saying it's my fault for allowing him to have too much of an imagination. Honestly he's three years old of course he's going to have an imagination, we weren't all brought up in a strict environment and posh boarding school.

It has crossed my mind that Frank could be spiritual, and maybe very sensitive to the old lady that lived here. I've heard stories about young children talking to people and describing someone from a past life.

I dare not have that conversation with Bobby, I can imagine his reaction to his very scientific black and white life. Maybe I'll have a chat to mum.

Hannah and John picked me and the boys up and took us to the local park near the town centre. It's so beautiful around here. The boys had a great time running around the adventure playground. There was a big wooden ship that was perfect to play hide and seek. Zip wires, swings and slides. We then played crazy golf. Frank was so cute running to each hole checking if Stuart Little the mouse was living there. He didn't want him to get hurt so had to make sure everything was safe for him. It was so good to see Frank having a great time and it took his mind off the Ghost Lady.

Robbie was loving having a go at 'golf', he did really well. John was showing him how to hold a club and putt. He was taking it all in, even John was impressed and told him that if he wanted golf lessons he would take him to his club.

The boys then found it very amusing when they decided to attack their Uncle John, although I'm not quite sure he enjoyed it that much. He was walking a little bent over by the time they were finished.

The weather was glorious sunshine. So, we sat on the grass with the biggest ice creams ever and people watched.

I've never understood why Hannah and John haven't had children; they would make amazing parents.

Bobby was working late again so Hannah and John came back to ours and we had fish and chips for tea with Dandelion and Burdock. - That's a really strange combination but I enjoyed it.

Thank you for a beautiful playful sunny day. Thank you Hannah and John for being there for me.

Sometimes I get a little bit lonely and very emotional. I don't understand why because I have everything.

Wednesday 31st July 2002

I have no idea what is going on at our GP practice. The new young nurse is such a dozy ditherer. I went to get my blood pressure checked and my blood test results, and she informed me I was pregnant! She then congratulated me. CONGRATULATED me for heaven's sake.

I was furious how on earth could she have made such a shocking mistake. Do I look like the type of woman who would indulge in such lewd behaviour?

I didn't tell Michael what had happened, heavens knows what he would have thought. We have never shared a room never mind a bed. He would have been terribly shocked and angry and poor Seb would have been horrified to imagine we would indulge in such fornication.

The thought of going through that again made me shudder. I can't even tolerate thinking about it. It is just unbearable, simply unbearable. The last thing I would want to experience.

I was so furious with the nurse; she burst into tears and ran out of the room like a snivelling child. Pathetic as well as stupid. I did not care how upset she was or who heard how inept she was. All I could think of was the repulsive idea of pregnancy.

Dr Walton came rushing in and ordered me to calm down, calm down how dare he.

He profusely apologised saying the results were an error of filing and clearly not mine, some address confusion, a simple misunderstanding. It was just all to appalling for me.

Eventually the practice manager brought me a cup of tea, unfortunately in a mug, not in a decent china cup with a saucer, with a biscuit on a chipped plate, and between them talked me down.

The good thing that has come of today is Dr Walton feels I could go for some Psychotherapy at the new clinic.

I am thrilled as it is very exclusive and only a certain type of patient is lucky enough to be treated there.

I have read about a few famous people who have stayed there as a retreat when their famous lives have worn them *out.*

I am so looking forward to going.

I decided not to take my complaint about the surgery any further as it was not Dr Waltons fault, he had such a useless employee.

I think I have made my feelings quite clear and expect the nurse will be sacked, so no hard feelings there.

I'm not going to mention the clinic appointment to Michael it can be my little pleasure, like next doors garden adventures.

I will have to buy some nice outfits to wear to my appointments so that it is obvious I am of some importance. After all you never know who you might meet.

Friday 23/8/2002

We had a lovely gardener today to cut back the massive hedge between us and the neighbours.

An unusual business name 'Trim your bush by Barry', but he was recommended to us.

Barry parked his van on our drive, I did notice underneath his signage on the van in small lettering 'Happy to trim more than your bushes.' I couldn't stop giggling. It must be the Yorkshire sense of humour.

Christine walked past and I could see her looking at the van as Barry was unloading his tools, and then within minutes he took his shirt off!

A very pleasant view. I think Christine enjoyed it too. She just smiled and said, "it's a lovely morning". It certainly was. I have to say it's been a while since I've seen a bit of eye candy. Although far too young for me, and I honestly have not got the energy for another male in my life. In fact, I haven't got the energy for very much at the moment. Still, it's nice to look.

It didn't take long before Barry got carried away trimming our privet.

It's amazing how much garden we have gained.

We then noticed a little fence between us and the neighbours. The gardener has levelled the hedge off to the same height. I can now see Clarissa and Michael's garden. It's so beautiful. It's like looking on to Kew Gardens. Certainly, an inspiration.

Frank and Robbie were helping the hunky gardener. Barry gave the boys a little wheelbarrow and some kiddies gardening tools. They loved it, until the gardener asked the boys to go into the overgrown end. Robbie couldn't open the gate, so he jumped over the fence and was straight in. Frank just stood by the fence and stared. I'm getting quite worried about him. I'll speak to Bobby and see what he thinks we should do.

I still don't feel quite like myself. Then seeing how upset Frank was and I didn't fancy making hundreds of cups of tea for Barry all day.

I decided to take the boys to a local pet shop. We needed more rabbit food, and I thought it would be nice to see the other animals.

After a long discussion about not buying a snake. The boys ran off, the next thing I saw was the pet shop owner looking very angry trying to hoik Frank out of the fish-pond covered in water lilies, knee deep with fish swimming around him.

I took the boys straight back to the car. Then the pet owner came out accusing me of not paying for the rabbit food.

I apologised again, gave him £20, most expensive rabbit food ever and burst into tears.

Why do these things always seem to happen to me?

Shouted at the boys all the way home.

Got home to find Barry the gardener didn't get to finish the bottom end, that's another days work (lucky me), it really is very overgrown. Although I thought it odd that he asked if I'd been digging up plants and cutting branches off the Lemon Cypress tree, I hadn't a clue what he was on about.

Bobby came back with some news. He'd got the results of my blood test.

It turns out I'm pregnant. I don't understand as I am still regular. Or am I? Did I miss a month with everything going on?

He said they took longer to get back because there was a mix up with my results and they'd been put on to another patients records.

What if somebody else had been given my blood test results.

If I am in shock can you imagine how they would be feeling.

At least that explains why I feel like I do.

Well, you know what they say new house, new baby. Let's hope it's a little girl. As much as I love my boys it will be nice to have some balance of female company. And we've always talked about having three children. Well, I have.

I couldn't read Bobby's face, I hope he's happy, he seemed to be more concerned about the mix up of the blood results than us having another baby.

Ordered a very large trampoline and a big football net for the boys.

Still waiting for cooker.

Note to self... pasta does not work in a slow cooker.

Thank you for our wonderful news. (I think).

Friday 23rd August 2002

I am furious. Those terrible people are clearly invading my privacy. They have lowered the hedge to a height where I can clearly see into their unkempt garden. The only possible benefit is that I noticed closer to the house are a few more plants I really ought to acquire at some point soon.

It was terrible to watch the hedge massacred down to the level of the original fence Michael had had put in.

The young man who cut it down was almost naked. He wielded his power tool like a weapon. He must have smelt terrible because under his tan he looked very sweaty.

I felt I had to watch him just to keep an eye on things.

When he saw me watching him, he waved and shouted hello and asked if I was ok. I suppose he thought his nice smile would have an effect on me! I mean really, as if I would answer him.

I felt quite overcome by the sight of the destruction to the poor hedge.

I wanted to tell him to put his clothes on but was too shocked and embarrassed by him. I went upstairs and continued to watch the destruction from my bedroom. He made very light work of the job, clearly his arms must have been very strong, and he is used to manual work but really, he was so naked!

I also noticed that there is some kind of rodent animal bouncing around a cage attacking a football in a very unnatural way.

I really was shocked at how it was behaving with the brat's ball. I mean really no morals these people are just disgusting.

What a good job Michael has been busy with Seb all day. I am sure he would have had plenty to say about the naked man flaunting his body and wait until he sees the hedge.

I went down to the tree at the end of the garden when he had finished to check he hadn't interfered with my way into next door. Happily, he has not touched it.

Luckily, it is well hidden by the foliage at the moment.

I was tempted to slip through and check the summer house and for more plants but decided to leave it until it's easier to get in without breaking branches.

The whole new area I have designed is looking splendid and the plants I have rescued so far are flourishing. It really has been a most beneficial plan salvaging them. By September, the area will be stunning.

Thursday 5/9/2002

We've been so lucky with the weather. Warm evenings and not having to worry about taking a coat with us during the day. It always makes life easier when trying to get out of the house not loaded up with waterproofs and jumpers.

There's definitely something special about September, a calmness after summer, a settling down. Maybe it's because the boys have gone back to school and it's quiet!

I'm so pleased that they have both settled into their new school and nursery.

They seem to be making lots of new friends and I really appreciate the time I have without them. Does that sound like

I'm a terrible mother?

I am just so exhausted with this pregnancy. I've actually got time to put my feet up for five minutes and do a positive meditation. Bobby laughs when I tell him what I've done during the day. He said it's a posh description for a Nanna nap.

Our cooker finally arrived! It turns out they have tried to deliver it three times and each time the delivery drivers have turned up; someone has told them they have got the wrong address. So, it's had to go back to the depot and go through the system. Well, that was their explanation for the delay.

They must have got the address so wrong because I'm sure most of our neighbours around here know I'm desperate for a cooker.

Oh, and the rabbit escaped again. We have covered almost every part of our garden with chicken wire to keep Paul in.

Where he goes I have no idea, but it amazes me as he always comes back. We often see him hopping down our drive then he sits by the back door waiting for the boys to give him a bit of toast or biscuits. Not sure if rabbits are supposed to eat toast or biscuits but he looks happy to me. The other thing I love about Paul is we don't have to cut the grass as often.

I find it quite amusing watching Paul play football - well I say play football he's actually doing what rabbits do, it's the boys who think he wants to play with them. They kick the ball while he's in full action and all three of them go chasing after it. Hours of entertainment.

I'm feeling a little bit stressed about planning Robbie's birthday.

Not sure if we just invite a few friends over or the whole

class. I need to find out what the norm is at school.

Christine is so lovely she came round with a plateful of buns that she just made. She told me that her only son lives abroad and misses him very much. I'm not sure if she has grandchildren, she's never mentioned any, but she seems to have taken me and the boys under her wing.

We sat and had a lovely cup of tea, and she has offered to baby sit for us. I'm not sure she actually knows what she will be letting herself in for.

The last time we had a babysitter, one of my friends daughters, she tried to read the boys a story. But they wanted an action story so were trying to climb out of the window.

She couldn't wait until we came home and never offered again.

Bobby had another meeting after work.

It was just the boys and me for tea. It was so nice to use the hob.

I got the boys sorted for bed and I am going to have an early night.

Thank you for our new cooker, love it! And thank you Christine for sharing her lovely buns.

Thursday 5th September 2002

The lovely weather has meant that my garden still looks colourful. I am so pleased to be hosting the WI garden party, especially as its on my birthday. I haven't mentioned my birthday, one doesn't discuss these things and besides there is no one to particularly note it.

Michael has certainly chosen to ignore it, and so shall I.

Michael is going to take himself off to Sebs for the

weekend. They are going to a golfing tournament.

I was a little disappointed that Seb hadn't thought to invite us for a meal in the evening after it, but I suppose the tournament will keep them busy.

I noticed that some of my carrots appear to have been disturbed by something. Perhaps the birds looking for worms. What a terrible nuisance, I will have to put netting over them until the party.

I do hope the weather holds.

I noticed Mrs Wade heading next door earlier, I really need to catch her and suggest she doesn't become friendly with them. It's really not appropriate.

I also noticed the delivery van pulling away, filthy white thing. I'm not sure how many times I am going to need to tell them nobody on this street would dream of using such a filthy looking vehicle for a delivery.

I have managed to pop through the hedge to the potting shed and salvage some more pretty planters. I've realised going through at the break of day not only does the air feel fresh and invigorating adding to the excitement, but the only sign of life from the house is perhaps the bleary-eyed little brat who watches me from the window. I've discovered if I stare at him, he turns and runs. I am quite enjoying the effect I have on him and make a point of looking for him each time I pop in.

I thought he would tell that awful woman but clearly, he doesn't as no one comes. I do love scaring him. It's as exhilarating as the excursions.

Wonderful fun.

Monday 23/9/2002

Woke up in such a panic! We had all slept in.

Grabbed chocolate bars for the boys' breakfast to eat on the way to school and nursery.

Thank goodness they have short hair, and I didn't need to brush it.

I dragged them out as fast as I could.

The school run did seem unusually quiet. We got to the main road and noticed the lolly pop lady wasn't there either. I couldn't believe how late we were.

Dodged a few cars, only one driver hooted their horn. Honestly, some people are so impatient, couldn't they see I was late!

Got down the school drive and still didn't see anyone in the playground. It was all very odd. Then I saw the lovely Miss Shutt.

She asked if I was all right. I just apologised for being late.

She smiled and very kindly reminded me it was a teacher training day.

I felt so stupid! I'm blaming the pregnancy. Baby brain must have kicked in.

I then had to do the walk of shame back up the school drive. Thought there was no point in taking Frank to nursery, so we went home.

Robbie has just gone back to school, why are they having a teacher training day?

Although it gave me a good excuse to get Robbie to write out all his birthday invitations.

I have been told it is normal to invite the whole class.

Going by his last school twenty children didn't seem so bad. But when I asked for the class list there are thirty-three in his class plus some of his friends from the other class! I thought government guidelines had a maximum number of about twenty-five children. Rules obviously don't apply in Yorkshire.

I haven't told Bobby yet; he will have a fit since we decided to have the party in our garden. I just pray it does not rain!

Need to get my thinking head on and organise something. Honestly, I'm having sleepless nights about organising a children's party and there are countries at war or worried about when they are going to eat. Come on Seren get life into prospective. It can't be that hard. Anyway, I'm sure not all will come. People have busy lives.

I do wish my parents where here to help. Bobby's parents are great but it's not the same.

One positive I did have a lovely day at home with the boys after their morning exercise to school and back!

Thank you for a lovely productive day.

Monday 23rd September 2002

This morning while on my way to my hair appointment I passed that stupid woman and her gaggle of offensive brats, filthy as usual, trying to cross the road opposite the school.

I could have stopped but speeded up slightly and blasted my horn to make her wait. I don't even think she noticed it was me.

Clearly, she was late as there was no crossing person in attendance. So, her own fault I didn't let her cross and caused her to be even later!

I was dismayed to come home and find them in their garden this afternoon.

I had hoped to have a proper look in the house to see if they were actually doing anything. Discreetly of course! I have the keys but have been terribly consumed with salvaging the plants so never quite found the time to go back in. I can't imagine there is much improvement as it seems she spends an awful amount of time in the back garden, which now resembles a play park.

Not at all in keeping with our standards. She really could do with adding a few nice formal flower beds and the bottom end near the summer house is becoming very overgrown and difficult to traverse. I have left several deep holes while digging up plants and they are quite hard to spot in places where the weeds have taken hold.

I would be very annoyed if I fell, or twisted my ankle in them, it would be entirely down to her lack of garden maintenance.

Michael had a wander down the garden to have a look at my vegetable patch, he feels that perhaps there is a rodent interfering with them. Of course, if it is it will be coming from next door. I have called in pest control. Can't possibly have the ladies here with that kind of problem. I stressed it is a matter of urgency and high priority that someone should come and that they need to park their vehicle outside next door so that no one suspects they are here. After all it would not do for people to think I had rodents.

Michael didn't notice my way into next door so hopefully no one will when the ladies are here. It would be awful if it was no longer a secret.

Saturday 28/9/2002 - Robbie's birthday

Last night I suggested Bobby needed to relax so I plied him with drink.

I thought it was a good call giving him a very large whiskey. You know one for the road, to help him forget our conversation.

Thinking this would give me the ideal opportunity to actually tell him how many children were coming to Robbie's party.

Not one person said they could not make it. Everyone is coming!!

I told him we have thirty-six children arriving at two o'clock.

He didn't respond, so he must have been ok with it.

This morning, I regretted giving him any alcohol. He spent the night throwing up and neither of us got much sleep. He was like a bear with a sore head.

Then Robbie jumped on our bed so we could sing happy birthday to him.

Thank goodness the bouncy castle man turned up. It gave Bobby something to focus on.

I had also organised a children's entertainer. And I was sure all the other parents would come and help me serve the food and supervise as we all helped each other at Robbie's last school.

It turns out this is not the case. Once your child gets to a certain age, you are then the babysitter for the rest of the class.

One mother left her son with his little brother saying, "I hope you don't mind, I have to dash into town". Cheeky mare!

The cooking and serving took forever, some of the parents who were there, I'm sure they just wanted to be nosey to see our home and who the new doctor in town is. They did sweet FA to help!

Saying that there were a couple of lovely mums who did. I was so appreciative.

I decided to get paper tablecloths and crayons, so while I was cooking hot dogs and chips the children could sit and colour.

The artwork in this area is not quite Vincent Van Gogh. I have never seen so many willies of all sizes and colours in one place.

The girls were loving the disco, all dancing away in their pretty party dresses. Until the entertainer produced a very large water pistol and lined the kids up to be soaked and then proceeded to give them loads of sweets to make them even more hyper and louder.

What kind of entertainment goes on in Yorkshire? The entertainer must have been in his seventy's. He seemed to be loving it as much as the kids.

The boys were a nightmare! Running, screaming and climbing everywhere.

I do hope this baby I am carrying will be a girl. I am not sure I could cope with another boy. Especially after today.

Bobby just kept glaring at me and shaking his head.

I have to say it was the longest few hours of my life. And then some of the parents were half an hour late. The mother who left her younger child who was not invited turned up an hour late!

Some of the mum's came back asking for water and a scraper. Someone had put big no parking stickers right across their car windscreens.

Have we got parking restrictions on this road?

Bobby and I did not speak for the rest of the day.

But at least Robbie had a fabulous time, and I did meet a few really nice mums.

Thank you for no major injuries and a sunny day.

Saturday 28th September 2002

I am beyond furious.

For heaven's sake, today should have been my grand party, but that terrible woman had some kind of rave verging on a den of inequity going on next door, even involving the awful children, who appeared to have multiplied to at least thirty.

Most unacceptable.

It began just after lunch.

The street was full of cars and so many people coming and going up their drive. All just as my WI ladies were due to arrive. I made notices and took them out sticking them on the windscreens of all the cars, stating this is a private street and no parking is allowed.

Not that it freed up any spaces for my visitors. Fortunately, they parked on our drive or outside on the other side of my drive.

Then I had to apologise to the ladies as they arrived for the carry-on next door. During our cup of tea some of the ladies were very distracted by children bouncing up and down shouting Hello at them. I tried to tell the awful brats to Shoo but they just kept laughing and bouncing so that they could peer at us over the fence.

The ladies kept trying to say it wasn't a problem and how lucky I am to have a young couple next door.

Really what is lucky about having them there as a constant reminder of how happy families are meant to be.

I started to say I disliked the family intensely, but Mrs Abbott said she had heard they were very good friends with the Smythe's, so I kept quiet. After all the Smythe's are very popular people.

Mrs Edwards did sympathise that as I had no children or grandchildren, I possibly found it all a bit much. Stupid woman, what does she know.

I nearly told her I was glad I hadn't had the ordeal of bringing up a child.

But then, I do wonder now and again how life could have been.

It was all so dreadful. I felt quite exhausted by the whole ordeal.

To ruin the day more, Mrs Warbottom told me in no uncertain terms I have a problem with rabbits eating my vegetables. How ridiculous. We don't live in that kind of area. If only the pest control people had come when I told them too.

I called Michael to see if he would come home and go next door to complain but his phone went straight to voice mail.

I have no idea what he can have been doing as he keeps it on even on the golf course. I tried Sebs phone but that was also turned off. I will be giving them a piece of my mind as it could have been urgent.

It is so typical of Michael to be unavailable when I need him. Sometimes I wonder if he even appreciates how trying life can be for me.

I thought he might possibly have wished me a happy

birthday this morning, but he was much too preoccupied with The Financial Times and getting ready to go to Golf.

Seb, bless him, did bring me some flowers and mumbled that he hoped I enjoyed my day. Really, he is quite kind.

I had to end today with a large gin and tonic. It was a relief when Michael called me to say he was not coming home so I did not need to cook dinner. I suppose he has completely forgotten it was my birthday and I am alone apart from the continual racket from next doors children still trying to sing Happy Birthday loudly and out of tune!!!

Saturday 5/10/2002

The day started with a crisp and sunny morning. Bobby left me a cup of tea by the side of the bed, then went off to play his tennis match. The boys were up and out early in the garden to play on their trampoline.

Robbie, his usual hundred miles per hour, and Frank, well at Frank's pace. I think if the boys were animals Robbie would be a Border Collie and Frank a Sloth.

Robbie didn't play too long with Frank, as he decided he wanted to play football on the drive, while Frank was away with the fairies.

Frank then came running in ever so upset, in fact hysterical telling me that the old potting shed had collapsed, and the ghost lady was there carrying a big blue pot.

I ran out to the garden. I couldn't believe it. The potting shed had gone. Total destruction. Frank stood by the fence, all colour drained from his little face, drip white, just staring. He then wet himself.

I asked him what had happened as I looked at the wooden

mound and saw Frank's large remote-control car. It must have gone through a gap in the fence and crashed into the potting shed.

He just kept saying it was the ghost lady.

I asked him to tell me the truth, if he'd been playing near the shed, but he gave me the same answer. I was so cross with him. Which I feel really bad about now. He could have been injured. I don't know what's going on. It's so unlike Frank to be quiet, he used to be the one that talked for hours, and I couldn't get him to shut up.

Bobby got back from his tennis match and said enough was enough about old ghost ladies. He's obviously trying to get attention. Bobby said he would speak to one of his colleagues and get him some help.

I am really worried about my little Frank.

I thought it would be nice for us all to get out of the house and go on a long walk. The weather was changing so we got wrapped up. Bobby still seemed annoyed. He drove the car in silence until we got to the local woods, it seemed to calm everyone down as the boys ran around, climbed trees and played hide and seek.

It was beautiful to watch. I love this time of year when the leaves start to change colour. Especially when it's windy like this afternoon and it feels as if it's raining leaves.

Got back home with colour back in our cheeks, boys exercised, fed and watered, then sat in the front room, snuggled under our duvets with hot chocolate and watched a Disney film. Then Christine popped round with a lovely chocolate cake and joined us. She is just so kind.

Frank finally fell asleep. I decided he needed to sleep with us tonight, so I can keep an eye on him. He's not settled at all in our new home. Perhaps it is attention, but I'm not convinced.

Thank you for keeping everyone safe, having a lovely afternoon and Christine's fabulous chocolate cake.

Saturday 5th October 2002

It was imperative today that I popped next door. I wanted to get the largest of the pretty pots from the potting shed. I've finally managed to clear a path to it and the weather is fine.

Unfortunately, the pot was heavier than I anticipated and as I staggered back out of the shed, I stumbled into the door frame. The whole shed groaned and creaked then began to sway. I just managed to get clear when the entire shed caved in.

It made a terrible sound. I could have been hurt, really you would think they would have realised how dangerous it was!

As I turned to run clear of the debris, I realised the blue-eyed brat was standing at the dividing fence staring at me. He looked as horrified and shocked as I felt.

I burst out laughing.

How must I have looked to him.

Possessed by a mischievous whim and still hugging the pot, I went to the gate and stepped toward him as if I was going to go through it, he screamed and turned tail and ran.

Strange child but how I laughed.

I was back in my garden when I heard the stupid woman telling him off for going near the poor potting shed. She entirely placed the blame for the carnage on his small shoulders.

I would have felt sorry for him if the whole thing hadn't

been so funny.

At least I have all I want from the potting shed, so it doesn't matter its gone.

I must admit I now have an impressive array of plants and pots from next door. I am almost running out of space. I think as the winter creeps in I may need to be more careful and cut the trips down a little.

My appointment came for the new clinic. I am quite excited to go and check the place out and wear my new outfits. I will be sure that my hair and nail appointments coincide with the dates.

Michael informed me that he and Seb are going to be away for a few days. The peace will be wonderful.

Friday 18/10/2002

I dropped Robbie off at school, then Frank and I went to the surgery.

Bobby had booked us in with a psychologist Dr Burns. He said she was a lovely lady and the best in her field.

We sat in the waiting area, Frank thought it was great not going to nursery, having special time with me and more importantly he could stand and watch the colourful fish in a very large round tank in the waiting area. He was so good until he turned round and shouted, 'Mummy it's the ghost lady.' Then screamed so loud that the receptionist came dashing out with two doctors, one I recognised as posh Chris.

The waiting room was full of ill people. I dashed over, but then felt a very uncomfortable feeling of something coming out of my trouser leg. I looked down and noticed my red lace thong sat for all to see in the middle of the floor. I wanted the ground to open up and swallow me.

Frank was inconsolable, bless him he couldn't stop sobbing. My heart was bleeding for him. He then wet himself.

From the corner of my eye, I'm sure I could see a woman smirking. But I couldn't be one hundred percent certain. She was then called in for her appointment which seemed to help Frank settle down.

Bobby dashed out of his consulting room looking very concerned and then saw everyone looking at us with my underwear lying there. He straightened up to look professional and in his doctors voice said, 'someone will be with you soon.' Then he walked away kicking my knickers under a chair.

How dare he act like a total pillock!

We were then called into Dr Burns consulting room.

I hugged Frank and carried him past all the nosy patients who were shaking their heads in disgust.

He was still sobbing about seeing the ghost lady.

Dr Burns was lovely, she managed to calm him down and let Frank talk to her. He was much better after she gave him a lolly.

Bobby knocked on the door and joined us. I glared at him. As he stood there all nice like a concerned father.

Dr Burns was more concerned about how Frank reacted in the waiting room.

This should've been a safe environment. She also asked the question if somebody had triggered his emotions, maybe someone he recognised?

Then it dawned on me was that it was that woman in the waiting area, Clarissa?

Bobby heard me say her name under my breath. He was

quick to interrupt and told me, 'Not to be so ridiculous.'

I threw him one of my looks. How dare he belittle me in front of his colleagues!

It did get me thinking about Frank. Has he actually been describing the woman next door all this time?

I had Frank's nursery bag with me that had some of his spare clothes, changed him in the surgery staff room then took Frank into town for a treat. I let him choose a new toy car and got Robbie another football, then we went to a cafe for hot chocolate.

When we got home, I asked Christine to watch Frank for five minutes, while I went to check the bottom of the garden.

I couldn't open the gate as it was padlocked so I stepped over the fence. I noticed the grass to the side was trampled down.

It would have been impossible for Frank to firstly open the gate and then to make a path to the bottom corner near the Cypress tree. I then spotted a little bit of material caught on a rusty nail by the fence. I wandered around and noticed holes in the ground, from a distance I thought there were rabbit or even mole holes until I fell down one and twisted my ankle really badly. The hole was far too large for an animal.

Someone must have been digging in our garden! And recently as the soil looked freshly dug. I started to crawl back towards the main garden and noticed a big blue button with gold circles, really unusual, lying near the old potting shed.

Christine must be a mind reader as she was coming out of the back door walking towards me with Frank, she helped me hobble back to the house and then checked my ankle. It was like a balloon and already starting to turn black and blue.

She rang Bobby, although I really didn't want to talk to him.

Left Frank and I on the sofa with the T.V. on and then went to pick Robbie up from school.

Christine looked after both the boys while Bobby took me to A&E.

I gave him the silent treatment, I'm too sore and upset to deal with him. Luckily, it's just a bad sprain, nothing broken. But I am on crutches.

Bobby made tea for us and sorted the boys for bed. We are still not talking.

Note to self, check the garden for holes and my jeans for underwear in leg before putting them on and maybe get a new husband!

Thank you Christine, where would I be without you.

Friday 18th October 2002

I was sat in the waiting room at the doctors when she arrived with the blue-eyed brat. She looked very pale and tired but was obviously putting on a show for the waiting room by attempting to sound and look like a perfect mother.

The child seemed happy enough and had quite rosy cheeks as he wandered to the fish tank to watch the fish.

It was when he turned around and our eyes met that the rosy cheeks disappeared, and the pale terrified expression returned with the inevitable tears. I was at first disappointed, then elated. Even though I haven't seen him for a few weeks he is clearly still aware of who I am.

He even wet himself, there in front of the whole waiting room. It was wonderful it made me want to laugh, then annoyingly I felt a small tinge of remorse.

I do feel perhaps a little sorry for him. I seem to continually get him into trouble and cause chaos.

Fortunately, I was called into see Dr Walton.

I stepped around the wisp of what clearly seemed to resemble red underwear, I'm sure that had come from that terrible woman's trouser, clearly she must be some type of floozy, even perhaps on the game, something else to add to my notebook. There was hardly any wonder she had lost her underwear they were so insubstantial, for heaven's sake, hardly worth wearing in the first place.

Even in the consulting room I could hear the commotion I had left; it was quite entertaining. Dr Walton even commented I was looking happier.

I told him I was feeling much happier in myself now the clinic appointment had come and if I could only rid myself of the terrible family next door my life would be perfect.

I have no idea why that made him frown.

He asked me what the problem was with my neighbours, and I explained how rowdy, uncouth and out of control they are. Not suitable for our neighbourhood at all.

I described that terrible woman and her inability to care for the children and then told him she was in fact the useless mother in the waiting room with the screaming brat at that very moment.

I think I may have described her in a little too much detail as on a few occasions as I spoke, he looked quite worried.

While I talked, I realised that she in fact reminded me in looks of someone I once knew. Many years ago. Someone best forgotten about. Someone I had to stop any thoughts about.

Yes, she had to go and soon.

I told him all I have been observing and about my notebook.

At that he started to look as though he was going to question me further, so I stopped him with my newest allegations. The one that could possibly rid me of her.

The drug abuse. Oh yes that made his ears prick up.

He dared to ask me if I had proof. I explained I didn't need proof my word was good enough.

Talking to him has given me such a good idea.

He is so kind always looking out for me. He has offered to arrange to bring my clinic appointment forward, which is wonderful.

I wanted to tell Michael about the visit but as usual he was busy with Seb and didn't come home until late.

I feel so much happier having formed a new plan to rid us of next door.

I popped through to their garden to see if there was any sign of the blue-eyed brat, but all seemed very quiet and dark in the back of the house, he must, I suppose, be sleeping after his eventful day.

Thursday 31/10/2002

I keep forgetting things, feeling sick, needing to sleep and then wanting to cry. Perhaps it's because I'm still so worried about Frank. I have to say since he's had a few more sessions with Dr Burns he does seem to be more settled.

Being pregnant and on these stupid crutches, hasn't helped. I feel so useless. I don't remember feeling this rubbish when I was carrying the boys.

Ginger biscuits were my saviour last time. Now I need

to carry a pot of Vick vapour rub to keep having a sniff. I also have a massive craving for Fisherman's Friends throat sweets. Bobby has gone out at all hours to get them for me. Happy wife Happy life! - Not sure that's the case at the moment, he still seems to be really grumpy with me, I did point out he is part to blame for my condition.

It maybe because he feels very awkward when he's purchased ten packets of Fisherman's Friends at a time!

Beth has been amazing over the last week, she has helped with the boys and taking me around the supermarket. It's been so lovely to see her again. I have really missed her.

I think she must be seeing someone as there's a little glint in her eye and is just looking even more radiant, but she's been very secretive. I wonder who he is?

Had a good rest this afternoon and arranged for some of the nice mums to come round with their children so we can all go trick or treating together.

I'd planned a few games, apple dunking and picking sweets out of flour.

Christine came to help. I don't think she thought it would get as loud and messy as it did.

It was funny seeing the children in their fabulous halloween outfits covered in flour. We left a white trail down a few drives. They had a great time. And so did Hannah. Who turned up with so many sweets that sent the children hyper!

There weren't many houses with pumpkins outside. I don't think they are used to children in our area, so the kids walked up and down the street several times making lots of spooky noises.

Bobby and Beth both arrived at the same time to help out.

Thank you for my lovely friends, where would I be without

them?

Thursday 31st October 2002

I had my first appointment at the Clinic today, following yesterday's phone call from Ms Georgina DiFiore's personal assistant, Wendy.

It's such a lovely, elegant building, with all the latest security, one really felt that once you stepped over the threshold, they planned to keep you.

Ms DiFiore is wonderful. Very tall and elegant wearing a black Dior dress and perfectly manicured.

She remembered to ensure I was seated and comfortable before she sat down. A clear mark of respect to my status.

She was very interested in who I am and Michael's position in the community. She asked how we had met and for a terrible second, I felt as though I was looking into a deep black hole. She must have realised she was being far to inquisitive when I pulled myself together and suggested she was perhaps asking too many personal questions for our first acquaintance, she had the grace to look concerned.

I think she will possibly be glad to strike up a good relationship with me as she is clearly interested in my social status. Perhaps I could introduce her to Seb at some point. They would make an interesting couple. I might suggest it next week when I see her again.

Michael arrived home at seven this evening he said as he was pulling into the drive, he noticed next doors brats trawling the streets howling and leaving flowery footprints all over the paths. He thought he saw Mrs Wade and another woman who he almost thought was Jo-Hannah Smythe.

I suggested he was quite mistaken.

He raised his eyebrows at me, so I didn't pursue the subject as he so dislikes being wrong. But honestly what a ridiculous idea.

As for Mrs Wade perhaps I should ask her for coffee and have a chat about the amount of time she is spending next door.

Friday 1/11/2002

Dropped the boys off at school and nursery, then dashed up to the hospital for my first scan. Bobby couldn't make it as he had a full clinic.

I really wish he was with me. Especially when the radiographer said congratulations on your healthy twins!

I just burst into tears. I can't cope with two, how am I going to cope with four?

I sat on the hospital toilet for about half an hour crying.

Finally got home after trying Bobby several times. Sniffing my Vick as I was driving. Sometimes I wish he would put our family first before his patients. He's been working so many extra hours lately.

Walked into the house to see a letter on the door mat. The envelope had beautiful handwriting. Thought it may be something exciting, maybe an invitation to cheer me up.

Sat down with another packet of Fisherman's friends and read.

I am still in shock. How can a beautifully written letter be so vile. It was from that woman next door. That nasty, nasty woman! I felt really angry at first but then so upset.

I tried Bobby again, but he was still busy.

Went to get Frank from nursery and cried all the way there.

Got back home and Bobby finally rang,

I struggled to read the letter to him, especially the part about.

"I have seen you sniffing drugs and unless you want me to notify the police I suggest you take notice of this letter. There is no wonder your children look so unkempt; I will have no choice but to report their neglect to the appropriate services if I see you doing it again!"

My children are my world. I could not survive if anyone took them away.

Who does she think she is? The Ice Queen next door. I blabbered to Bobby.

Frank overheard and thought we now live next door to an Ice Cream lady! At least it wasn't Clarissa the Cow he overheard, which is what I really wanted to say.

Finally finished sobbing, took a breath and them mentioned we were having twins.

The only response I got was 'Thank you very much for letting me know. Unfortunately, I have to go as my next patient is waiting'.

End of conversation!

At least I had Frank to give me a big hug.

I felt like I had to sneak out of our home to do the school run. Making sure I avoided that woman.

I want to move. I want to go back to our lovely old home. I want things to be as they were. I want my old Bobby back.

I wonder how my real mum must have felt when her life was turned upside down. There is one thing for sure I'm never giving up on my children or this pregnancy. I will never do to them what she did to me.

Christine must have seen me looking upset because she was waiting for me when I came back from school, bless her. I showed her the letter and read.

'I have decided to write to you, as I can no longer tolerate your behaviour.

I feel it needs to be said you are a disgrace to our neighbourhood with your unruly, filthy children. You need to respect that this is not the type of area for trawling your brats around the streets during the day and especially not at night.'

Christine didn't say a word, she just got up and gave me a big hug. I think it must have upset her as well.

Note to self never having sex again! Pregnancy is not all it's cracked up to be.

I really wish mum and dad were here. Not a good day.

Friday 1st November 2002

I have decided that as Michael feels unable to confront next door I will. After all it's for her own good.

They made an absolute mess on the street parading up and down making wailing noises and leaving flour prints at Halloween. Luckily, they did not come here.

I also saw her, several times sniffing a substance from a container, both on the street, in her car and in the garden. I knew she was on drugs now I have the proof. Probably her husband is supplying them!

Seb suggested I should not make that kind of accusation, but he's always prepared to give people the benefit of the doubt. I told Michael they need reporting to the police again, but he just grunted and changed the subject.

So, I have taken it on myself and written a very stern letter, telling her I know she's a drug addict and she should be ashamed of herself. Pointing out also that her brats are out of control and are not welcome to trawl up and down our street. I have made it clear the street is not a public car park and her visitors need to park elsewhere, also any deliveries need to be made more discreetly.

I mentioned that I will be speaking to Mrs Smythe and telling her that she is passing herself off as a friend and that Mrs Smythe will be mortified as she is an upstanding member of our community so would not fraternise with the likes of her.

My letter was her opportunity to realise she needed to move before I involved the police.

I was, therefore, very surprised when Mrs Wade, obviously very angry, came banging at my front door! She was quite oblivious to the fact she could be seen and heard by the entire street!!! She said that she had seen my letter, and I ought to be ashamed of myself. She had the audacity to tell me I do not speak for the street, and I have an entirely wrong opinion of the family next door.

She was so angry that Michael came and asked what on earth I had done to cause such a fuss.

Mrs Wade felt she would tell him in her own words. She made me sound terrible and I'm quite certain I was just pointing out the facts. As if that wasn't bad enough, Seb arrived in the middle of it all. As usual he had a calming effect but ordered Michael to remove me into the house.

I was very angry when he came in and suggested I had acted maliciously and needed to apologise before the situation got worse. Sometimes I do think he has too much of an opinion. Michael as usual sided with him. Men what do they know. I don't know why the stupid woman didn't keep it to herself instead of causing all this upset.

I certainly won't be apologising! Although I suppose I do feel a little sorry that she has reacted so badly instead of just moving. I didn't expect her to react by discussing me with the neighbours.

I will mention the scenario to Georgina at the clinic, I am sure she will agree that this was the only way to deal with this situation without involving the police. She will understand the importance of not letting situations slide.

Quite inappropriate.

I have been thinking about her and the brats all day, it completely ruined what could have been a nice day. If only they would just MOVE

Needless to say, there was no sign of her all day she kept very quiet and out of the way.

Monday 11/11/2002

Feeling so drained after a terrible weekend.

Bobby and I argued over next doors' letter. I've told him he needs to go round and defend us. He says he's not allowed!

Not allowed, more like he doesn't want to confront the evil cow.

He's told me I have to rise above it. How can I rise above it. She's a sick and twisted woman.

Why has she made all these horrible accusations about me. What have I done so wrong to upset her?

If I had married Bill Long he would have gone round and

planted her one. (Although that is the reason why I didn't marry Block Head Bill). Why has that thought just popped into my head? I know violence is not the answer. I just feel so hurt, angry, upset. I don't know what to do with myself.

Last night I dreamt that I gave the Ice Queen a piece of my mind. She apologised and we became best friends. Then I woke up.

Told Bobby about my dream and he told me I was getting obsessed and went to work without telling me he loved me. He's never done that before.

Spoke to mum earlier. She told me to meditate and believe in Karma. I asked her how long Karma takes to kick in?

She told me to calm down as getting upset over something you can't control is not the way forward. I know she's right. But it's so hard.

I told mum I hate living here, apart from I love our new house, I love the garden, the schools and Christine. She just told me to focus on the positives.

When Bobby came home he told me not to stress as it's not good for the babies. (More like not good for him), I was still upset.

It's ok for him he's not here during the day and having to sneak out of the house. I feel sick in our own home. I never want to see that woman again.

Bobby then produced a lovely bunch of flowers with a new pot of Vick vapour rub in the middle. He then said he'd arranged a treat with Hannah to help me feel better and gave me a big hug. I felt better. Making up hugs are always the best. But I still feel a mess inside.

Perhaps everyone is right.

I'm going to have a long bath then fall asleep to my positive affirmation C.D.

Tomorrow is another day.

Thank you for my lovely flowers - staying positive is not always easy.

Monday 11th November 2002

Letter printed out for Georgina

To My Neighbour

I have decided to write to you, as I can no longer tolerate your behaviour.

I feel it needs to be said you are a disgrace to our neighbourhood with your unruly, filthy children.

You need to respect that this is not the type of area for trawling your brats around the streets during the day and especially not at night.

I have had to send away white, unmarked vans, attempting to park outside my house and put notes on all the cars using the street as a car park while partying in your back garden. This is quite unacceptable completely lowering the tone!!!

You are wasting taxpayers' money by causing me to have to send for the fire brigade to assist you in putting out your smelly fire and prevent you from setting fire to the boundary hedge and fence.

I would also add it is quite unacceptable for you to have naked men working in your garden, while you blatantly ogle their body. I was appalled and shocked at the sight of him wielding his power tool. I am very unhappy you have lowered the hedge to the height of the fence as your garden looks more like a play area than respectable garden. Again, I stress lowering the tone of our area and unacceptable.

I would suggest that as you have no sense of decorum, nor the ability to bring the property back into keeping with the rest of the street, you consider moving back to where you came from or an area more suiting your status.

I have seen you sniffing drugs and unless you want me to notify the police, I suggest you take notice of this letter. I am aware your husband must clearly be supplying you with them as no one in this area would dream of doing such a shameful thing. There is no wonder your children look so unkempt; I will have no choice but to report their neglect to the appropriate services.

It has also come to my attention you are passing yourself off as a friend of the Smythes. You need to stop this at once as they are friends of mine and hold an important social status which you cannot possibly aspire to.

I hope you will take note of my advice as I'm sure you cannot be happy as you look worn out and on days quite ill.

Your Sincerely

Mrs C. Devonshire

I had another meeting with Georgina at the clinic today.

She started to dominate the meeting by asking me about my relationship with Michael.

I had to remind her it is none of her business and I quickly suggested what I had to say was far more important.

She looked very curious as I handed her the letter I have

sent to next door, the authorities and Dr Walton. I had copied it for her to have.

The expression on her face as she read it showed quite clearly her distaste and sympathy for my situation, but her questioning if I was aware of the consequences of such a letter and its accusations was quite unexpected. I suppose she felt concerned for me.

Of course, I know there will be repercussions, but they should not be directed at me as my part in this is complete. I have aired my concerns now they just have to move. It really is that simple.

She looked very concerned and kept trying to interrupt me, most annoying. I really expected her to be more supportive instead she was more interested in why I felt that that woman shouldn't have involved Mrs Wade and that I was no longer involved.

Honestly, I feel she has just made me out to be the villain, not at all what one would have expected from such a distinguished professional.

I have spent all day wondering why on earth everyone seems to be shocked by what I have done, after all it's for their own good and that of the area.

I spent a while looking into their garden. I seem to have most of what I need for mine, but I do miss the excitement of popping round. The silly blue-eyed brat has not been seen since the surgery.

I must say I have quite missed entertaining him with my wickedness.

Saturday 30/11/2002

Felt very sick first thing this morning. I'm sure it wasn't just from my pregnancy as my Fisherman's friends and Vick sniffing didn't help.

Struggling with horrible flash backs to that evil letter she sent. I sat and cried. Am I really such a bad mother? Is that what people think of me?

And to add to my upset I was getting into a right flap about tonight.

Bobby has insisted we should join Hannah and John at the golf club for an early Christmas event and have some time together without the boys. I wasn't sure. I'm really not in a great place. But Bobby thought it would do us the world of good. Christine agreed with Bobby and offered to babysit.

I think Christine has been checking up on me and reporting back to him. Any excuse to come round. Bless her. She's so lovely.

Then Hannah turned up about eleven o'clock for my surprise Bobby had organised.

John went to pick Frank up from nursery and kept him entertained until it was time to collect Robbie from school.

We went out for a light lunch, then Hannah took me to her friends dress shop, and I chose a fabulous knee length black dress with long chiffon sleeves and a few sparkles that fitted perfectly over my growing boobs and little bump.

She then took me for a make-over. It was so lovely to be pampered. I felt a million dollars, my hair was curled, and my make-up was like a movie star. I felt so much better.

By the time I got back home, Bobby was feeding the boys. I told him not to look until I was dressed.

Didn't fancy wearing high heels as my ankle was still sore,

so I wore boots and socks. Not quite the image Bobby was expecting with my new dress. But I love my pink and green striped fluffy socks. Anyway, there's only me and Bobby who knows what I'm wearing. Fur coat and no knickers springs to mind!

It's been a long time since I saw him look at me like he used to. I was really worried he'd forgotten me.

Hannah and John were waiting at the door of the golf club to greet us.

I was impressed. I never thought that a boring golf club could be so ornate. It was like walking into an old mansion with its mahogany panelled walls, an amazing stone fireplace with a real fire. All tastefully decorated with beautiful Christmas garlands, and a huge show stopping Christmas tree, it was amazing!

I've told Bobby I want a fabulous tree like that. He smiled and nodded.

Then I spotted The Ice Queen and her miserable other half.

I felt sick again and couldn't stop shaking. I really wasn't expecting to see that nasty cow.

Hannah must have seen my face as she introduced and surrounded me with a group of her friends.

I thought they would be all talking about hitting a little ball with a stick and speaking their own language, Bogey, Birdie, Eagle. But actually, they were chatting about babies and how amazing I looked. They were so kind. I really needed that boost.

There was a really good-looking man stood with Ice Queen and miserable Michael. He made a move over to Bobby and John. It was so weird. I thought he was going to have a go at Bobby, but all he did was smile and kept touching his arm.

Hannah introduced me to the man, he's called Seb.

I said how impressed I was with the Christmas decorations. He said he organises and decorates the tree every year and was more than happy to help me with ours. He's lovely.

He passed Bobby his number and said call me. I winked at Bobby and said of course he will. John turned away choking on his drink.

I said to Bobby I think you've got an admirer. Bobby just gave me one of his looks.

To make my night you should have seen the faces of them next door. I didn't see them after that.

Excited for getting a big Christmas tree. Thank you for an amazing pamper and actually a pleasant evening.

Saturday 30th November 2002

Today began wonderfully. New dress, nails manicured.

I was so excited to be getting dressed up for a lovely evening with Michael and Seb.

Seb picked us up in the Rolls Royce, he looked immaculate and dapper as usual, and Michael looked charming.

I must admit I looked very well groomed for the occasion, not at all how I have been looking as I have gone through the hedge to next door, the comparison made me smile.

Seb, bless him did take a moment, as I got in the car, to tell me I looked lovely. It was very kind of him as I'm never certain Michael even notices.

At least I knew I was up to Sebs standards so that was good enough.

The Golf club was terribly busy.

I don't know what on earth was wrong with Michael, his gout must have been playing up as he became very grumpy when Seb joined The Smythe's and was formally introduced to the new GP, who incidentally is genuinely nice looking and looks as if he plays a lot of sport. Seb didn't introduce us or include us in the conversation, so we stayed with the Carrick's listening to their rather boring story of their recent cruise.

It was unusual for Seb to wander off and leave us and could in some ways explain why Michael felt a little put out. After all we are his closest and most important friends

I was looking for Jo-Hannah Smythe so that I could impress her with my dress, but she seemed very deep in conversation with a group of ladies, and I was completely unable to catch her eye. I almost felt she was excluding and avoiding me, though why she would I have no idea. Just me being silly I'm sure.

Seb spent so much time chatting to John and the new GP that Michael in the end wandered off to the bar and then just as I was speaking to Mrs Giles who was wondering who Jo-Hannah's new friend is, who was entertaining her circle and keeping her so busy, Michael announced he had booked us a taxi and we were leaving, so frustrating and so intriguing.

I must try and find out more about who her new friend is and perhaps invite the new lady to coffee.

I will ring round tomorrow and see who has met her. It was so difficult to get a look for myself. Perhaps she is someone new to the area.

Friday 13/12/2002

Woke up to a cup of tea beside the bed. Feeling so much better about life and my morning sickness seems to be settling. I've not heard or seen them next door. But I'm still keeping a very low profile.

Played my positive affirmation C.D. while I got ready as needed to be organised for school and nursery. Robbie wanted to give all his Christmas cards to his friends in the playground before school started. So that gave us a little more time to get to nursery for Frank's first Christmas Nativity play.

I asked Christine to join us as she's been amazing as always, helping me with Frank's costume. She is so good at art.

Frank was very excited to be an Italian flag!

I get Joseph, Mary, angels and shepherds. But not an **Italian flag**! It would have been so much easier for Frank to wear a dressing gown and tea towel on his head rather than an attempt at making him into the only flag. Maybe there were some hidden flags in baby Jesus's stable.

I'm so pleased Bobby managed to slip out of work to join us. I could see him stood by the doorway. There wasn't a spare seat available.

I probably shouldn't have giggled, but when Frank walked onto the stage carrying his very large toy fire engine passionately singing 'Away in a manger' with the sirens and flashing lights. I found it quite amusing.

Unfortunately, some of the other parents didn't and I got quite a few unpleasant glares. Am I the only one with free spirited children?

I glanced over to Bobby who was suddenly looking a bit

cross. He then sloped off.

Well, it is Friday the thirteenth.

It was so lovely seeing the play and seeing Frank like his little old self. A moment in time that will never be relived.

Christine invited us back to hers for lunch.

Frank loved his costume so much he kept it on until bedtime.

Mum called again and said she was very disappointed she couldn't join us. I can't wait to see them next week.

She gave me a little more advise, that at the end of every day write down three positive things that have happened even if you feel they are very small.

Thank you for my cup of tea in bed.

Thank you for Franks amazing nativity performance.

Thank you Christine for making the best Italian flag ever.

Friday 13th December 2002

Well today has been very interesting.

I met with Georgina at the clinic, although she is very reluctant to engage with me about herself, she did manage to persuade me to tell her about my up bringing. It was most strange to hear myself telling her about my rather rigid childhood.

I have not really thought about my parents since mother died ten years ago. It occurred to me today, what a terrible bitter and twisted woman she was. I would hope to goodness I never end up so cantankerous.

Father, on the other hand was always so strict and unapproachable I had very little to do with him until he introduced me to Michael shortly before we married, but he clearly had my best interest at heart. I see that now, although at the time I would have disagreed.

Georgina wondered why I would make that comment. Silly young woman should be able to answer her own question just by looking at me.

I have a good social position, a beautiful home and I am the perfect wife, yet her question has quite unsettled me for some reason.

Heavens knows what Michael would say if I told him about her questioning. He would probably stop me from seeing her again. I find her so curious that I would quite miss going, besides, I really do need to get her to open up about herself so that I can assess her suitability for Seb. She just has this uncanny knack of keeping me talking about myself, then that leads me to question things in my life that are best left alone and forgotten.

I saw the blue-eyed brat while I was looking out of the window. He was laughing and appeared, for some strange reason to be dressed as the Italian flag. Heavens knows what that woman was taking to prompt her to do that to him. At least Mrs Wade was with them so he was with one responsible adult at least, I really don't approve of the amount of time she spends with that woman, but she clearly has concerns for the children, or she wouldn't do it. She will be very lonely when they go.

If I had been his mother, he would not have been out in public dressed in such away! It makes you wonder what kind of parents that woman had.

I am terribly frustrated that I didn't realise there was no one home next door. I do keep meaning to pop round and perhaps slip into the house to see if there is any sign of them leaving.

Michael has been hanging around the house such a lot since the do at the golf club it is quite annoying. I can't even pop through the hedge as he might notice.

At least he is spending a lot of the time in the study. I know better than to interrupt him when he is in there.

I tried to contact Mrs Giles today to see if there was an update on the Smythe's new protégée.

Everyone seems to be so terribly busy preparing for family Christmases that it is impossible to catch anyone. Most inconvenient. I can't imagine what all the fuss is about.

Such a relief it is always just Michael, Seb and I, all quiet and civilised, just as Michael likes it. Seb once commented Christmas is a time for children and Michael said he disagreed. Children were an encumbrance and germ riddled expensive accessories. Judging by Seb's expression I don't think he quite agreed.

Saturday 14/12/2002

I do think the positive affirmation CDs are working. I'm feeling much better about our home and the boys are back playing in the garden, when the weather allows it!

Frank seems to be doing really well. He's not mentioned the ghost lady for some time and his therapy sessions are almost finished.

I got a phone call from Bobby saying to look out for a surprise delivery.

I thought he meant mum and dad. As I've been so excited to see them again. I really do miss my parents.

But it turns out the surprise came on an incredibly large lorry. How it got down the road I have no idea. Driving an articulated lorry is one job I would hate to do. I struggle with our family car at times. I imagine I'd be knocking most of Britain's fences down if I was a truck driver. Although at the moment there is one person's fence I feel I'd like to knock down!

Anyway, stop the negatives Seren, this drop-dead gorgeous driver got out. I did think maybe he was my surprise, dare not mention that to Bobby!

(I hope he doesn't read my journals)

He smiled nicely and said, "Where do you want it love?" There were a few answers that popped into my head. Then he lifted his cover up and showed me his Christmas trees.

I stood open mouthed. I know I said I wanted a big tree, but I wasn't expecting one to come from the Sequoia forest.

The driver just flung this big tree over his shoulder and said, "Shall I follow you love?"

I was very tempted to say yes please, forgetting about the boys jumping up and down with excitement.

Luckily mum and dad arrived with Bobby.

Bobby was grinning ear to ear. It turns out our tree was a gift from Seb.

All that flirting Bobby did at the golf club paid off.

The driver kindly left the tree in the hallway.

I took great pleasure in watching him walk back up the drive. (I must stop these naughty thoughts. Blame my hormones).

It was wonderful to see mum and dad, they look so well. I'm so excited to hear about their travels.

Hannah and John popped round. I know Hannah has been

checking up on me. Bobby must have told them about the letter and how upset I was.

Hannah in her graceful way was asking me if I was alright and implying Clarissa the cow is really not worth it and isn't very popular at the golf club. It's nothing personal with Clarissa she's like that with everyone.

Perhaps I need to be more accommodating. I've been so focused on me and the boys. She's maybe going through some terrible trauma in her life.

We then spent the rest of the day playing Christmas music and decorating our massive tree.

Thank you mum and dad for coming to stay with us.

Thank you Bobby and Seb for organising our lovely surprise.

Thank you to the hunky lorry driver for delivering our lovely big Christmas tree and giving me something nice to look at.

Saturday 14th December 2002

I was very excited to see the lorry arrive on the street today with the Christmas trees.

I was sure it was the haulage firm Seb uses, but it wasn't for us, most disappointing.

I watched from the bedroom window as the driver lifted the cover. He was very tall and clearly used to manual labour as he made light work of lifting a good eight-foot tree off the back.

She was at the end of the drive with the out-of-control children, smiling very flirtatiously, when she managed to close her mouth and stop fawning over him it was clear, she was attracted to his physique, she was quite unable to take her eyes off him when he slung the tree over his shoulder.

He really was quite a sight.

I don't know how her husband puts up with her continual flow of men built like hunks parading around for her.

In the midst of all this, her poor husband arrived home with a couple who looked like they had flown in from somewhere exotic as they had very nice luggage and looked wonderfully tanned.

I thought the husband looked vaguely familiar to me, but then the lorry driver came back to the lorry and stood exchanging pleasantries with them before leaping back into the cab.

I was very angry when as he pulled forward to reverse back down the street, he pulled up onto the grass verge, so I have taken the number of the company and will get Michael to phone and complain about the damage to the grass.

My letter to next door, seems to have had little or no effect, which is most annoying. Although I am not unreasonable, I suppose they can't really move this close to Christmas with children. Let's just hope that she continues to stay out of my sight.

Mrs Wade has continued to be overly involved in visiting, perhaps I can catch her and see what they are planning.

I won't be able to slip into the garden while she has visitors which is such an inconvenience as I do like to visit just to keep an eye on things.

Monday 16/12/2002

Mum and dad went to Hannah and Johns by taxi last night

but decided to stay over as it snowed. It was a shame they missed out the boys snow fun today. Love snow days.

It was announced on the radio that school and nursery have been closed.

Everything picture white. So beautiful. The boys were super excited, rushed breakfast, wrapped up and off into the back garden.

Bobby couldn't get the car out of the drive, so he worked from home telephone triaging, which was brilliant. That meant he could sneak out and play with the boys. They spent all morning making a massive igloo. It was amazing.

I took them out some little stools so they could sit and have crisps and hot chocolate in it.

It got a bit cold and wet for me, and Bobby had to do some work. The boys were having so much fun, we just left them playing.

Robbie and Frank then went to the front garden to build snowmen. Bless them, I gave them some carrots and potatoes, hats and scarves.

I did have to remind the boys to avoid yellow snow. Why would any mother make that comment to their children.

It turns out Robbie is a bit of an artist. They came dashing in to show us their master pieces.

I was a little shocked to see that the potatoes and carrots were not used for eyes and a nose. Instead, we have an orange-coloured penis with potatoes for testicles!

How do you tell them off when they tell me they have built daddy! I don't think I can look at carrots or Bobby come to that, the same way again.

Homemade carrot soup for tea, bath and bed. The boys were worn out.

Very large glass of wine for Bobby and an herbal tea for me, then mum and dad joined us and commented on the amazing sculptors!

Thank you for a lovely snow day.

Monday 16th December 2002

Michael was furious today.

I had watched the brats rolling around in the snow in the back garden and making a terrible amount of noise, then I thought they had gone in, after all it was very cold, what kind of mother lets her children out in snow.

Apparently, he could hear the brats next door out in the front garden and wondered what was going on as they were shouting about yellow snow. When he looked, he was most shocked to see a large orange penis on a snowman, I mean really what kind of mother allows that sort of thing and in the front garden.

What will people think when passing?

Poor Michael was nearly apoplectic over it, I thought he was going to go around and make a complaint but instead he forbade me to look out of the window at the front garden, saying it was not something I should see, it was an obscene sight and he had closed the curtains so that I couldn't see it and be offended.

He was so put out he phoned our local MP who seemed to suggest he might be overreacting somewhat. That just made Michael angrier, and I was glad when he said he was going out after he had slammed the phone down.

Of course, when he stormed off to go to Sebs, I had to

look, I mean how could I not, it was just all so disgusting as Michael had said. I took some photographs in case it melted so that perhaps someone from the council might pop around and take Michaels complaint more seriously.

Tuesday 24/12/2002 - Christmas Eve

Despite all the stress of organising everything our house looks amazing and even smells of Christmas! I'm so excited about our first Christmas here.

I've put decorations in almost every room, including all the boys Christmas artwork. Even the windows are covered.

I've got Christmas cinnamon and fern toilet sprays for the bathrooms, Father Christmas soap dispensers and Christmas bathmats. Mum helped me change all the bedding, so we all have Father Christmas quilt covers and Christmas tea towels with matching oven gloves. Not sure how impressed Bobby was, but it makes me smile.

The boys had finished their chocolate advent calendars on the 5th of December, so I'd bought them both a chocolate Father Christmas which they ate for breakfast.

Everyone has admired our big tree. Mum commented on how artistically talented I am. I don't know why but I did wonder if my real parents were artists.

I've put the boys Christmas decorations they made at school and nursery to the front the tree so everyone can see them. I'm still not sure if an Italian flag is an actual Christmas decoration. But who cares. Frank loves it.

Hannah in her wisdom has advised me the best way to deal with Clarissa the cow (I really must stop calling her that) is to invite all the neighbours round for Christmas drinks and to include Seb, as he's a really lovely man and seems to be a calming influence on Clarissa.

Bobby was very proud of me sending the invite, well I actually got Robbie to post it with a Christmas card. It is the season of goodwill after all.

I want to give our boys the perfect memories like I had as a child.

I've been telling them for weeks that the alarm sensor in the hallway is Father Christmas checking in on them to make sure they are behaving themselves.

I've caught Robbie quite a few times scaling over the banister and sliding down the wall to avoid the red sensor, so he wasn't spotted by Santa.

Am I a bad mother, telling my boys some random man in a red suit is watching them. I hope they don't have nightmares about it.

But it has been a brilliant way to blackmail them.

The Turkey was delivered at mid-day.

Peter, Helen and Beth all arrived early afternoon.

Christmas music blasting and mulled wine.

We all sat around the table peeling the veg. Although the shape of the vegetables did vary by the time they got to their fourth bottle of mulled wine.

It's quite amusing being sober watching your parents and in-laws get absolutely hammered.

Mum had brought the traditional Christmas Eve pork pie and Helen had made a very alcoholic pudding! I did try a spoonful. It would have been rude not to. I'm sure it wouldn't harm the babies. After all it would be diluted between the two of them.

I was a little bit worried at one point that Father Christmas may not be able to deliver all the presents. Especially as they were hidden in the attic.

I haven't seen Bobby this drunk for a long time. It was so good to have my Bobby back having fun.

The boys then started to run a riot! They were so excited. So, we put a Christmas DVD on to try and calm the boys down. That didn't last too long as Mum had brought some reindeer food for them to spread all over the garden. Which just hyped them up again.

Our drive looked beautiful with all its sparkle, although not quite sure about the porridge oats. But on a positive the wildlife will have something nice to eat.

We decided Father Christmas and his elves were drinking Peter's 30-year-old whiskey. It was quite amusing to see six whiskey glasses lined up on the fireplace next to carrots and minced pies.

Trying to put the boys to bed was a nightmare, constantly up and down checking if Father Christmas had been.

Everyone had to wait a long time before they could drink Father Christmas's whiskey. I had a glass of milk.

How the men did not wake the boys up climbing around the attic, I have no idea.

2am Bed!

Thank you for our first Christmas in our fabulous new home. Thank you for my wonderful family.

Thank you for keeping Father Christmas safe in the attic while getting the presents.

Merry Christmas.

Tuesday 24th December 2002

I was surprised and extremely annoyed, to receive an invitation, clearly from next door, addressed to Michael and I, inviting us round for Christmas drinks.

Really, she has no dignity. I don't know who she thinks she is, gossiping about me to Mrs Wade and then asking us to some do, as if she is a suitable neighbour for us to fraternise with.

Needless to say, I dropped it into the bin and did not bother Michael with it.

I suppose the street will turn into her personal car park again. If it's not to icy, I will pop out and ticket the cars, or maybe I should advise the police that her house is full of drunk drivers. After all that would be the right thing to do.

I watched the brats outside, laughing and jumping around with the older woman, probably her mother-in-law as she looks nothing like her.

Maybe I should try and ask Mrs Wade to introduce me to her so that I can fill her in on the problems with them living there. She may understand this is completely the wrong area for them and get them to move on. It's unlikely she will be happy with that woman being married to her son anyway. So, she is bound to be understanding.

The blue-eyed brat looked quite perky and happy. Shouting about Rudolph, I presume the reindeer, and throwing some sort of food around the garden, no doubt we will be infested by rats before the new year.

I've spent all day preparing for tomorrow.

I asked Michael to source a Christmas tree, but he was very grumpy and at teatime appeared with a very worn out looking artificial tree, that apparently belonged to his mother when he was a boy.

It's terrible, I can't possibly put it up and he flatly refused to go out and buy one saying it was too cold and who was I planning to impress.

I pointed out that Seb always has a beautiful real tree and would be appalled by ours this year. Michael was very churlish and suggested Seb provide and decorate the tree if he was so good at it.

I do wonder why this year Seb hasn't sent us one like he usually does, it's most unlike him and I haven't seen him to ask. I was so sure the tree delivered to next door was for us. I expect she pretended to be me so she could steal it as a retaliation for all the times I sent her stupid oven delivery back, saying they had the wrong address.

I really don't know what the matter is with Michael, since the golf club do, he has been so much grumpier and at times quite rude and unkind to me. Seb obviously feels there is a problem because he has been noticeably absent.

I have tried to discover who the mystery new woman is from the golf club, but no one seems to know who I am talking about, and Michael has been less than talkative. Perhaps I will ask Seb to enquire on my behalf when he comes for lunch tomorrow.

I was quite disappointed that Michael refused to go to Mass this evening. I couldn't possibly attend alone.

I have another visit to the clinic between now and new year perhaps I could ask Georgina if she can suggest something to cheer Michael up, after all she is extremely fascinated by us and our lives.

Wednesday 25/12/2002 - Christmas Day

5am wakeup call! Robbie and Frank were so excited. We told them that Father Christmas had left us a letter saying his toys were magic and if they went downstairs before 8.00am they would turn to ash. The boys went back to bed.

Bobbie crept downstairs to set up the video camera, so we could capture the magic on their faces.

Honestly, I've never seen so many presents in one room. It looked like Santa's grotto.

Bobby chuntered away. I hope that's not captured on video. He was a real bah humbug. I don't suppose his hangover would have helped.

Mum and Dad, Helen, Peter and Beth all joined in.

Everyone had their own Christmas stocking. The front room was a mass of wrapping paper. You couldn't see the floor.

The boys thought it was hysterical that their Papa, Grandad and Bobby all got a potato, carrot and a large stone in their stockings.

It was magical!

My parents took the boys to ride up and down the street on their new scooters and use their walkie talkies. I think they missed the point of a walkie talkie because all they did was shout at each other. I could hear them in the dining room.

Turkey in the oven. Bobby and his dad were in charge of cooking Christmas dinner. So, everything was at the ready with all the timings written down.

I was really looking forward to our day, but I still had my reservations about The Ice Queen and her husband coming round. I just hoped Frank does not ask her for an ice cream.

11.00am on the dot. Christine and Seb arrived at the same

time. Both producing a bottle of Champagne. Hannah and John came by taxi not long after.

I thought The Ice Queen and Michael would have been prompt but there was no sign of them.

Once the Champagne was flowing for everyone. I didn't give them a second thought. We were all having such a fabulous time, we invited everyone to stay for Christmas dinner. Obviously all the timings went out of the window.

My only job was to make the gravy. I thought I'd got this to a fine art. So, I'm not sure what went wrong. One lump or two? Maybe because I've usually made gravy with a glass of wine in one hand.

Christine, after laughing at my efforts nipped home with Seb to get her large sieve to de-lump the gravy.

Seb's really funny, lovely to talk to and extremely charming.

At one point Christine and Seb were sat giggling in a corner like two naughty children. You'd never have thought Christine is in her 70's.

It also turns out that Peter, John and Seb all went to the same school. It was like the old times for them, remembering the good old days. I think even Bobby was quite shocked with some of their stories.

I still don't understand why Beth is still single. I'd hoped she may have caught Seb's eye. But I'm not sure Beth is what he's after.

She was very quiet, and I noticed she wasn't drinking as much. Beth seemed to have lost her sparkle. Very out of character.

We all played Pictionary but had to stop once the drawings were getting too rude. I think Robbie knows a lot more than we think about life! So, we changed to play charades.

Frank loved it trying to act our Thomas the Tank Engine. He went to pick up the video cover and pointed at it. He was so sweet when Papa shouted out Spider-man and Harry Potter. He kept saying 'Oh Papa, it's easy.' Robbie shouted out the answer and Frank jumped on Papa, poor dad and then he fell asleep.

At that point, the rest of the adults just kept drinking until 2.30am!

I am shattered!

Thank you for my wonderful family and lovely, lovely friends and neighbours. Thank you for Clarissa and Michael not turning up. Thank you for an amazing magical Christmas day.

Wednesday 25th December 2002

Here we are yet another Christmas day. It did begin so well. I was so excited that Seb was due for lunch I gave in and put the tree up.

It was a glory of pinks, purples and blacks and really looked quite eye catching despite its age. Michael raised his eyebrows and said nothing, he appeared quite speechless at my talent.

Seb arrived at his usual time but oddly didn't even come in. Michael muttered something about him already having had a drink or several and said he had no idea what he had been talking about. I don't know why he is so grumpy with Seb.

Seb left before I could see him, he didn't even wish me Merry Christmas I was so very disappointed.

I had cooked a marvellous dinner and now it's just Michael and I. Not at all how I had planned today.

Michael bought me a wonderful new watch, well I chose it and bought it myself as is always the way, but then when Seb left Michael slapped an envelope down on the table containing a luxury weekend away at The Chimes Hotel voucher.

I'm not sure why he did that, perhaps new year new start.

I'm thrilled. I can't wait to share that piece of information with Georgina, I'm sure she will be envious and ask lots of questions about how that made me feel.

As part of the package is a show called the Rocky Horror Show. I thought that was a little out of my taste but it's so wonderful after all these years that he actually bought me something, so I am very grateful.

I really must thank Seb as Michael would never have thought to buy me such a gift without his encouragement of that I am sure.

We watched the Queens speech over our sherry, then Michael started on a bottle of whiskey. I thought I had better not comment that it was early in the day to be drinking. He is, after all, his own man.

I don't know what on earth was going on next door but there appeared to be some kind of adult party with all the laughter and raised voices.

Those poor children were riding scooters up and down the street with the grandmother, clearly, she was keeping them out in the cold so that they weren't party to the goings on inside. The blue-eyed brat was laughing very loudly on his bright blue scooter, and I was tempted to go out and see how he would react when he saw me but decided not to as it was quite cold.

I also resisted the urge to slip into their garden and take some more books from the summer house. I have amassed quite a collection of books on modern art and portraits from the boxes stored there. After all no one else seems to have even been in there since they moved in. I have hidden them in a case in my wardrobe because I know Michael will not approve of my renewed interest in art.

I have grown up and come so far, but sadly do not seem to have outgrown this interest which the discovery of the art supplies, books and easel in the summer house has reignited.

It is so difficult to resist the temptation to draw and paint especially when I have so much free time from the gardening.

I am so tempted to set up the easel. The blue-eyed brat is a very tempting candidate for a portrait. I really must resist, if Michael discovers this, he will be furious, and heavens knows what will happen.

I will speak to Georgina and see if she can suggest some therapy to cure me of this temptation, after all that is her specialist field.

Thursday 26/12/2002 - Boxing Day

Helen and Peter were first up and had everything tided and organised, while mum and dad entertained the boys.

Bobby was not long after them as he was on call. I've no idea how he managed to get up so early, especially after having an excessive day with Dad, Peter, Seb and John. I hope his patients appreciate him working today and all the extra hours he does.

I'd overheard Bobby on the phone to his colleague. He was chuntering about one particular patient that has been testing his patience. Always the professional! My Dr Williams.

Beth came downstairs just before lunch. Not looking her best. I did notice yesterday she wasn't really drinking with the rest of them, yet I think it's the first time I've ever seen her look this bad. She must be coming down with something.

I felt quite smug not having a hangover. It's very entertaining watching your friends and family get absolutely out of their heads while you are stone cold sober.

Mum and dad took the boys out again in the afternoon. They were so excited to play on their scooters.

I think Bobby must have drunk far more than he let on, because he left the car in the drive, and I saw him out of the window talking to Christine.

He still makes my heart flutter, especially when he's wearing his work suit and his round dark rimmed glasses that give him a very sexy look.

Just as well he was there as he stopped Frank scootering in front of a car with Robbie not too far behind him!

When Bobby came back he was looking very drained and was unusually quiet. He seemed lost in thought.

I can only guess he must have had to deal with a terrible emergency, as he went straight for the whiskey bottle.

I do hope that it's not bad news for a family especially during the Christmas festivities.

It's really sad he can't talk to me about some of the things he has to deal with due to patient confidentiality. Talking always helps me, whereas Bobby seems to bottle everything up.

I told Bobby I am not inviting Clarissa and Miserable Michael for New Year's Eve, or anything else come to that, I think to be snubbed once without an apology is enough. I'm not going to be snubbed again.

He didn't answer which is quite unusual for him. He's normally got an opinion about them next door.

He then suggested that maybe we shouldn't have a party on New Years Eve but have a quiet family evening instead.

When have we ever had a quiet New Year's Eve? I'm wondering if he's coming down with something too.

I'll speak to him tomorrow. I'm sure a good night's sleep will help him change his mind. Besides, I've already organised for our friends to come and join us.

Thank you for my cup of tea in bed. Thank you for mum and dad looking after the boys. Thank you for Bobby saving Frank from being run over.

Thursday 26th December 2002

This has been such a stressful day.

Michael had been drinking for hours, such a disgusting habit and somehow it appears he found the invite to the Christmas drinks at next doors.

It looked like he had tipped over the kitchen bin, it was a dreadful mess and naturally down to me to clean it up.

He was so angry that I hadn't told him about the invite and muttering and mumbling about Seb having been there without him. AS if Seb would lower himself to fraternise with people like that. Really!!!

I got so concerned about his slurring I rang for the out of hours GP. I simply couldn't understand what he was trying to say to me, and he looked so terrible, I thought he was having a seizure.

The doctor arrived very quickly. Dr Williams, the new GP, he looked very smart dressed in a very well-made suit and was clearly an intelligent man, one can always tell these things. Not very old but his glasses gave him an air of experience. I wanted to ask him how he was settling at the practice, but he was more interested in Michael than speaking to me, typical doctor.

I explained we have the most awful neighbours who had sent the invite and that seemed to have worked Michael up. I explained how the wife was a drug abuser and neglected her children. He looked quite annoyed at that, as well he should.

He was very thoughtful and didn't say much, but after examining Michael thoroughly, suggested he should have something to eat and head off to bed.

I said he would be lucky to sleep as listen to the racket coming over the hedge, they are clearly having a drugs rave. He looked very shocked. I told Michael to get some toast while I walked the doctor out. I was curious to see what sort of car he would drive.

As usual the street was next doors own personal car park, so I apologised that he had not got parked close by. He shook his head and said he had walked. He did look rather annoyed, obviously not with me. I left him at the gate as he seemed rather preoccupied.

I went upstairs to turn Michael's bed down and noticed the Doctor talking to Mrs Wade and those terrible children from next door, he even had to stop them being run over by a car, I wonder if Mrs Wade is a patient.

Odd how like the husband of next door he looks. Perhaps they are distant relatives and that's why he rented them the house. I really ought to have asked.

I was on my way to rescue him from being detained, when the phone rang, and Mrs Ivory invited us to a new year's party along with Seb. Most inconvenient timing.

In the evening Seb rang to speak to Michael but he told me to tell him he was too unwell to come to the phone. Most worrying, as usually he is very keen to speak with him.

Poor Seb went very quiet and didn't seem to know what to say.

I did manage to thank him for the wonderful hotel gift, and he seemed very surprised that I had guessed his involvement, even going so far as to ask where I was going and what the play was.

He is such a darling. I invited him to the New Year's Eve party, but he said he thought he couldn't make it. Most unlike him as usually he would go anywhere with us.

I am beginning to wonder what on earth is going on.

Monday 30/12/2002

Bobby was back in the practice early this morning and left a thermal mug of tea by my side of the bed.

I love sitting in bed with a mug of tea, is that an age thing? Anyway, it's just such a lovely way to start the day.

Beth disappeared, not sure where she went, she said something about unfinished business. She was still not looking herself.

Peter and Helen took themselves off to that fabulous Victorian cafe in the town centre to meet Hannah and John.

Mum had the boys doing yoga poses in the front room while dad cooked breakfast for us all. It was so nice just to be with mum and dad.

I sat and had a lovely dad to daughter conversation about travelling, how he met mum and how he finds some of her 'Spiritual' experiences quite interesting as he was brought up in a very different environment, looking after his mum when my grandfather died at such a young age.

It was so nice reminiscing about my childhood. Such happy days being out on magical walks, that always ended up with some adventure climbing a tree to look at the world, jam jar fishing by pretty streams and picnics in the middle of a field, every day was like Christmas and that's what I want to give to my children and hope one day they will look back and feel the same about their childhood.

I also talked to dad about Frank seeing the ghost lady, the professional help we were getting from Dr Burns was great, but I was concerned that there may be more to it. Did he think I should speak to mum. Bobby thinks spiritual experiences are bonkers, so it's so difficult to talk to him about it.

I told dad I have a gut feeling that there's something more going on with next door and I wonder if Frank had seen Clarissa because the ghost lady he describes is very similar. And there was the unusual blue button I found in the garden. It was too clean to have been there for a long time.

He quietly took everything in and said to leave it with him. He had that clever thinking look about him.

Dad also said that if I ever wanted to find out who my biological parents were, they would be a hundred and ten percent behind me and understood there must be so many questions I would like to have answered. He gave me a big hug.

If I was ever to choose my parents, I would always choose

them, they are the best!

Dad then told me he was very proud of Bobby and I, and how amazing our wonderful polite, happy boys are.

My heart was bursting with pride. I love my parents so much.

Bobby came home mid-afternoon and asked to speak to me. I am still very worried about him; he's not been himself again.

Mum and dad must have a second sense as they took the boys out on their scooters again.

Bobby was acting very strange and started asking me questions about the letter I received back in November. And what I thought had happened for her next door to write the letter and make lots of allegations, especially about me taking drugs?

He then questioned me about the boys, and asked if anything had been going on while he was at work that he didn't know about?

This was the first time he's really spoken to me about the letter.

It was all very odd, then he said he didn't want to tell me what to do, but he strongly advised that I kept well away from them next door.

At that point mum and dad came back with the boys. Frank was screaming and blood was everywhere as he's taken a nasty tumble off his scooter. Bobby cleaned him up.

Peter and Helen came back with lots of wonderful cakes, and we all sat down for a lovely teatime treat.

Then Bobby suggested we have a big party tomorrow night. (I daren't tell him I'd already arranged it).

Thank you for my lovely mug of tea. Thank you for my

lovely chat with dad. Thank you for Helen and Peter for the delicious cakes.

Monday 30th December 2002

I popped into town to my appointment at the Clinic today. It's so wonderful. When I arrived, I was ushered in to the waiting room and Georgina came straight to collect me, it makes you feel terribly important.

I told her about the strange Christmas and the silly woman asked if I thought Michael and Seb had perhaps disagreed over something. She really has no idea they are such firm and fast friends nothing comes between them. Their friendship extends so far back they are almost joined at the hip.

I suggested perhaps she could see him. But she was very non-committal saying appointments by referral only. I thought by now she would have realised he is much too important to be bothered with that kind of thing.

I remembered to ask her for some advice about the urges I have been having to take up art again. She looked very surprised that I would want to suppress them, saying art is a recognised form of therapy.

I suggested she is mistaken; art is for dreamers and not appropriate for women of my standing.

She dared to contradict me. Suggested I was wrong for suppressing my emotions, for heaven's sake for someone so well educated she sometimes seems to know so little. If she only knew how much trouble I had ended up in all those years ago, because of my obsession with art, and its associated lifestyle, she wouldn't be condoning it now.

I told her that fortunately Michael had stepped in, at my father's request and subsequently made me a respectable woman.

She seemed very surprised at that, and wanted me to explain...

I told her she really does ask to many questions that are absolutely none of her business. She merely raised a perfect eyebrow at that.

I don't know why I continue to see her; except I do think it's my duty to perhaps introduce her to Seb.

She really could be perfect for him if she wasn't so nosy. Of course, I didn't tell her that!

When she continued to ask me about Michael stepping in to save me from that terrible time, I said it was time I left. I don't know why she was so put out my time is very precious, and I won't have her invading my privacy.

Michael didn't go to the golf club today, he shut himself in his office again. I have no idea what on earth is wrong with him and know from experience there is no point asking.

I spent the afternoon wondering about art therapy. Perhaps when he is more approachable, I might mention that Georgina thought it was a respectable type of therapy. After all, I'm sure now I'm older if I am discreet it can't hurt. Before I speak to him, I might just try a pencil portrait or something as he told me I had no talent for art.

Next time he is out I think I will go up into our attic and look for the box I hid there all those years ago when we moved here. I don't want to make a fool of myself thinking I can paint if I really was so bad at it. Perhaps I could move it into next doors summer house and go through it there.

After all they don't use it and it's just sitting there empty. The box is full of the very last of my life as a student. I rescued it from the trash the day before Michael and I married, when mother insisted grownups did not need sentimental clutter and emptied my room of everything that would remind me of years past.

The terrible blue-eyed brat appeared to injure himself on that dangerous scooter today. For heaven's sake she can't even get responsible people to look after him. He cried piteously; it really was most disturbing. Something really should be done about getting them out of our area and quickly.

Tuesday 31/12/2002 - New Year's Eve

Can't believe how big my bump as suddenly grown. I felt quite neat before, now I feel like I'm waddling not walking. Everything is really uncomfortable especially trying to get my socks and boots on, so I've resorted to wearing flip flops. I'm passed caring what I look like.

A very different pregnancy to the boys. I was still playing tennis at this stage. Now I'm thinking about reinstating the Stannah stair lift.

Bobby was up and determined to get everything organised for tonight.

I had to confess that I'd already asked Hannah, John and Seb round, but unfortunately they were all going to a friends from the golf club, but it will still be a lovely evening. He seemed absolutely fine about it, especially as I offered to cook.

I then mentioned that I'd asked Paul the footballer, not the rabbit, and Beth. He surprised me when he said he wasn't bothered for them to come.

It's been my tradition for years to be with Beth on New Year's Eve.

I've no idea what's going on with him. He was happy chatting to Beth the other night and she's been staying here most of the week. I did say to Bobby that maybe he needed to check Beth out as she's not been herself. He then told me to mind my own business and he was sure Beth was absolutely fine, which is really out of character for him.

I went off in a huff and he went out in the car somewhere.

I think mum and dad must have heard our squabble, so they took the boys out with Helen and Peter for the last walk of the year. No doubt Robbie and Frank will be coming home hyper with all the treats they get.

I'm so lucky to have them around. I'm dreading them all going. I will miss them dearly and I am worried about being on my own in the house especially with her next door. I still do not know what I've done to upset Clarissa the Cow and miserable Michael.

Decided to make time now to write, as the house feels very quiet. I don't think I like it. Going for a rest and to do my positive meditation as I've put everything in the slow cooker and finished off my non-alcoholic trifle.

***

Slept a lot longer than I intended to.

Bobby woke me up with a large bunch of flowers with a packet of Fisherman's Friends in the middle and apologised for being so grumpy. That was so sweet of him. I hate falling out.

Everyone was downstairs waiting for me. Hannah, John

and Seb had changed their minds and come to join us.

I was so pleased I'd made extra food; I thought I was being really clever using the slow cooker. But it turns out Lasagne really doesn't work in a slow cooker and my image of this beautifully prepared dish was slopped onto our plates as Lasagne soup! We had to get rid of the forks and replace them with spoons.

Everyone was being super lovely and told me how delicious and unusual my cooking was.

Then I got the trifle out of the fridge.

That was even more of a disaster. I've no idea what I've done. Perhaps it's because I didn't put alcohol in it. We needed a soup ladle to dish it out and to make it worse Robbie went to get everyone a straw to eat it.

I felt so embarrassed.

Luckily, everyone saw the funny side and said it's one way to remember 2002.

Christine was to the rescue again and went and brought over a very large selection of cheese, biscuits and a Bingo game!

Bobby suddenly seemed a little on edge as everyone was getting louder. I thought he was annoyed with me for not getting everything right this evening but then seemed more relaxed when Christine commented on seeing 'them next door' leave in a taxi. It looked like a huge cloud had been lifted from Bobby.

Who would have thought we could have such fun playing Bingo!

John read out the numbers. He was hilarious, not the normal two little ducks or legs eleven expressions, he had some very rude rhymes. The boys thought it was hysterical and I thought I was going to go into labour from aching with laughter!

We allowed Robbie to stay up. Frank had already fallen asleep on the sofa.

Put the BBC on to listen to Big Ben and sing along to Auld Lang Syne. I still do not know the words. I'll add that to my New Year's resolutions.

Beth and Paul didn't turn up, so I called Beth, but it just went straight onto her answer phone. I hope she's alright.

2002 has been a very busy eventful year. I can't believe how much my life has changed and will be changing again in 2003!

Thank you for a wonderful year with my wonderful family and friends.

Tuesday 31st December 2002

Michael was much better today, but still very frosty with me for not telling him about next doors party.

I do wonder what on earth all the fuss is about we wouldn't be associating with them anyway. He made it clear from the start they were persons non gratis.

Apparently, I should have remembered my place and that he has the final say in our social activity.

There was really very little I could say. I felt very chastised and ended up apologising as he expected me to do.

He got very smartened up for the do at Mrs Ivory's tonight. Actually, he looked almost as dapper as Seb would have done. It was nice that he had made an effort.

It was quite a shock, when on arrival Mrs Ivory told us she was so sorry Seb was unable to come, apparently, he was asked to a party with the Smythe's in attendance and had felt he couldn't refuse.

I asked Michael why we hadn't been invited to that one rather than this, and he snapped that he and Seb were not joined at the hip, nor were we always expected to be seen with Seb we had our own friends.

His reaction was quite uncalled for.

Mrs Ivory had been at the golf club do, so I asked her about the mystery woman and apparently, she is the daughter in law of a friend of Johns who also attended boarding school with Seb, that was an interesting snippet and in some ways explained why Seb had been preoccupied.

How wonderful to know she is well connected; I must try and track her down. Seb could introduce us, as he has a connection.

Michael decided we should leave before midnight.

As the taxi dropped us off on the street it was very apparent next door were having another wild rave.

I am sure I recognised Jo-Hannah Smythes car, but it's extremely unlikely it could have been hers. It's appalling the amount of partying that goes on, no wonder she hardly seems fit to be a parent.

Wednesday 1/1/2003 - New Year's Day & My birthday

First New Year's Day in a long time that I haven't had a hangover!

Although I'm now slowly creeping towards the thirty mark, I have to keep reminding myself I'm only in my late twenties.

The thought of turning thirty does not appeal to me, it's sounds so old. But the thought of being a mother of four is far more daunting.

Come on Seren get life into perspective!

Bobby and the boys brought me breakfast in bed with my cards and presents. Bobby got me a beautiful necklace and matching earrings from the boys.

When I finally got downstairs mum and dad, Peter and Helen were waiting with a pot of tea to sing happy birthday and more cards and presents. I'm so lucky.

We then all met up at the golf club for a birthday lunch. Hannah and John's treat.

Tried Beth again, still no answer, there wasn't even a card to open. I am really starting to worry about her.

Bobby told me not to be anxious, just enjoy my day and he'll try and get hold of her later.

Seb had popped into the golf club for a drink and then came to join us.

He's a very interesting man. And some of the stories he told us, well I'm now looking at my father-in-law in a different light. It is funny listening to their school day tales. I didn't realise how posh Bobby's family really are.

Mum and dad are talking about their next adventure. Going on a short break before the twins arrive. Mum has said there is a hot yoga course that her and dad want to do in India.

It all sounds very exciting. I really will miss them.

The boys were surprisingly well behaved in the club, there was an area where they could sit and watch cartoons, which was perfect as they were so tired. They lay on very large cushions with their pop and crisps.

We came home and everyone had an early night.

Helen and Peter are leaving first thing and mum and dad are leaving after lunch. I'm feeling really sad that everyone is going after such a wonderful festive time.

Too tired to write anymore.

Thank you for a wonderful birthday. Thank you boys for being so good. Thank you for my lovely family.

Wednesday 1st January 2003

Heavens another year.

I spared a moment to remember all the years since I finished school and married Michael.

They have been so interesting. I have come so far. I have tried so hard to be a perfect hostess and wife.

It has not always been easy. It was not the life I expected or even planned, but as father said Dreamers are fools. I suppose he was right.

Reality has kept me grounded and today is not the day to hash up foolish fantasies. I am extremely lucky that Michael took me in hand.

Michaels interests and life are very regimented. He has always just liked to do as he will, and my place has always been at his side as his hostess or running our home to the standards he likes it kept.

I was so pleased, that for the first time in all our time together, he bought me a real Christmas gift, and not just something for me, but for both of us.

I wonder if this year we might start to spend more time together privately instead of just appearing socially as a couple.

I haven't minded too much that he has left me to my own devices but now I feel we are getting older and should perhaps be more settled and get used to each other's company and become better friends.

I am sure there should be something more to our relationship than just social politeness, it's probably Georgina putting ideas in my head with all her questions and subtle insinuations.

Perhaps I should be happy as we are.

Of course, Michael has his work and friendship with Seb, and they are often off together but every man needs a woman to come home to.

I've never understood why Seb has never settled down, it's not as though he is not well respected and liked. He is so kind and caring. I wonder if perhaps I shouldn't try and suggest a suitable wife for him, like Georgina for instance.

I'm sure Georgina would be grateful to have a man like Seb, so much more respectable for her to be a Mrs than a Ms.

I will have a think how to broach the subject delicately with Seb.

Saturday 11/1/2003

Bobby got up super early this morning and was dressed as if he was going to work. I just assumed he was on call or having to go to Saturday surgery, but he seemed far too excited for work.

Bless him he brought me up tea and toast and then entertained the boys.

I went downstairs about ten o'clock to find Bobby gone and the boys sat quietly watching T.V. My first thought that went through my head was he must have drugged them!

Then Robbie let it slip that daddy had a surprise for us and they had to be very well behaved.

I do not know what is going on in my own home at times.

Then Bobby came rushing into the house and put a blind fold on me, took me outside and left me on the drive. It was very strange just standing there on my own.

I have to say I had an awful feeling he was going to run me over because I could hear a car engine. I've no idea why that popped into my head. But I dare not ever tell him that, and then I felt really guilty for even thinking it. I'm blaming the hormones again!

I could hear the boys giggling as Bobby took hold of my hand and told me to guess what it was.

Well, I told him I thought he'd brought home an elephant from the zoo which made the boys laugh out even louder. Then I heard Frank very excitedly shout "Mummy it's a new car!"

At that point Bobby took my blind fold off and there was a brand-new Renault Espace. It was the size of a minibus. Silver grey with blacked out windows. Perfect for our growing family. A big seven-seater, with car seats already fitted.

He's just so thoughtful. Perhaps that's why he has been a little distant trying to keep this a secret.

We went for a test drive, and I then dropped Bobby off at the garage. He told me he needed to finish off some paperwork and he would make his own way back.

It was lovely to drive. So much space.

I tried to ring Bobby but no answer which was really odd for him. Then I got a call to go out onto the street.

I spotted Seb with Bobby and this two-seater sports car.

I thought Beth must have come round at first, but it had Bobby's personal number plate on. I didn't know Bobby liked sports cars. Why was his number plate on this one?

He asked me if I wanted to take it out for a test drive but there was no way I could get in it. What is going on with him? Is he going through a mid-life crisis. How are we going to go anywhere with the kids in his two-seater. It's the most impractical car ever.

Then he tells me he's always wanted one after he'd been for a drive with Beth, so he bought hers.

I asked him when he met Beth. He was very vague and said sometime over Christmas.

I also mentioned to Bobby that I have left several messages on her answer phone, and she still hasn't got back to me, but she has managed to make time to sell her car to him!

My surprise was very bittersweet. I honestly don't know what's going on.

I got the impression Bobby felt I should have been more excited for him, as I struggled to muster up a smile.

I told him I felt really tired and overwhelmed by everything, but incredibly grateful for my new car and needed to lie down.

I should be thankful for our new family car and cup of tea in bed and I'm really trying to stay positive, it's just very difficult. Instead, I've come to bed for a little cry.

Saturday 11th January 2003

I dropped Michael off at the golf club this lunch time. I didn't go in but noticed Sebs car there. I'm relieved that he has finally found some free time to catch up with Michael. He seems to have been terribly busy and Michael has been quite neglected.

When Seb dropped him off after lunch Michael still seemed

very grumpy.

Apparently, Seb was coming in to wish me Happy New Year, when he caught sight of someone he needed to speak to. I was most surprised to realise it was Dr Williams looking very smart as usual. He has a very nice sports car that Seb was interested in.

I wonder what he was doing next door. Poor man, but as a doctor I suppose he has to go where he is sent.

I'm terribly excited to have had an invitation from Jo-Hannah Smythe to meet for coffee at the golf club tomorrow. Perhaps now I will get to find out who her mystery friend is. She even hand delivered the invitation so clearly It is an important gathering. I've been and had my hair and nails done, I do want to look my best.

I asked Michael if we should have got an extra ticket for the show, in February so that Seb could have come when we go to the Chimes.

It seems odd, but exciting to be going away without him. Just the two of us after all these years.

I wondered if perhaps I ought to pop into Marks and buy a new night dress. Something cotton rather than flannel. It's been so long since I shared a room with anyone I am not sure what to expect. I would imagine the room will have twin beds but still I should look my best.

It appears that things have quietened down next door. I think all the party goers have left. I saw her taking the children out for a walk. She looks extremely tired and waddling like a duck. Perhaps that's why the Doctor was there today.

I noticed Mrs Wade caught her as she was coming back,

and they stood and chatted. I really do need to speak to the silly woman. She shouldn't be making her feel at all welcome. We want them to move out not get settled. I suppose Mrs Wade is just glad to have a friend.

I haven't managed to visit the summer house again yet, but I did pick up some art supplies from the little shop near the gallery and have put them with the art box.

I am sure I do not know why I feel so guilty about drawing and painting a few silly pictures, it is just I know Michael will be shocked and angry if he finds out.

Georgina really is a bit of a bad influence; she wonders what harm it can possibly do to have taken it back up as a hobby.

Sunday 12/1/2003

Bobby brought me a cup of tea up and wanted to know how I was feeling.

I really want to tell him he's been an absolute prat, can't believe he bought himself a single man's pulling car, I hate living next door to them, can't cope with the boys, feel like a blob and I want to go back down south to be normal again.

But I did my usual answer of 'I'm fine!'

He then questioned me about the other day when Frank was nearly knocked down.

I wasn't sure what he was on about at first. Then he said I'd been spotted off Whitten Lane.

I'd forgotten about that, so I explained I'm so tired all the time, Frank had fallen asleep in his car seat, so I pulled over on this little side road and had a sleep myself.

I only woke up when I heard a car beeping it's horn as

Frank had managed to open the car door. Thought the child lock was on.

When I told Bobby what happened he got really cross about that too.

No one was hurt. I don't understand. And who told him?

I can't seem to do anything right. It's like walking on eggshells.

Bobby went to clean his new car. He's never cleaned a car in his life.

He has been acting very strangely again especially since his call out on Boxing Day.

Something must have really bothered him because he's mentioned about changing jobs. I thought he loved his new job.

I'm so scared about losing him.

I left him to it for a while then thought I'd better do the right thing, so I took him a cup of tea out and asked if he's ok. At that point Clarissa the cow and miserable Michael were stomping down their drive. Her face was like thunder!

She still makes my stomach churn.

Bobby looked up and smiled at them. The next thing I saw was Michael diving towards the fence and shouting 'Are you a Voyeur?'

Bobby threw his sponge into his bucket, grabbed me by the arm, tea went everywhere and muttered something about we need to move.

If he wasn't in the professional position he's in. I'm sure he would have squared up to Michael. I have never seen Bobby react so badly to anyone.

I'm not sure what to do. I can't talk to Bobby he's told me that I'm not the only person struggling at the moment. Then he apologised and said that work was getting him down.

Is he really stressed at work or is there something going on?

I had a mad thought of ringing Beth up to see if she has any advice, after all her and Bobby had seemed to be getting on rather well over Christmas and I know they've been in touch because of the car, but I've still not heard from her. Deep down I really want to ask her when she went for a drive with my husband! I don't understand, she's supposed to be my best friend.

Sod the three positives for today!

Sunday 12th January 2003

It's been a disastrous day, I made so much of an effort getting ready to meet Jo-Hannah at the golf club. I expected a few of us to be there. When I realised it was just myself, I was thrilled to have been singled out to spend time with her, but Jo-Hannah was so sharp and angry with me. I was absolutely astounded.

The stupid woman next door is only her new protégée and the lovely Dr Williams her husband. How regrettable!

I am shocked that it is even possible. He looks nothing like who I thought her husband was. What on earth does she have to make a man like that be attracted to her.

I can't believe Jo-Hannah actually spoke to me as if I was in the wrong for sending my letter pointing out the error of her ways and reporting her and her husband to the authorities.

She has totally hoodwinked Jo-Hannah and if I don't apologise then I will not be welcome to any more of her dos.

Well, I will not be backing down. I have done absolutely

nothing wrong.

I will need to think carefully how I manage this as I don't want to lose my social standing with the Smythes.

When I told Michael what had transpired, he was extremely angry and it turns out Seb has known all along that they were our neighbours, even going so far as to fraternise with them over the holiday.

It is all just so sickening; we have been completely betrayed. No wonder Michael and Seb had fallen out... He was deceiving us by knowingly spending time with them.

As if the day hadn't been distressing enough, Michael and I were going down the drive to the car to pop into town, suddenly Michael began to shout at the Doctor, who was outside, calling him a voyeur and angrily cursing him.

I was most shocked at his uncharacteristic behaviour in a public place for anyone to see or hear.

He was very rude to me when I asked what on earth had provoked him, muttering about Seb and betrayal.

I wondered how much he had had to drink at the golf club earlier, and if he should in fact be driving if he had been drinking.

Of course, I am sure he wouldn't if he had had too much, after all he isn't stupid.

Friday 31/1/2003

I don't know what to do. I'm exhausted and worried. My hair has gone greasy, I've got spots breaking out all over my face. I can't sleep on a night; I can't function and now that woman from next door tells me she's seen my Bobby with a beautiful blond. Has Bobby met someone else? Especially as I look so big and horrible.

I tried not to show any emotion towards her, as she stared me in the eye. I turned my back on her and walked into the house, I couldn't respond.

The sad thing is I thought she was going to be nice, so I let my guard down. I think she gets great pleasure out of wanting to hurt me.

I still to this day do not know what I ever did to that woman for her to behave so badly towards me.

At one point before she dropped the bombshell I caught a glimpse of a smile, and I suddenly imagined her to be a beautiful attractive lady. She actually has striking features. She apologised for upsetting me and said she didn't realise we were so well connected. Then it just went downhill.

The problem is I've only seen her nasty side, and beauty comes from within which makes her quite ugly!

Although Bobby has been very defensive about her. He's told me to be kind. How can you be kind to someone who hates you for no reason. Maybe he's saying that because he knows that she knows about this blond.

I tried to call Beth, but I'm still getting her answer phone. It's been a month and she's still avoiding me. I then tried to get hold of Bobby.

He's on call again or is he?

Christine must have some sixth sense. She came over to see how I was, and she'd made a stew, as she thought it would save me cooking. Bless her she also brought over five packets of Fisherman's friends and a new football for the boys, as she knows next door won't throw the boys ball back.

I just hugged her and sobbed. I don't know where I'd be

without this wonderful lady, she's like my adoptive grandma. I reassured Christine it's because I've got double the hormones with expecting twins. She gave me that look, I really don't think she believed me.

Bobby came home on time this evening, so I plucked up the courage to question him about the blond. He told me not to worry and he'd explain later when the boys had gone to bed.

Later!! I want to know now.

By the time the boys had gone to bed, he'd fallen asleep, I didn't like to wake him! I'm so frustrated!... And to make things worse I'm feeling very constipated.

Why is nothing going right for me? There are some days I wish I wasn't pregnant. No, I take that back. My children are my world and I have to keep believing everything is for a reason.

I swore I would never be like my real mother. I am better than that.

Still can't stop crying. So, I've come to bed early to listen to my positive meditation music. I feel I need to go back to basics and look after myself.

Thank you Christine, you are my guardian angel.

Thank you boys for being so good and especially Frank who seems settled in our home now, no more Ghost Lady.

Thank you for having a roof over our heads.

Friday 31st January 2003

Today has been quite strange to say the least. I popped into town to get my hair and nails done.

While I was there, I called for coffee at Latinos and was very surprised to see Dr Williams or is it Dr Williams De Lacy, whatever name he goes under. He is such a charlatan, with his double names and now sat with a very attractive blonde it appears he also leads a double life!!

He had hold of her hand so tightly and they were talking quite intimately, the woman appeared to be hanging on his every word. I think she saw me looking and took her hand back, but he was so intent on her he didn't notice me.

I sat and watched them for some time before I remembered I was on a meter.

How lucky for me that as I pulled onto the drive, I saw next door struggling back from somewhere so pregnant she looked fit to burst.

I almost felt sorry for her, there was no comparison to the lovely woman sat with Dr Williams.

How typical of the man to leave her in the state she was in, and already with the two brats to care for.

I saw a chance to perhaps make amends with Jo-Hannah Smythe and intercepted her as she got almost to the drive.

I'm sure I almost managed to sound convincing when I apologised for having upset her and pointed out she really should have made more effort to be the kind of suitable neighbour and wife as befitted our street.

I explained that I had no idea she was so well connected.

Of course, I explained that socially I was far too busy for her to be seen with me, but that we might pass each other if the occasion arises.

She just stood looking at me as if I was speaking in a foreign language. It struck me that she could actually have been quite reasonably attractive if she took more care of herself and had *kept herself from being so pregnant.*

It was most odd, she really does have the greenest eyes they reminded me of someone I had once known, they gave me a quite unexpected jolt, with their intensity.

Perhaps that's why I told her I had just seen Dr Williams with the most attractive woman, they looked very cosy, I hoped that everything was alright between them at home...

She looked, for a second like a startled animal then walked away as if I wasn't there, so rude after I had made the effort to extend the olive branch and offer my apology.

Perhaps I shouldn't have mentioned seeing the Doctor with the blonde as that woman looked a little upset.

However, I had a duty as a friend of Jo-Hannahs to point out the indiscretion, after all anyone could have seen them together.

Michael arrived home late from the golf club and announced our weekend away was cancelled. He has an important business trip with Seb.

I'm a little disappointed but I suppose business is far more important than pleasure.

Saturday 1/2/2003 - Bobby's birthday

I couldn't sleep last night but I made myself get up extra early to put my make-up on and try to look more glamorous, incredibly difficult to do when you can't see your toes and feel like a great humpback whale.

But I put on a smile, took Bobby breakfast in bed and got the boys up to sing happy birthday and help him open his presents.

I just wanted him to feel special and see what he's missing

if he's with another woman.

I'd got him some new aftershave and a nice designer shirt but all I could think of was him wearing them for her. I had to look away a few times to hide my tears.

Bobby didn't seem to notice my effort this morning or my tears. He was just acting as normal snuggling up with the boys and telling me how much he loved his presents and then jumped in the shower and went to work.

I was in such a daze I told the boys to get ready for school, they laughed at me and reminded me it was Saturday. But then why had Bobby gone to work? I thought he was on call last week.

My head was all over the place, I told the boys to sort themselves out. I made myself a cup of tea and just sat at the kitchen table staring at it.

The boys had a pillow fight in the front room. I could hear them giggling, then a loud smash, at the same time there was a knock at the door. I felt sick, was this Clarissa coming round to tell me off for my badly behaved children or tell me she'd just seem my husband with the blond again?

Luckily, it wasn't it was Seb all smiles with a red box with a lovely bow on top. He was hoping to catch Bobby to wish him happy birthday.

Such a relief, I invited him in for coffee, but he said he wasn't stopping.

A few hours later Bobby was back home. I asked him how work was, and he said he'd got his days mixed up so didn't actually see any patients so caught up with paperwork.

Paperwork is that what they call it nowadays!

He then asked if I minded if he could go to the golf club and meet John for a few holes. I replied it was his birthday and he could do what he wanted.

He seemed to be in such a good mood, almost giddy, then grabbed his clubs and left again without getting changed.

What am I to do. There's no way I can tell him about my conversation yesterday. Do I pretend it never happened? Do I risk losing him. Or if he leaves me how do I cope with twins on the way, two boys, where do I live and can I get a job to financially support us.

It was all too much so I phoned Christine and asked her if she could help me with the boys while I went for a lie down.

Bobby came home late afternoon with Hannah and John and a takeaway for his birthday tea.

He said he's had a lovely day. I wanted to tell him I'd had a horrible one.

But instead, I invited Christine to join us and thank her again for helping me with the boys.

Everything was all very civilised. What am I to think?

Saturday 1st February 2003

I wondered if I should have let Jo-Hannah know I had spoken to that woman yesterday about her wayward husband.

I thought perhaps she could have checked on her and perhaps suggested she keep her husband under control in public places and ensure their private life remains just that.

As it was I didn't get chance to make the call as Seb arrived and said he had had a visit to make close by so called for a coffee.

It was so lovely to see him and have a nice catch up.

He managed to avoid the question of where he had had to go prior to visiting us. I wondered if perhaps it was to see The

Smythes and hesitated about telling him about the Doctors indiscretion with his new woman. I caught Michael looking very suspicious about Sebs lack of information so decided the best course of action was to move the conversation along to safer topics rather than risk another bout of anger from him.

By the time they went off to golf I had to dash off to meet Mrs Warbottom to hand over the paperwork for the upcoming trip to Kew Gardens in the Autumn. I told her I couldn't possibly go, as I had not travelled by bus for many years. She said it would be a luxury executive coach, not a bus. I wondered how she could split hairs; a bus is a bus and really not acceptable transport for ladies such as ourselves.

Michael rang early evening to say he would be home tomorrow as a few of them at the club were going to play cards.

Thank goodness he seems to have sorted out his differences with Seb.

Perhaps now life will settle down again.

Wednesday 12/2/2003

It feels like Bobby, and I have been skirting around each other. He's been so distant. I can't seem to talk to him. I feel so insecure. I asked him about the blonde as I can't get that image out of my head, he still hasn't given me an explanation.

I managed to take the boys to school and nursery without crying this morning.

I have a constant churning in my stomach and it's not the twins.

Christine keeps popping in to check on me. I'd be so lost

without her.

Mum rang from India; we had a lovely chat about her Hot Yoga and spiritual adventures. When she gets back she's going to come up on her own to help me with everything.

I then explained I can't think at the moment, I'm really struggling. I poured my heart out to her about what's been going on. Mum suggested that I have everyone round to our home to talk about it.

We can't throw away our relationships without a fight and ask a few home truths.

So, feeling very brave I've invited Beth round tonight for dinner.

I was surprised when she even answered and said she is staying local. She was lovely on the phone and surprised me when she asked if she could bring Paul. I didn't know she knew Paul that well that she would have asked him. When I said that, she just laughed and said we needed to catch up.

Too right we do!!

I sent a text to Bobby and asked him to pop into the takeaway and pick up some different curries.

I didn't want to make the effort of cooking if I was to find out my husband has been having an affair with my best friend.

Bobby thought it was a great idea for us all to spend the evening together, which I found really odd.

Beth and Paul arrived early together.

Paul had two great big bouquets of flowers. One for me and one for Beth. A signed football for the boys and a new Leeds kit each, as well as a stack of kids videos. He's so generous.

Beth was really giddy and helped me set the table, chattering away and completely oblivious to my fuming silence.

I couldn't stop shaking until Bobby came in with the takeaway, all smiles and hugs, as if nothing had happened between them. I felt like a spare part.

We all sat down together, then Paul and Beth made an announcement.

It turns out they are an item! Beth is going to become a W.A.G.!

But even more surprising. She's only having his baby!

When did all this happen?

Beth said she was desperate to talk to me about all her problems but could see I wasn't coping. She was so apologetic and explained she needed to sort her own head out.

At the time she didn't know what was happening and had asked to meet Bobby in the cafe to ask his advice, to find out what he thought Paul's reaction would be as she wasn't sure how to tell him, and to ask Bobby if he wanted to buy her car because it will be so impractical for her and the baby.

She was so grateful to have such good friends that she could turn to.

I did not see that coming! But I am so relieved this horrible situation is now resolved.

Paul is over the moon to become a dad. You could see him glowing. We all had a big hug and a fabulous evening.

Thank you for my husband not to be having an affair. Thank you for having my best friend back and thank you for Beth having a baby! I'm so excited for her.

Wednesday 12th February 2003

Michael hardly spoke to me when he arrived home tonight.

He was very distracted by his short notice trip away with Seb. It was all quite a surprise, first they are hardly speaking then they are rushing off.

I suppose business is business and when I tried to ask any questions Michael was extremely short with me.

He packed his bag and said he wasn't sure which day he would get home but that Seb was picking him up first thing in the morning.

I asked if he would cancel the hotel and perhaps rearrange it for us to go another time, but he just said not to worry about it. He had more important things to think about. So disappointing really, but then I suppose business always comes first and it's not my place to complain.

It's just more and more since meeting Georgina I am beginning to wonder if there shouldn't be more between us. More to life as she puts it. We are after all not getting any younger.

Still, him being away will allow me more free time.

I missed a call today from the new chairman of the gardening club, her message was actually to remind me I have not been in touch and was everything alright. She hoped it wasn't because I didn't want to go with them to Kew, after all that was entirely my choice.

I have been so preoccupied I forgot all about renewing my membership. I can hardly say that I have lost interest in the club I really will have to try to keep up some pretence of normality and call her back with an excuse.

I have been so caught up with painting and my visits to the Clinic that my other life has been rather eclipsed, oddly I have *not missed it and in a strange way feel much happier.*

Even the deception to Michael comes with no guilt. I am sure I can continue to be suitable and artistic at the same time as long as I keep the art secret and continue to do it next door in the summer house out of everyone's sight.

Friday 14/2/2003 - Valentine's Day

I got all excited when I saw the florist standing at the top of the drive with a beautiful bouquet of what looked like wildflowers. Bobby knows they are my favourite.

Unfortunately, they went next door. Can't imagine miserable Michael sending flowers to her. Well at least I got three valentines cards this morning left by the toaster.

It's so cute that the boys made their own. I have to admit I was very impressed with Robbie's picture of football boots hanging from a tree. Obviously illustrating the true meaning of Valentine's Day.

Frank was really clingy this morning, he didn't want to go to nursery, I felt awful leaving him there, but the staff reassured me it was quite normal for young children to have their off days and he would be fine once I'd gone. But he wasn't fine. My poor Frank sat all morning on a chair in the cloak room looking out of the window, waiting for me to collect him. He refused to join in with anything. Is that normal? Am I a bad mother?

He's definitely his father's son, stubborn!

When we got home Frank was exhausted, so he fell asleep in front of the T.V.

I felt weird, as I had a massive urge to clean the kitchen cupboards and Paul's hutch! Did the cupboards but decided not to clean the rabbit hutch as I didn't want to see that horrible woman in her garden.

So, I continued cleaning the kitchen windows. As I was busy wiping away the cleaning solution, I noticed some movement down by the collapsed potting shed. I thought I saw Frank's ghost. I'd maybe over done it, so I called Christine to join me for a cup of tea.

We sat in the kitchen just generally chit chatting, then she got up to the window and said she thought she'd seen someone in our summer house.

We both walked down the garden, I was carrying a rolling pin (what on earth was I thinking, and what would I have done with it anyway. Rolled someone into pastry?)

When we got to the summer house there was a slim woman wearing a bright blue overcoat, like Frank had described, she was painting on the old easel that had been left and was singing away to herself in the most dreadful pitched voice. We must have stood there for a good few minutes when Christine gave a very loud cough and the woman span round.

I couldn't believe my eyes. It was her from next door. I was speechless. I just stared at her, then I looked at her painting. It was Frank, she had painted my son. She didn't even flinch. In fact, she looked annoyed that we had disturbed her.

I gave my sternest look of disdain and looked her up and down. That's when I noticed her unusual buttons on her overcoat. She had one missing. I couldn't believe it. I had found her button months ago.

How dare she come into my garden; how dare she sit in our summer house. How dare she paint my son. At that point I doubled over with massive stomach cramps.

Christine held on to me. Clarissa turned back to her painting and finished off what she was doing. I can't believe her cheek, acting like she was quite at home in OUR summer house.

Christine angrily said, 'you need to go, and we will deal with this later.' I've never seen Christine so angry. Who knew she had it in her.

I was trying to breathe deeply, then I felt a trickle down my leg. Out of all the people in the world, I had wet myself in front of that woman.

That cow, Clarissa, calmly walked past us not saying a word and left.

At that point I then heard Frank from the back door shout loudly 'Ghost lady, ghost lady!'

Christine helped me into the house to lay down on the sofa in the front room, Frank lay with me and just cuddled me so tightly while he sobbed. A hot chocolate and Thomas the Tank engine seemed to help settle him.

Christine then went to call Bobby. I told her it couldn't possibly be the twins as I've another 6 weeks to go.

Bobby wasn't too long, by that time it was the school run. Christine took Frank to go and meet Robbie.

I then felt absolutely fine and sat up with a nice cup of tea. I told Bobby about what had happened, and he just seem to dismiss it, by telling me not to worry about her, I need to look after myself, he then asked if I liked the flowers.

I didn't find it very funny. He looked quite shocked and said he had ordered me my favourite.

He's going to have to do better than that. I'm really not in the mood for jokes.

So, I've come to bed early. It's all been too much. Can't think anymore.

***

2.22am I've just woken up feeling very odd. With painful contractions very close together. It can't be the twins, can it? Bobby said we need to go as soon as Christine arrives.

Friday 14th February 2003

I was so thrilled to receive a wonderful bouquet of colourful scented wildflowers, delivered by the florists with a simple card that read Sorry we don't seem to have had much time together much love. Most unlike Michael, he has never sent me flowers before.

Perhaps he realised how disappointed I was not to be going away. The flowers are not the selection I would have expected from him, but they are quite stunning, perhaps next year I will buy some plants and make a corner of the garden to remind me of them.

I have also just realised it's Valentine's Day; he really is making an effort to change our relationship for the better. It's not that I particularly want attention, but it is rather nice to feel appreciated.

Our marriage perhaps didn't quite get off to the right start as neither of us were quite expecting it, but we have got along and grown used to each other.

It's so obvious love is a ridiculous sentiment that is quite unattainable and clearly should be left in fairy tale books.

I tried to call Michael, but his phone went to voice mail. I didn't leave a message as I know he will be terribly busy.

I wonder if Seb has been talking to him about how valuable I am and how lucky he is to have me.

I felt so happy with the flowers I decided I could go to the hotel and go to the show myself, but oddly I couldn't find the tickets and booking.

Michael must have taken the envelope so he could contact them to cancel the booking.

Never mind I am sure we will go sometime and perhaps to a better show.

It's been such a sunny crisp day I decided to take my paints and go to the summer house.

In my mind I have a very clear picture of the little brat from next door, I want to commit him to paper, he has such good bone structure and eyes that remind me of another painting from long ago... but that's not the point!

I don't know how long I had been working there, the light was perfect when I was so rudely interrupted, I felt quite dazed to tear my eyes from my work and find myself confronted by Mrs Wade, I was just adding a crucial stroke to the picture, when she was suddenly in my face ordering me to leave and that terrible pregnant woman being all dramatic about me being there.

I was surprised at the tone of Mrs Wades voice, I mean really, she is normally so mousy. Honestly, such a performance, it's not as if they have ever used the place and what harm was I doing.

I was so shocked I left in a bit of a hurry but noticed the brat bawling at the door. Really their whole lives are such chaos!

It was all so inconvenient, such a good job Michael is away, I had to creep back over and retrieve all my things from their summer house in the dark. I suppose she is going to stop me using it as a studio so I have hidden all of my art things in my *green house until I can find another place to paint, but the picture I have put on the easel to study it.*

Truly, if I say so myself it is quite endearing, I have truly captured his eyes. It stops my heart to look at them. I wonder what Georgina will say about it, I think I will take it in to show her.

Saturday 15/2/2003

Christine was over in no time; Bobby was flapping which surprised me. How's he supposed to deal with patients if he's having a flap? Good job I've been here before. Luckily I'd packed my case the other day, I must have known.

Bobby drove like an idiot to the maternity unit. I'm amazed I didn't give birth in the car.

The journey was a complete blur, it didn't seem to take too long to get there.

When we arrived, I do remember everything seemed loud. I could hear someone screaming in labour, I could hear moans and groans of discomfort, snoring and fingers on keyboards tapping away by the nurses station. It was weird, like a calm before the storm, then the hospital smell hit me it was so strong I threw up all over the nurses station. They were not too happy.

Straight to a bed for examination and the most wonderful pain relief ever! Sod the breathing through pain, for heaven sake I'm married to a doctor!

I hope they didn't think I was one of those pampered princesses. I then slept for a while. I've no idea how long but then woke up with immense pain.

Bobby was with me but didn't look happy. The next thing is I'm in theatre and the anaesthetist was doing his checks singing along to the radio.

"I bet you never thought childbirth would be like this."

Everyone was jolly around me. I think he was referring to his singing.

I'm sure I slurred my words to answer. "No, I thought I would be sitting in a birthing pool, listening to Abba singing Dancing Queen, wearing a nice bikini top."

Where do these thoughts come from? I tried to smile; I don't think I could move very much at this point.

"Abba, you like a bit of Abba. Sarah love, do me a favour and ring reception, ask them if they can ring up the radio station to put some Abba on for us."

The next thing I remember is 'Knowing me Knowing you' being played and then the cry of a baby.

That noise, that alarm bell of I am here, I have arrived.

They took the baby away, I didn't know what I had, then a second cry.

Bobby was wearing scrubs and just grinning. He was then handed the first baby while they took the second baby away. There was lots of happy noise. And I fell asleep.

I woke up in a private room with Bobby and the nurse holding a baby each.

We have a boy and a girl. I can't believe we have two beautiful babies. I cried with joy as Bobby handed me our little girl, he then held our beautiful boy and sat next to me on the bed.

Thank you for my healthy beautiful babies. Thank you for all the wonderful hospital staff and drugs. Thank you Bobby. I love you so much.

Saturday 15th February 2003

It has been very quiet next door, lots of comings and goings of cars and I saw Mrs Wade hurrying over quite early on, but no sign of that woman or the brats. I am a little curious about what's happening there.

I half expected some type of apology for half scaring me to death in the summer house, or at least some kind of acknowledgement of my presence there. It is most strange there has been nothing.

I sat for a long time in my greenhouse studying the painting, I feel quietly quite pleased with it.

Michael will be furious when he finds out I have taken up a hobby. I know he will say I should not have time and that if I need something else to fill my time, I should join the Bridge club.

The problem is Georgina has actively encouraged me to explore my own interests and honestly, I do blame her for this rekindled fondness of art.

I can't tell Michael it is entirely her fault as I would not like to have to stop seeing her and until I can find a way to match her up with Seb I will need to be careful.

Michael rang to say that the trip has had to be extended until Wednesday, strangely I was quite relieved to have a few more free days.

I want to try and find somewhere to continue my art with good light and out of Michaels sight.

I don't feel I can continue in the summer house next door as there will be no privacy now.

I suppose I will quite miss scaring the little brat.

Monday 17/2/2003

I've got five minutes to myself before the night feeds start.

It amazes me how tiny our precious babies are. I still can't believe it as I watch them sleeping peacefully. We have two beautiful healthy babies. It does feel like a miracle.

I felt I needed to reflect on today. I want to remember every precious detail while I can, as I'm not sure I am going to be able to keep up with my journal for a while.

Bobby has not left my side and I've just cuddled and fed the babies while Bobby has changed their nappies. I'm still very sore and can't get out of bed too easily at the moment. I thought giving birth naturally was painful, but this is a different level and I have to wait six weeks before I can drive.

Peter and Helen arrived this morning to meet their baby grandchildren. They brought a pink and blue teddy bear. I think Helen is so excited about buying baby girl dresses, although so am I. They stayed a while then went back to help Christine with the boys.

Christine sent some beautiful wildflowers. How did she know?

Mum and Dad arrived later in the afternoon and brought the boys to meet their brother and sister.

They had to wait in the family room while I was being examined by the doctor.

I could hear mum whispering very loudly 'Frank get your pants on now or you are not going to get that special present from Papa.'

I love the way mum always manages to bribe the boys. I think she's given up on positive talking to them and realised boys can be very different to reason with than girls.

Next thing the door flung open and there stood Frank

completely naked holding his willy. What is it about little boys and their willy's? They always seem to have their hands down their trousers.

Mum and dad, Helen and Peter, followed.

Frank was ready to pounce on the bed but was grabbed by mum. Robbie stood quietly by the door. I could see him looking at all the medical equipment around me, then he looked at the twins in their plastic cots and burst into tears. Bless him, it must have all been too much.

Frank in all his glory dashed over to him and said it's ok. We are getting a present. That put a smile on his face.

Skylet woke up. I asked Robbie if he wanted to hold his little sister. His beautiful blue eyes shimmered and he nodded.

He came and gave me a big hug then sat down in the hospital chair next to my bed.

Mum passed him Skylet, and he gently cuddled her. It was so lovely.

Bobby walked in and just smiled at me. My heart melted until the biggest fart you'd ever heard, and the most horrendous smell came from Skylet.

Robbie almost dropped his baby sister. He couldn't get rid of her fast enough. Bobby dived towards them both and caught her.

"I'm not touching a girl again! They are smelly."

Bobby placed Skylet in her cot and proceeded to change her nappy.

Frank stood holding his nose then squealed looking down on Skylet and shouted, "He's not got a willy."

At that point Tommy woke up crying. Dad picked him up as runny poo started seeping out of his nappy all over his white baby grow and clean bedding.

Robbie then screamed, "Send them back, I don't want them!" at that point a nurse came dashing in to see what all the commotion was about.

This happy beautiful image of the boys meeting the twins turned into a nightmare and I just burst into tears. How am I going to cope with everything, when I can't cope with what I already have.

Helen walked over and said, "It's ok. I have an idea and don't worry we are all here to help."

Maybe this is why my real mother gave me up. She just could not cope!

I'm so glad they are keeping me in for few days. I'm having nightmares about going home.

I can hear Skylet stirring, that lovely baby noise. It must be time for the next feed. I feel all over the place. I'm sure everything will be better tomorrow.

Thank you for Skylet and Tommy. Thank you for my wonderful family. Thank you hospital staff for keeping me in longer.

Monday 17th February 2003

I have had a very strange day.

My appointment with Georgina was most disturbing. I explained the events leading up to and including finding myself interrupted in next doors summer house. She was actually quite unsympathetic and had the audacity to suggest I had actually been trespassing and breaking the law. Honestly, there is no pleasing some people.

She even went so far as to say I should be apologising to the awful woman and what on earth had she done to deserve to be held in such contempt.

When I stopped being so angry by Georgina's reaction, I did actually think which particular incident had triggered such dislike in me towards the stupid woman. It's just there is something so familiar about her ridiculous smile...

Anyway, I had wandered down to the green house and was busy wondering what to do with the brat picture when Mrs Wade appeared at the door. She was incredibly angry with me and most rude considering she had barged in on me in the summer house, she was in full flow when I stepped to the side, and she caught sight of the brats picture.

I almost laughed as she stopped mid flow and her mouth flapped on silent words and her eyes widened in surprise then narrowed. She was quiet for what seemed like a long time, and I was so mesmerised I couldn't speak. She finally broke the mood with, "Oh Clarissa what have you done."

I didn't even know she knew my name but before I could correct her, she continued telling me it was a beautiful picture and she had no idea I was interested in art, well why should she, after all I hardly knew her.

Before I really had a clue what to say to her, she squared her shoulders and said in a very firm voice I clearly needed somewhere to paint that was more appropriate than the green house and that she had just the place. She ordered me to follow her, and my foolish legs obeyed.

I really don't know why I did. Clearly, I was on auto pilot and behaving quite out of character.

Through a gate at the side of her house she showed me into what clearly has been a space designed to paint in. There were canvasses against the wall and the heavy smell of turps brought back long repressed memories of the school art room.

For a moment I thought I was going to cry. Georgina being so sharp with me must have upset me more than I realised.

It has definitely been a day of changes and strange emotions. I didn't remember to correct Mrs Wade, Christine, about using my first name. She was very firm with me that I was not to bother the awful woman next door and that my using the studio could be a temporary thing until I get sorted out and it would remain our secret.

Of course, this is all well and good, but I am not happy that Mrs Wade speaks down to me, or that she assumes she is permitted to call me by my first name.

I also do not plan to apologise to that awful woman next door for upsetting her. After all I was not doing any harm and they certainly never used the summer house.

Mrs Wade dared suggest I should hand over the picture of the brat to his mother. Well, that is not happening. I have hidden him in my room so that he is safe.

I will need to pretend to have been contrite over my behaviour so that I can use Mrs Wades studio.

When Michael returns I will need to think of a way to get to Mrs Wades without him knowing as he would not approve of my fraternising with her.

Friday 21/2/2003 - Coming home with the twins

Bobby came on his own with the two car seats. The lovely midwife Lizzie, who has been amazing looking after me, helped us carry Skylet and Tommy to the car.

I mentioned to Bobby, that we must remember to send all the staff a thank you card.

Bobby grinned and said he was one step ahead as he's already sorted it with a big box of chocolates. He's so good.

Bobby also suggested as Skylet and Tommy were a good weight both weighing five pounds six ounces and doing well we may have got our dates wrong.

I came home to a lovely welcome from mum, dad, Helen, Peter, Hannah and John, with lots of pink and blue balloons on the gate post and a big banner the boys had help make saying 'Welcome home mummy.' Although their artwork of the twins was very graphic with a penis and breasts. I'm guessing that was Robbie's artistic talents again.

We also had another addition to the family which was a little bit of a shock. In the corner of the front room was a budgerigar. Beautiful bright blue feathers and a very loud shrill!

I glared at Bobby; he shook his head as if to say nothing to do with me.

The boys were more excited to show me their new pet than to acknowledge their brother and sister.

It turns out mum and dads special present for the boys was to get a goldfish.

I know I have baby brain, but I still know the difference between a fish and a bird.

I was far too tired to take on board the explanation about having to set up a tank for a week and the pet shop wouldn't allow them just to buy a fish.

We had a goldfish at home that we won at the fair. I remember carrying it home in a plastic bag. It lasted for years. Although it did change colour a few times. Still, I don't understand what a budgie has to do with anything.

Robbie and Frank wanted to call it Thomas, after Thomas the tank engine. (not even Tommy after their brother). But then the shop keeper told them he thought it was female so now it's called Clarabel after one of Thomas's carriages.

It was all too much so I crept off to bed. Knowing I'll be up in a couple of hours for the next round off feeding.

Oh, and I can't stand the smell of Vick or the taste of Fisherman's Friends.

Thank you for bringing my children home safely.

Thank you for everything and anything. Too tired to think.

Friday 21st February 2003

Michael has not even noticed that I have been popping over to Mrs Wades, he has been so busy with golf and Seb. He has hardly had anytime at all, and poor Seb has not been anywhere near on social calls. Clearly something important is taking up their time.

In some respects, I am actually quite relieved that they are both so preoccupied.

I have been back over to the summer house and managed to move all the art things into Mrs Wades and have quite successfully made the space my own. Fortunately, I have had very little need to speak to her, although I am curious why such a dowdy little woman should have an art studio. She certainly does not appear the type who would have any artistic talent.

I mentioned that to Georgina, and she had the audacity to raise her eyebrows and ask me what an artist with talent looked like. Honestly, if she wasn't such a qualified therapist with impeccable credentials and so perfect for Seb I would not waste my time with her.

All I want to do at the moment is paint, and I blame her for that too. I have even lost interest in the garden, and I have increased the cleaners' hours to free up my time. I know I shouldn't be so interested but it is so familiar and engrossing. It gives me the same rush as popping next door, knowing I shouldn't be doing it but what harm is it doing.

I try not to remember when I was younger, and it was my all-consuming passion.

Georgina is so nosey she actually asked me to talk about why I had stopped painting. I couldn't possibly tell her if she ever shared that snippet of our acquaintance with Seb he would, as Michael warned me, find me socially quite unacceptable and I dread to consider how Michael would respond. He was very clear on our wedding day that our arrangement hinges purely on my not painting or discussing my past.

It was all so long ago, but the stigma remains.

Mrs Wade mentioned that the woman next door had had twins. How awful for the poor doctor. He seemed such a nice man. How on earth he has got mixed up with someone with four children I don't know.

Friday 28/2/2003

Haven't been able to keep up with my journal. I'm exhausted.

How am I going to cope? It's really worrying me, even the thought of getting the boys to school and nursery as I can't drive yet. How do other mothers do it?

At least I still have Bobby around for another week. I really don't want him to go back to work.

Mum and dad are going to stay for a few more days, Helen and Peter went back home last week.

Hannah and John have been helping with the boys and Christine is just my guardian angel helping with her amazing cooking.

I stood in the kitchen for five minutes yesterday just wondering where I was going, then I remembered I just needed the toilet. My brain feels like mush.

And to add to my confusion I feel like a milking cow and all the twins seem to do is cry, feed, poo, repeat.

Beth came round with Paul the other day. She is looking amazing. Just glowing. I'm not sure how hands on Paul will be when their baby arrives. He was very reluctant to hold either of the twins. But it is very different when they are your own.

The midwife said I'd done really well as Skylet and Tommy have both put on an ounce. Which really doesn't sound very much at all.

I'm sure the midwife has never had children and definitely never felt that excruciating toe-curling latching on. Tummy to Mummy, nose to nipple rubbish. My boobs are going to look like spaniels ears by the time I've finished.

Bobby said I'm doing really well. What does he know. He's a man! I've decided in my next life I'm coming back as a male!

Bobby has suggested he does the last feed using some ready-made baby milk. He's bought a dozen little milk cartons. Who knew there was such a thing.

Finally, some quality sleep and allowing my sore nipples time to stop throbbing. I'm not telling the midwife. She's a bit scary and if Bobby's agreed to do it. I can say the doctor said it was ok.

Thank you for ready-made baby milk.

Thank you for all the wonderful support from mum and dad, Peter and Helen, Hannah and John and of course Christine.

And just thank you, despite how I'm feeling I am very lucky. I must keep on reminding myself.

Friday 28th February 2003

Mrs Wade has been spending a terrible amount of time with next door and there have been people coming and going in a variety of different cars.

I thought about reminding them the street is not their personal car park and took the notices outside to put on the cars, but Mrs Wade caught me and suggested, in a very sarcastic tone which I did not appreciate, that I was not the traffic warden, and my time might be better spent.

Something in the way she said it was indicative of a veiled threat and the only reason I stopped was because I do not want to lose the use of her space for painting.

She really can be quite formidable; I don't know how I ever thought she was mousy, and she has the sharpest most intelligent eyes. Such a shame Michael would not approve of her, she is so beneath us.

I had to go to the surgery this morning. Dr Walton was very interested in how I was getting on with Georgina. Of course, I didn't mention my plan to introduce her to Seb, but I did say she asks rather a lot of personal questions and that perhaps he might suggest to her, discreetly of course, that I feel uncomfortable with them. He also asked how things were next door. I told him the poor Doctor now has four brats to care for and his useless wife, but that all in all apart from the inconvenience of having to stop using their summer house everything was not acceptable but tolerable.

I am sure he looked disapproving about the summer house incident, perhaps he agrees with me it is a shame to leave it standing neglected and unused. Of course, he was much too busy to go into a great deal of detail.

I did add I hoped that they would soon have no choice but to move to a more suitable area and he looked very thoughtful and nodded his head, so I take that as an agreement and acknowledgement of my predicament.

Michael and Seb are going to a conference in Amsterdam over Easter, I do wish I could have gone along too. I would so love to see the place. I could have gone to the Van Gough Museum and the Rjks Museum to see the modern and contemporary art. They would never have known I was there, and they could have been at their conference without my interfering.

Michael did not even let me finish suggesting I join them; it was a very categoric NO.

Truly he seems to have lost the drive for igniting our relationship.

Later when I tentatively suggested I had hoped to spend more time with him he suggested I should remember my place and that I am a woman not a lovelorn teenager... It was on the tip of my tongue to remind him that where he was concerned, I had never been a lovelorn teenager, then I remembered my place and let the subject drop.

At least I can paint while he is away without worrying he will find out.

I will perhaps speak to Georgina.

I feel most out of sorts with my life beyond my painting.

Monday 10/3/2003

The twins are almost four weeks old. It's been an absolute blur.

With Robbie and Frank, I knew to the hour how old there were and how much they weighed.

I've no idea what day it is, or what I ate for tea.

We made a decision to stop breast feeding. That has taken so much pressure off me. The twins are now sleeping through, so I do wonder if they weren't getting enough from me.

After mum and dad went back home the other week our house has seemed relatively quiet.

Saying that mum has come back on her own today for another week to help out as I thought Bobby was going back to work. Bobby's paternity seems to be going on a lot longer, which I'm really pleased about.

I have asked on several occasions when he's planning to go back but I've not had a proper answer. He's been very quiet, I guess we are just both tired.

Peter and Helen keep coming up at weekends to help with Hannah and John, which has been great, so Robbie and Frank are being entertained and not feeling like they are getting their noses pushed out.

Bobby suggested we had some time to ourselves this evening and go for a walk with the twins. We've not actually been on our own with them or our new double pushchair.

I wrapped them up, so they were warm and snug and left Robbie and Frank with mum.

I'd forgotten how much how I love the feeling of cold fresh air on my face and filling my lungs. It was good to feel a little more human.

Then Bobby produced a hip flask.

I felt very naughty, but it was lovely as we walked and talked swigging whiskey. It was like date night.

The twins just slept and by the time we got back home the house was in darkness, so we just carried the twins into their cribs.

Thank you for a lovely evening. Thank you mum for babysitting. Thank you Bobby for the hip flask.

Monday 10th March 2003

Michael insisted we had to go the golf club this evening.

Seb was very pleased to see me and asked how I was and what I had been up to. For a horrendous moment I thought he had found out about the painting, but he was just being polite.

I was very flattered when he commented on how lovely my hair looked until I caught Michael's very disapproving eye. Michael responded, very sternly that I have begun to let myself go. Before I could respond Seb burst out laughing and said not at all it made me look quite charming. Secretly I was thrilled to have him step in as Michael always listens to him.

My hair has grown considerably, and the red is very obvious because rather than time in the hairdressers each week I have been painting.

The talk shifted to the captain's dinner, and I am quite sorry I will have to cut painting time down to organise that,

I suppose.

Seb hasn't actually asked me too, but I usually act as his hostess. What a shame I can't get him to meet Georgina. She could have saved me the trouble of having to juggle my time.

It was terribly nice to spend quality time with Seb. I did comment on his notable absence but before he could respond Michael reminded me, he was his friend not mine so why would I expect to see him. I was most embarrassed, and Seb looked quite uncomfortable, luckily Mrs Warbottom chose that moment to spill her drink all over her husband, so the commotion acted as a distraction.

On the way back at about 9.30 pm we drove past the Doctor and that terrible woman out walking with the new brats. How ridiculous at that time of night and giggling like school children. I should report them.

Michael slowed the car down enough to make his disapproval clear by glaring at them both then mumbling very unflattering comments about their behaviour. I am sure he called the Doctor a relationship wrecker, I wondered if he knew about the affair with the blond that I had caught the Doctor having, but when I queried his comment, he snapped at me to shut up.

I really do resent how he speaks to me at times, it must be the drink!

Sunday 30/3/2003 - Mothering Sunday

Bobby got up to sort the twins and told me I had to stay in bed. I wasn't going to argue, I'd forgotten how much sleepless nights take it out of me. Although the twins have slept through until the early hours of the morning. Fingers crossed this will continue and go for a few more hours.

So, I propped my pillow up and sat quietly for about five minutes looking at our walls and counting the large sunflower heads on the brown and yellow wallpaper. Fifty-one and a half along and twelve and a stem down. I wonder how long this wallpaper has been here. It's funny how fashion changes. I'm sure in its day it would have been all the rage. Looking at it now, it feels quite depressing. I don't understand why Bobby would rather decorate the attic room first. We have enough rooms on this floor for everyone and once Skylet and Tommy are about six months old they will both be sharing the nursery. Who knows what goes on in his head.

My peace and quiet didn't last for long as Robbie and Frank came charging in and jumped on the bed with a slice of cold half eaten toast, half a mug of milky tea and Mother's Day cards that were made at school and nursery.

I love looking at their artwork. I actually think Robbie has a talent. A bit early to tell with Frank and I have to be realistic he is only three.

We had a lovely cuddle then they disappeared and left me to enjoy my breakfast in bed.

After about five minutes I could hear talking outside and thought I could hear Seb's voice. Then I could hear the boys saying, 'leave it, no you leave it, Daddy tell him, no boys you need to be quiet, or you will frighten him.'

Then I heard a bark. I was hoping I was just hearing things. But I was wrong.

The boys came bounding upstairs with puppy in tow.

O.M.G. I can't believe it. They have got me a puppy for Mothering Sunday!!!

Can I cope with a budgie? Can I cope with a rabbit? Can I cope with four children? How the hell am I supposed to cope with a puppy as well???

I was happy with my half-eaten toast and lots of cuddles, maybe we could have all gone out for Sunday lunch. But no, a puppy that will need training and time spending with it. What was Bobby thinking?

My face must have said it all. I really did try to look excited, obviously I didn't do a very good job as I saw the disappointment in Bobby. He's been really trying over the last few days. Something's not right with him. I felt so guilty for not being grateful for my present.

The boys were running around our bedroom with the golden Labrador puppy chasing after them.

I have to say it was wonderful seeing the boys playing well together the puppy does look very cute. It reminded me of the toilet roll adverts. How can I possibly get rid of him? The boys would be heart broken.

Bobby was holding Skylet while Tommy was still in his crib, he took the boys out of the room while I got dressed.

I carried Tommy down and fed Tommy while Bobby fed Skylet while the boys and the puppy were having a great time in the garden.

I didn't really talk to Bobby. I wasn't sure what to say until he said he's not back at work yet, so don't worry, he'll help with the boys and Charlie. I looked at him and asked who was Charlie?

He pointed to the dog basket and cage.

There wasn't a lot else for me to say and why is Bobby still on paternity leave?

Rang my mum and Helen to wish them Happy Mother's

Day.

Pottered around the house trying to feel happy. I didn't hear a peep out of the boys as they were having so much fun with Charlie.

Had a takeaway for tea as the rest of my Mother's Day treat then went to bed early feeling very overwhelmed with everything.

Come on Seren think of three positives.

Thank you for the twins sleeping through.

I guess thank you Charlie for keeping Robbie and Frank entertained.

And thank you for takeaways so I didn't have to cook.

Sunday 30th March 2003

I do not know how long Mrs Wade had been sat watching me paint today. I had not even heard her come in; she made no sound until she sighed as I put the paint brush down after the final stroke.

Oh, my Clarissa. She said standing up and coming towards the painting. Childishly I wanted to hide it.

Some people do not appreciate abstract art, but I do and judging by the rapt expression on Mrs Wades face she did too. We stared at the canvass in silence.

I had painted the hardest period of my life onto this canvass and not realised what I had done until the final stroke.

Silently Mrs Wade walked out but still I sat there seeing the mess of colour, anger, hurt, and yes betrayal.

A few minutes later Mrs Wade handed me a very large whiskey. I downed it in one and she refilled my glass, then sat down.

I have not talked about art to anyone so knowledgeable for many years and so enjoyed her company. I was quite disappointed when she had to go to answer a phone call from her son who was calling to wish her happy Mother's Day.

I hadn't realised it was Mother's Day until then, and the knowledge made me quite sad. I wondered what kind of mother I might have been in a different life from this life that I have now.

Michael was still not back when I crept home thank goodness. I am glad to have the peace and time to think without him here.

I have an appointment on Tuesday with Georgina and need to tell her about the painting and the content of the boxes I hid. It seems as though she has been leading me to this point from our first meeting. I do hope she knows what she is doing, and that I can trust her.

Michael will be furious. I am not supposed to have any life other than the one he has created for me.

Tuesday 1/4/2003 - April Fool's Day

The day started off really well. Bobby helped with breakfast then sorted Charlie, Paul and Clarabel, (not quite sure what he did for the rabbit and budgie), while I walked the boys to school and nursery and got them there on time. It was quite an achievement especially with the double pushchair. I then decided to walk into town with the twins and just have time to myself wondering around. It feels like an age since I last went into town, besides, I have to get myself used to doing it on my own.

While I was outside Marks and Spencers, I bumped into

one of the partners of the practice. The one from Winchester college, Chris who was very polite. It was strange that he didn't ask how I was or the twins, he just said it's terrible what's happened to Bobby, and he's been so badly treated. Tell him they were all thinking about him, and they know the whole system is wrong.

What kind of sick joke is this? I know it's April fool's day. But this is not funny.

I hadn't a clue what he was on about, so I came straight back home and quizzed Bobby.

When I told him about my bizarre conversation with Chris, he looked away from me, shuffled his feet like a small child needing his mother.

I've never seen him in this light before, he's always been the strong tall man, assertive and pragmatic. It was the first time I'd really looked at him that way.

Bobby then told me he's been suspended from work.

He said he was suspended at the end of February due to allegations made by a patient of professional misconduct.

I knew we were both exhausted, just trying to cope with our expanding family. I had no idea he was struggling with anything else.

I asked him what he'd done to this patient? He said he really didn't know and wasn't given the name of the patient until further investigations.

How do you defend yourself when you don't know what you've done wrong?

Bobby is so professional; he always does everything by the book. I know he wouldn't take any short cuts with anything because he would never want to jeopardise his job or more importantly our family. He told me not to worry as he had a meeting with Dr Walton this afternoon.

Just when I thought Bobby and I were getting on so well. I don't understand it. I felt I was getting on my feet and our family seemed settled. Although the puppy is doing my head in barking and peeing. But to be fair to Bobby he has been dealing with Charlie.

He said he was going to tell me about it but was waiting until he knew more from his meeting. But still I can't believe he's not told me. I am his wife for heaven's sake. What other things has he not said.

I've found myself talking to the budgie. I get more sense from her about my life. At least Clarabel listens to me.

I have to admit I did find myself talking to the washing machine as well the other day, saying thank you for all the extra work it's doing.

Bobby changed the subject and told me that the builders/decorators are starting to work in the attic tomorrow.

What happens if he loses his job? How are we going to pay for builders let alone our home. I asked him why he was so set on sorting the attic. He said his parents had a surprise.

As much as I love Helen and Peter and love it when they visit, I really do not want them living with us.

Bobby went for his meeting. I sorted the twins and then rang mum. As always she sees both sides and said he obviously didn't want to upset me and probably needed to deal with his own emotions.

Picked up the boys and made a nice meal for everyone.

Bobby came home looking more positive. He will find out more tomorrow.

Thank you for keeping us all safe, despite what is thrown at us.

Just had a thought, I still need to deal with Clarissa. I'd forgotten about her.

Tuesday 1st April 2003

April Fool's Day, and oh what a fool I feel.

My appointment with Georgina began quite well. I told her about the painting she was extremely interested, and I told her I had been into the attic and retrieved the box that contained all that was left of my life before Michael.

She asked me lots of questions about the contents of that box and foolishly I shared the answers with her and quite made a fool of myself by crying like a schoolgirl. So ridiculous.

There is no way now, I can possibly introduce her to Seb and when I said that to her, she just smiled and said we could talk about that some other time, that today she was more interested in talking about the box and my art and why Michael had insisted I gave up painting when clearly, I had loved it.

She was quite firm with me that I should in fact not allow myself to be so eclipsed by Michael. It has made me think. I was terribly pushed into our marriage, and I suppose while everyone concerned felt it was a good idea I did rather get lost in the process.

Oddly when Michael arrived home for his evening meal and discovered it was not ready and began to criticise me I felt as though I was someone else listening to him. I even dared to suggest we ate out. He turned me down saying he would call Seb and go to the golf club.

I was surprised at how pleased I was to see him go.

I wandered over to Mrs Wades hoping she might be around if she saw the light on in the studio, but she wasn't home. The house was in darkness. I came home more disappointed by that than being in trouble with Michael.

I really am not sure what on earth is happening to me!! I feel such a fool about so many things. I am beginning to wish I had never met Georgina. I am questioning all sorts of aspects of who I am.

Wednesday 2/4/2003

I got up early to make Bobby a cup of coffee and breakfast in bed, sorted the puppy, fresh millet for Clarabel and gave Paul a slice of toast.

I've been so wrapped up with looking after the children, I've neglected Bobby. I need to make more of an effort. Although Christine often reminds me that I'm not Wonder Woman.

As I was sorting the twins and boys out, the phone rang. I could hear Bobby's voice but couldn't make out his conversation as the children were just too loud.

Bobby then came rushing down the stairs picked me up and swung me around the kitchen.

It was Dr Walton on the phone. Bobby said Dr Walton apologised for what he'd put him through, as there were a series of serious accusations from a patient. The practice had no choice but to look into them. There were allegations that could bring Bobby's profession and the practice into disrepute by allowing his wife to be a drug addict and the neglect of their children.

I looked at Bobby with disbelief. We've been put through all this from one patient's lies?

They told him to enjoy a few more days at home and to be back at work on Monday 14th April.

Then it dawned on me. The letter from Clarissa. Could it have been that cow. I didn't say a word to Bobby. I'm so relieved he has kept his job, and I didn't want to take away his joy.

I suggested that Bobby took the boys to school and nursery, as the fresh air would do him good and I would tidy up so we could go out for coffee somewhere with the twins. Bobby agreed but took the twins with him as well to give me some time to get sorted.

When he'd gone I marched round to confront Clarissa. I was so angry that I was sure she had set us up, I just wanted to know the truth.

I knocked on her door took a few deep breaths; my stomach was churning and then she answered.

She looked at me as if I was not worthy. I couldn't stop shaking and I just blurted everything out. I was pathetic.

I asked her if she thought I was a drug taker, did she think my children were badly treated and how dare she trespass onto our property, use our summer house and have the liberty to paint our son.

She just looked me up and down and seemed to smirk. Then she said, in her cold tone, "I am not saying anything to you unless it is in writing," as she didn't want to speak to me.

I told her she was an absolute disgrace, then out of the corner of my eye I could see Paul hopping down her drive, launch himself into her flower bed and dig. Followed by Charlie barking, I must have left the door open. He ran around her beautiful, manicured lawn, doing his stupid zoomies, then decided he'd had enough and did his business.

I don't think she noticed Paul, but Charlie. Her face turned red and ordered me off her property. I was mortified.

All of a sudden I was in the wrong. I grabbed Charlie and went back home with my tail between my legs. At that point two builder vans turned up and four strapping builders walked down our drive.

At least the distraction of the builders took my mind off my horrible experience.

I told the builders to follow me upstairs. Two of them looked at each other. One said with 'pleasure love and the other said where would you like us.'

It wasn't what they said it was the way they said it. This made me feel even more angry. I was so pleased when Bobby came back as I felt really uncomfortable in my own home. I left Bobby to explain to the builders what he wanted doing and we went out for coffee.

Bobby commented on how quiet I was. I just told him it was a relief that everything is going to be alright, but I dare not tell him about my awful encounter with Clarissa.

We stayed out of the house for most of the day while all the banging, mess and noise was going on. I hope I haven't made things worse, and Bobby still hasn't told me what the surprise is with the attic.

A bit of an exhausting day of emotions but at least I can say thank you for keeping Bobby's job safe.

Wednesday 2nd April 2003

I thought Mrs Wade had told my terrible neighbour that I would no longer be using her summer house, and that was the end of it. I am after all much too busy to be bothered with them, trying to sort out my own problems.

It was quite a shock to see the stupid woman looking slim and flushed, on my doorstep this morning, blathering and simpering like a spoilt child. I almost smiled at the effort she was clearly having to make to get her point across. No backbone was what came to mind.

I was tempted, for a second to relent, and tell her she should be proud I had painted her terrible brat, but then her ferocious wild dog came bounding up the drive, nearly scaring me to death, and proceeded to foul on Michaels prestigious lawn. He will be furious when he gets home, as I can't possibly move it.

I thought about the whole incident on my way to town and wondered what on earth Georgina would say. I am sure she would point out that the stupid woman was very brave, or foolish to dare to show her face. No doubt Georgina would make me feel in some way to blame for the whole embarrassing scene.

While waiting for my hair to be done, I caught sight of myself in the mirror. Or rather I caught sight of who I have become. It made me quite sad to see such an unhappy looking middle-aged woman staring back at me. I do blame Georgina for what happened next.

I realised that I liked the red in my hair and that it was growing again. (Partly due to several cancelled appointments) I decided to keep the look.

Marcus was delighted and in his usual flamboyant way snipped here and there and has quite created a much nicer look than my normal severe cut and colour. He made me feel quite feminine and was clearly delighted to be transforming me, as he put it. The lightness of his mood and his charming flattery actually made me feel quite happy with my decision. I have never seen him smile and be so happy in his work. It was quite wonderful.

Michael's reaction was furious. He looked fit to explode and has ordered me to go back and get my normal look back. I will think about it but not yet. A few more days won't hurt.

On my way to Mrs Wades to paint, I am sure someone actually whistled at me, honestly, I was shocked.

Of course, it had to come from the gaggle of builders milling around next door and cluttering up the street with their vans. Typically, it has to be the terrible neighbours disrupting the peace.

I told Mrs Wade what had happened regarding the whistle, and she laughed at me and queried my shock.

She said my hair made me look younger and less severe and unapproachable but then added I probably needed to rethink my outfits as I am adding many years to my age. I mean really, she does know how to cross the lines. I dress to reflect my status and position as Michael's wife. When I pointed that out, she merely raised her eyebrow and tutted. Such censor in her attitude that it hurt more than her words. I should stop seeing her, she is a bad influence on me. I am sure her and Georgina are conspiring to cause Michael and I to fall out.

She is so sure of herself I wonder how I ever thought of her as mousey. Sometimes I do find myself secretly smiling at her, she is a character.

I actually wish we could become friends, but Michael would

be so angry, and he must never know about the painting. I really must make sure she does not assume a friendship that we couldn't possibly have.

I WONDER what she really thinks of me. I know she is fascinated and loves my paintings but that's as far as we can go. I didn't feel I could mention this morning's altercation with that woman next door, I didn't want to see the disapproval in her eyes and spoil the mood.

Wednesday 9/4/2003

Thank goodness the builders and decorators have finished. We can have our home to ourselves again. Peace and quiet (well it's all relative) and no more running a cafe service for them. Can't believe how much milk and packets of biscuits we've been through.

I know they are busy working for us but it's such an intrusion of our personal space. And I didn't like the innuendos, "Come and see how much more banging you want me to do for you love." And, "Where do you want me to put your electric points, we all need a bit of electricity in our lives."

I'm sure one day I heard them wolf whistling out of the window at some poor passer-by. I thought wolf whistling was a thing of the past and I bet they never spoke to Bobby the same as they did with me.

Despite all their gross humour. They have actually done an excellent job. The whole of the attic looks amazing, so big, I can't believe the space. It's so bright and airy. The Velux window opens so you can stand on a balcony overlooking the back garden. There's a walk-in wardrobe with a built-in dressing table. The en-suite has two sinks and a walk-in shower that is big enough for two.

Bobby even arranged a super king size bed.

I can't wait to use it. But I am concerned about the children being on a different floor level to us. It makes our bedroom look so pokey and grim.

Did the usual running around after the Children.

Feeling really happy today. Bobby seems in a really good place too.

Had a lovely chat to Beth, she went for her scan, she said all went well but wants to keep it a secret about the sex of the baby. I'm so pleased for Beth and Paul.

Mum and dad gave me a quick call, but it was a really bad line. Not sure where they are this week. I can't wait to see them again.

I was about to phone Helen and Peter to say thank you for the attic. I'm guessing that was their wonderful surprise, but Bobby told me not to. Maybe he wants to thank them himself.

Thank you Bobby for organising our new bedroom and thank you Helen and Peter for our fabulous surprise.

Thank you for Beth's healthy baby.

Wednesday 9th April 2003

Today should have been my last appointment with Georgina.

I am thrilled that she had spoken to Dr Walton, and they have decided that in light of everything that has been happening with the terrible woman next door I can continue my visits.

I was a little wary about the new medication she prescribed, terrible side effects, but she assures me I will be very well monitored. As long as I can paint, I am quite happy.

I haven't told Michael the visits have been extended. He is so grumpy towards me all the time. I am actually quite thankful he is spending so much time with Seb, I do feel slightly sorry for Seb, as he is a kind man, but clearly more able to cope with Michael than I am at the moment.

Michaels absence has made me feel more confident about my art, I do think Georgina is right it has been terribly therapeutic and makes me feel actually quite fulfilled and happy. She did rather cross the line when she suggested Michael had suppressed my true personality.

I told her in no uncertain terms that I had a role to play that required me to adhere to rules of socially acceptable behaviour.

She looked horrified and I find myself wondering how I ever thought she could be a good match for Seb. She really has no idea. Which is probably why she is only a Ms.

I have been thinking a lot about that woman from next door. She really is tiresome. I have seen her a few times heading up the drive. Usually at most inconvenient times and had to shoo her away. I have no idea what she can think we have left to say.

Perhaps I will speak to Mrs Wade and suggest she mentions that she should stay well clear as Michael is terribly contrary at the moment and the repercussions of further irritating him will not be pleasant.

I wish they had never moved in; my life has been so completely disrupted. The only good thing is the painting.

I found myself going back through the gap in the fence to

just look at the summer house. I didn't dare go any further. Probably just as well as the vicious dog began to bark.

I will have to block the opening back up as I can't have it in my garden.

No sign of the blue-eyed brat though

Thursday 10/4/2003

I've tried to go into Clarissa's garden a few times to clean up Charlie's mess. I feel sick to the stomach about what happened but each time I've attempted to go down her drive, she's spotted me and shouted for me to get off her property.

I even tried sneaking into her garden when it was dark, but all her security lights came on, it was like Blackpool illuminations, and I could see her glaring out of her bedroom window. I really have tried to do the right thing.

Then today I went to put the children into the car. I could not believe my eyes. There was dog poo all over my windows, bonnet, and door handles.

Why would someone do that? Sick and senseless. Luckily, I spotted it before Frank grabbed the door handle. I stood staring at my car in bewilderment at what to do.

Christine was passing. (What is it about Christine, she's always there at the right time. It's like a weird connection, she just knows) anyway, she saw the state of my car and offered to take the boys to school and nursery. She really is my guardian angel.

I took the twins in and rang Bobby straight away.

The only person I could think of maybe capable is Clarissa. But would she actually do this? This is even low for her. I couldn't imagine her actually picking it up poo let alone smearing it.

I finally got hold of Bobby and he told me to take photos and call the police.

I wasn't expecting the police to turn up as quickly as they did, although he wasn't an actual a policeman he was a Community Officer. A young lad. (That's when you sound old when the police are younger than you). He was very nice and understanding. He asked if I knew of anyone that would do this. So, I was honest and gave him a brief history of them next door.

He went to talk to Clarissa and Michael, to ask if they had seen anyone vandalise our car or anyone they didn't recognise down our drive. He couldn't ask them directly if they had been involved.

He hadn't been gone long when he came back down our drive looking very flushed in the cheeks and was shaking, so I invited him in. I thought it was only me she had that influence on.

He said a male answered the door, and when he asked the questions the male said, "are you arresting me?" He explained no and said he was just making enquires. He was then asked if he was a proper police officer. He explained what he was and then the male shouted at him to get off their property. He had no right, and how dare anyone send an unqualified person round to their home to question them.

The poor young lad didn't know what to do. I made him a cup of tea. He had a few sips and then left saying he needed to write a report and would keep me posted.

Christine came back a bit later after the school and nursery run with a pair of rubber gloves and lots of disinfectant and fondant fancies from Latinos.

I couldn't have Christine cleaning my car. So, she offered

to make us a cup of tea and watched the twins while I sorted it.

She didn't say too much which is very unlike Christine. I then walked to pick up the boys, wondering what else are our neighbours are actually capable of.

When I got home the young Community Officer was at our door. But this time he was with his Sergeant. They were both looking very seriously at me.

It turns out that Clarissa and Michael went up to the police station after the young Community Officer's visit and produced a very large file on our behaviour with very serious accusations about our children, keeping dangerous animals, criminal damage to their property and I had deliberately covered my own car in dog excrement to make false allegations against them. The final straw was how I have manipulated Dr Williams to make him stay with me as I need him to supply me drugs!

I stood with my mouth open. Surely this was a wind up and Ant and Dec will come running through our front door with the rest of the camera crew.

But no. They suggested we avoid them at all cost, and we should keep a record ourselves. They were not following up on all the accusations. Only the ones that they had a duty of care to alert the dangerous animal enforcement office and social services. They then got up and handed me a card, saying if there is anything they could help me with, then to give them a call. With that they left.

I was in shock, then I was absolutely livid! And where the bloody hell has Bobby been all day.

Oh, playing golf with Seb. Since when has he played golf?

When Bobby finally got home, after I'd sorted Robbie,

Frank, Skylet, Tommy, Charlie, Paul and Clarabel. I started telling him the whole saga. At that point I'd reached for the wine!

Then there was a knock at the door before I could finish my tale. I got up to answer it and there stood a beautiful, slim, immaculately dressed woman. She spoke in a very posh voice telling me she was my Doubla and Mr and Mrs Williams have asked her to help.

What the hell is a Doubla?

Bobby came rushing to the door, gushing all over her. Saying, "It's so lovely to meet you in person".

That's all I need a posh professional woman, who probably has never had children of her own, telling me how bad I am looking after my children, my home, my animals.

Bobby took her bags and took her straight up to our beautiful attic conversion!

It was all too much so I've come to bed, with the wine bottle and my glass!

Can't believe after the day I've had; she's staying in the best room of the house.

My only positives for today are, thank you Christine for the delicious fondant fancies and all your support. And thank you to the maker of very large wine glasses!

Perhaps tomorrow I will wake up from this nightmare!

Thursday 10th April 2003

Michael got up this morning in a terribly foul mood. It seems he had wanted to see Seb and perhaps play some golf, but Seb had made other plans.

I tentatively tried to suggest he could still pop to the golf club himself, but he snarled at me that these days anyone could ask for membership to play and be accepted, there were no standards on who could be accepted. The day went downhill from there.

I'm not sure really quite what happened but someone came to the door while I was hoovering ready for Mrs Brown to come and clean, and the next thing Michael slammed into the bedroom obviously furious, for a heart stopping moment I thought he had found out about my art and trips to Mrs Wades, it was almost a relief when he demanded I hand over everything I had compiled about next door.

He snatched it off me then disappeared into his bedroom slamming the door behind him clearly not intending to give me an explanation or answer my anxious queries.

I am still in a terrible whirl about what happened next.

I mean it is one thing to complain to the relevant agencies about how terrible the neighbours are but actually to find oneself in a very uninviting police station hearing Michael rant furiously about them was most uncomfortable.

How I wished I had a stronger stomach and gone and removed the dog foul from the lawn. He made them sound so, so oh I don't know. But the dog foul seemed to have been the catalyst for us being at the station.

I could almost imagine Georgina's disapproving look at the allegations Michael was intent on sharing. I did try to say I had passed them on to the relevant people, but no one seemed to be listening to me. I suppose that is because I am after all just Michael's wife.

It was all most uncomfortable, especially when I recalled Georgina's arched eyebrow as she suggested I had been breaking the law by trespassing into the summerhouse and that actually I had stolen the plants I have so carefully nurtured. Whatever will happen if that all comes out.

Sat in that awful room with the sounds of shouting and ringing phones I was beginning to feel quite faint.

I have no idea why Michael has chosen now to be so angry. I really do not have time now for this.

How I wish they would all just move away, and Michael would just get back to his normal life with Seb.

I don't know what Georgina will say about all this.

Tomorrow I will have to try to speak to Mrs Wade and suggest she advises that terrible woman she needs to really consider the disruption she is causing and move.

Friday 11/4/2003

Bobby got up this morning and said I need to thank his parents for this amazing opportunity of introducing Bronwyn into our home. He said our life will be amazing with her, he was brought up with Nanny Gladys for many years before he went to boarding school. His parents went all over the world on various trips and holidays.

Then he announced he was going to make Bronwyn a cup of tea, show her the ropes, a tour of our home and take her on the school and nursery run.

I stayed in bed as I couldn't face the world, especially with what happened yesterday and now this woman, who calls herself a Doubla is in our home, with the new super king size bed and all the beautiful bedding I just bought thinking it was for us.

Bobby eventually came back upstairs, without a cup of

tea for me, to say how wonderful Bronwyn is. He was like a star struck child, raving over this woman because the boys did exactly what she asked them to do, and they even made their beds and own pack lunches. Breakfast and the school journey was a delight and the boys seem to love her already. Nanny Bronwyn has made a timetable for us all to create a perfect family home.

Well, she f---ing would, wouldn't she!

Then he proceeded to tell me lunch will be ready at around one o'clock and why wasn't I out of bed already.

I told him I felt unwell, and I really wasn't hungry.

I've not even met Nanny Bronwyn properly yet, but there's something about her, or perhaps I just want my home and family back to some sort of order my way.

I decided after lunch I'd better make an effort. I can't hide under the bedsheets all day.

The house was very quiet and then I spotted Bronwyn walking down the drive with the twins. To my horror she was stood talking to Clarissa.

When she came in I told Bronwyn she needed to be very careful what she said to that woman as she's delusional and has made up lots of lies about Bobby and myself.

She looked me up and down and said, "I found Clarissa to be very complimentary about Dr Williams and I was admiring her Corylopsis sinensis var. sinensis." (I had to look up the spelling!)

Was she speaking a different language? And then she tutted and said – "also known as Chinese winter hazel. You have to have well drained acid soil. It takes some skill to have it as beautiful as Clarissa's."

She's not just super nanny she's Percy Thrower

reincarnated! And to add insult to injury she thinks Clarissa is amazing and has told me she's been invited for tea at the next gardening meeting.

I asked Bronwyn where Skylet and Tommy were. She looked as if I was questioning her ability.

Her answer was they need routine and I've left them asleep in the back garden.

I said they don't usually have an afternoon nap otherwise they won't sleep through. All I got was, "In my experience this is exactly what the twins need, a proper routine".

I put on a false smile and turned away from her to make myself some toast. She then told me not to eat too much as she planned to cook Beef Wellington for dinner, and perhaps Dr Williams, when he's not too busy, might take a look at me."

I was seething. This woman is in my home, with my children, telling me what to do. And again, where was Bobby. I think she must have read my mind as she said, "I told Dr Williams that it was absolutely fine that he went to play golf as I have everything under control".

Is she a witch? And why can't she use our married name Williams De Lacy, I am his wife after all.

I can't cope with this woman and it's only day one. The problem is I don't feel like I have the energy to fight her. So, I've come back to bed hungry, I really feel like I need a good cry. And I've missed my morning cuddles from the children.

I'm hoping Bobby - when he can get off the golf course, will come and see me soon with the children.

Do Peter and Helen really think I am doing such a bad job? Am I a bad mother, wife, person?

I feel inadequate as it is without super nanny interfering in my life.

Forget my three positives, I can't think of any apart from wanting to shoot that bossy bitch for invading my home.

Friday 11th April 2003

Michael spent today in his study, only appearing for meals and had very little to say. I think he was drinking but the mood he was in I decided to stay out of his way and keep quiet. It has been another wasted day where I have been unable to paint. So frustrating.

I did start to head to Mrs Wades, but then was terribly surprised to see Bronwyn, Mrs Warbottom's niece, pushing next doors twins down their drive and out onto the street. I was almost speechless it was such a shock.

How on earth can they afford such a prestigious nanny.

Perhaps that terrible woman has decided to make some sort of effort to fit in after all. Such a shame she didn't try harder sooner. I expressed surprise that she should be in attendance to such a family and actually tolerating living with them.

Apparently, she has a beautiful room on the third floor, newly finished especially for her, small but adequate and I feel she is slightly enamoured by the Doctor by the way she was gushing over him.

She said the children are absolute darlings, a comment only someone in her profession would ever make about such terrible brats!

She invited me to admire the tiny bundles in the pram, but I couldn't bring myself to look, all this fuss over babies. I have never understood it when they cause you such pain.

I felt it was my duty to extend an offer of friendship as she will need someone of her class to talk too, so I have asked her to join us for afternoon tea when the garden club ladies come. That will please Mrs Warbottom.

We did actually have quite a pleasant chat about plants and gardening, so much so that I invited her to have a look at my Corylopsis sinensis var sinensis which is stunning with its lovely delicate yellow flowers. I am so proud of it.

Of course, I didn't tell her it was a plant I had relocated from next doors garden up by the summer house and how thrilled I am to be growing it in view of everyone and so successfully.

I didn't get across to speak to Mrs Wade as I was worried Bronwyn might notice and mention my visit.

Just as well really, as I doubt, Mrs Wade will be happy to learn of our visit to the police station. I have been worried about that all night, what if someone saw us there, whatever will people think. What on earth was Michael thinking of by being so in discreet. I really don't know how my life got so disrupted.

Sunday 20/4/2003 - Easter Sunday

I've not been able to keep up with myself let alone my journal.

I feel like I'm living in a nightmare, watching someone else's happy family. I don't think anyone has noticed me, not even the children. Even Charlie has stopped opening our bedroom door to see me in the morning to have his chin tickled.

Bobby is back at work working all hours, so I've missed him in a morning and I'm asleep when he comes home. I honestly don't know what has happened to my life.

Nothing feels right, I'm like an intruder in my own home as Bronwyn has taken over everything.

But I felt I had to make an effort for my children as it is Easter Sunday. She told me she has sorted out the most amazing bunny hunt for the boys. I told her I always do it.

She told me not to worry as she loves organising and didn't want to put on me, besides it's one of her specialities. She's baked and got lots of wonderful treats for the boys and everyone. I questioned everyone?

She replied saying she's invited Helen and Peter Hannah and John, and Christine.

Why has she invited our friends and family?

How does she even know them?

I asked her why she hadn't invited my parents? She said, she had but they were busy. When have my parents ever been too busy to see me and the children?

I really didn't want Bobby's parents or anyone to be honest as I'm not feeling up to entertaining, but she's already done it without me knowing. She said Bobby has agreed and thought it was a good idea. I don't want Bobby's parents seeing me like this. I think they think Bobby has married below his status as it is.

I didn't want to disappoint the boys as they were running around the garden having so much fun with Paul and Charlie finding all the Easter eggs that had been hidden.

I'm not sure if it's my imagination but has Charlie put on weight? In fact, are my children looking a bit chubby faced.

I could see how happy Bobby was and when everyone arrived he was introducing them all to Bronwyn as if she was his new partner.

I was about to go back to my room when Christine came

over to me and asked if I was ok. I started filling up with tears, so she took me into the kitchen, and I sobbed on her shoulder. How embarrassing that I can't cope.

Then I saw the delicious spread Bronwyn had made. Even her fondant fancies looked professional, just like Latinos.

I said to Christine, I didn't feel well, and I should be grateful for all the effort that Bronwyn had gone to. She didn't say very much. She just gave me a 'grandma look' of it will all work out.

I went back to my room, had a quick look out of the window and could see Christine talking to Helen, then Helen looked up at the window with a look of disdain. I'm rubbish! I've come back to bed.

I really don't know what to do or who I am at the moment. Perhaps they are all better off without me, I'm just a burden to everyone.

AGAIN, NO POSITIVE AFFIRMATIONS!!!!!!!!

What is there to be positive about these days?

Sunday 20th April 2003

I was so disappointed that I ended up sat next to Mrs Ivory in church this morning. She is such a gossip chattering on about the Smythes spending so much time with my terrible neighbours and quizzing me about Seb not being on the golf course with Michael, as he is so taken with the Doctor and seems to be on the course with him a lot. She even suggested he and Michael had fallen out.

I was quite at a loss as to where she was going with her inquisition. When I said she was mistaken about Seb and Michael as they are away on business in Amsterdam she laughed and asked if that's what they called it. I can only assume she is referring to the amount of golf they will no doubt play and that her husband is clearly jealous of Michael and Seb.

It was a relief to get home.

I went to Christine's to paint. She was out so it was wonderful to just get on with it. When she did finally come home, she asked me if I knew Bronwyn.

I told her of course, and that she is very professional and sought after. I am not sure what to make of Christine's raised eyebrows and now I wonder why she was so interested in her credentials and family. It is after all unlikely she would ever need to employ her or recommend her to anyone.

Wednesday 23/4/2003

Super nanny has taken over my home, my children and my husband. She's even been driving around in Bobby's car to meet friends; I've noticed she goes out at the same time every day.

Bobby said she's part of our family now!

I cringe when he mentions her name. How can I compete with this woman?

Bobby seems to have a sparkle about him. I hear them laughing on a night and him telling her what an amazing cook she is, how tidy the house is and how wonderfully behaved the children are.

I miss him. I miss my children.

I just don't know what to do. I find myself crying most of the day and I'm so tired. I avoid her as much as possible. I don't want super nanny to see I'm a failure.

I daren't say anything to Bobby about how I'm feeling or make any negative comments about her. I'm really worried I'm going to lose him.

It wasn't until Christine came round. I was still in bed, looking a mess. She suggested that maybe I had postnatal depression and may need medical help.

Christine said she would talk to Bobby as I didn't feel I could. In the meantime, she would keep an eye on the children and Bronwyn.

Am I ill? That was a complete shock to me. I don't have any history of depression, surely Bobby would have noticed.

I know if I say anything to the medical profession about depression then it can have an impact on our life insurance. Depression is what other people get. I have everything, a home, a husband, no financial worries and four healthy children.

I started crying again.

Christine said it wasn't anything to be embarrassed about, it's quite common after having children that a woman's hormone imbalance can make you feel very down.

She said she would go and make me some tea and toast to give me some strength and energy to get me going again. She also commented on how much weight I'd lost.

Apparently it was safe to go downstairs as she'd seen Bronwyn at Clarissa's with the twins enjoying her 'Garden Party.'

I sat at the kitchen table, and I continued to pour my heart out.

Christine is amazing.

I do believe she is my fairy godmother; she always seems to understand me.

I suddenly felt better, in a stupid way that I wasn't going mad, and I wasn't totally inadequate, I'm actually not well.

I nipped upstairs to wash my face and as I passed the landing window I could see Bronwyn with Skylet, she was passing her and a bottle to one lady while Tommy was being fed by another lady who I didn't know. They all looked very cosy in their little knitting circle in Clarissa's garden.

I didn't realise Bronwyn was such a good friends with Clarissa.

Has Clarissa set me up, to send me mad, to destroy and get rid of me. Maybe she wants Bronwyn to be my replacement as Bronwyn keeps telling me how wonderful our neighbour is and how much they have in common.

I went back downstairs, and told Christine, she told me not to be silly, it's just because of how I feel.

Christine said she had an idea on how to help me and not to worry, she's there for me.

With that she left.

I have to say I did feel better after a long shower and putting my face on.

Once back downstairs I checked the rest of my home. I'd forgotten how much work we'd done in such a short time and what a wonderful home we have.

I then sat and waited for Bronwyn to come back with my babies.

I asked her where she'd been. She said, "having a wonderful time with some friends. The twins were so well behaved. There wasn't a peep out of them they just sat and smiled at everyone and were now ready for their bottles."

She passed Skylet to me and said, "I'm sure mummy would like to feed you, as mummy is looking much better."

Was that a dig?

I sat with Skylet and proceeded to offer her her bottle, but she wouldn't take it.

I could see Bronwyn watching me, expecting me to get upset.

Tommy was fast asleep, which usually meant he'd just been fed, I said nothing and cuddled Skylet, I said to Bronwyn that Skylet would take her bottle when she was ready. I think she made a little scoff noise.

She then asked if I could leave the kitchen so she could prepare tea, before she picked up the boys.

I felt really tired again so went back to my room. I must have slept for a while as the next thing I knew Bobby brought me my tea on a tray. Beef Stroganoff.

I have to say it was delicious but it would have been nicer if he'd woken me so I could have sat with our family.

He was looking at me with kind eyes and didn't mention anything about the nanny, just asked how I was feeling and gave me a big hug.

He said everything would be ok and sorry for not being there for me.

Thank you Christine for your help.

And thank you Bobby for realising I am struggling.

Wednesday 23rd April 2003

Today was the Garden Club meeting at my house.

It was such a relief that Michael was out because Bronwyn arrived to join us with the two new scrawny brats from next door. Had he been home it would have been most embarrassing having them here.

I did expect her to come alone and had she voiced her

intention to bring them I would have told her they were not welcome; she had had adequate notice of the invitation and could have taken time off.

Mrs Warbottom was thrilled to see her and teased her that she was behaving like a doting mother. I almost pointed out that she was no more than the glorified hired help, and clearly unable to take time off, but I was distracted by Mrs Ivory asking for more tea and tucking in to the fondants that Bronwyn said she had made but looked suspiciously like the ones I love at Latinos. I am sure I must be mistaken as why would she try to pass them off as her own.

Of course, all the ladies were completely in awe when she began to pass the little bundles around as if they were parcels to be unwrapped and admired.

I felt quite uncomfortable with all the fussing and cooing and managed not to get to involved.

Quite unnecessary behaviour from Bronwyn. I am shocked that that woman next door would allow them to be displayed in such away. I suppose she can't be bothered with them herself but do rather wonder what her plan was by allowing Bronwyn to bring them. Perhaps she was deliberately trying to disrupt my afternoon and make me feel unhappy.

I must admit that I couldn't help but notice that the tiny baby girl has the most incredible eyes she reminded me of another baby long ago and for a terrible moment I was quite overcome, then she screwed her face up and began to howl with the most ear shattering noise coming from something so small until Bronwyn shoved a bottle of milk in the squawking mouth and handed her to Mrs Warbottom and another bottle to Mrs Kerwin for the boy.

It served to remind me she was nothing at all like the baby I remember; that child was perfect and quiet and content.

We really were terribly distracted from the point of discussing gardens and making our plans for the coming year. It was quite frustrating to have gone to so much effort for it to end up so disrupted.

Another wasted day where I could have been painting. Most annoying. I will be more selective about spending my time with Bronwyn, I have decided today she is rather odd. She is very full of how wonderful she is, and I tasted her fondants and am certain she did not make them as she claimed. There is just something not quite right about her.

Michael didn't come home for evening meal, just left a message saying he was with Seb, I was glad I hadn't started to cook as it was the perfect chance to slip to Mrs Wades.

It was a surprise to find her in the studio setting up more easels. When I asked her what on earth, she was doing she raised her eyebrow and politely reminded me it was her art studio and she had decided to start a therapy group. I was terribly dismayed at the prospect of not being able to continue to use the space and a little shocked when she said I should continue to come, and she would work her group round me. I suppose that is really the least she could do, after all she had said I could use the space.

I felt I have very little choice other than to accept her suggestion.

I just hope no one will recognise me, it would be terrible if they did, and it got back to Michael.

Almost as if she had read my mind, Mrs Wade said that it was highly unlikely the type of people, I associated with would attend.

Somehow, she managed to make the statement sound quite derogatory. She really has no boundaries. Yet I do find her quite refreshing.

Thursday 1/5/2003

Bobby put me on some medication last week. It's like life is in slow motion, my reaction times feel so sluggish but on a positive I am feeling better. Well, I was until this morning.

Super nanny was taking the boys to school and nursery, then taking the twins to a soft play. Can you believe it she asked me for money so she could buy herself a coffee as she was meeting a friend! Don't we pay her enough?

She had been gone half an hour when there was a knock at the door. To my surprise there was a very young - handsome I may add, policeman and a scruffy old man, without any front teeth hunched over next to him, with quite a stern cold stare.

They asked if I was the owner of a golden Labrador. Obviously, I said yes. They then went on to say there had been a serious report of a vicious stray dog called Charlie, and that lives at this address. The young officer said they needed to see the dog and have a discussion about its behaviour.

How can it be stray when they know its name and address?

The policeman was lovely, but the man it turns out was the dog warden, or whatever title he used, then proceeded to put on a very large pair of protective gloves.

I was told this was because the dog had been reported as extremely aggressive. The dog warden needed to take precautions and if the allegations were true it could lead to having the dog exterminated!

I just stared at them, was this a sick joke?? I asked who had made these allegations. But they weren't allowed to tell me.

How do you defend yourself against such a lie?

I took the men into our front room, before they could sit down Charlie came bounding in, jumped up at the policeman licked his face with his tail wagging, then rolled onto his back, legs in the air while the policeman bent over to rub his tummy.

The dog warden stared at the dog and asked its name.

I was so confused they'd already said have you got a dog called Charlie.

Then he asked if we had two dogs? I said no we only have one, Charlie.

He proceeded to question me on how old he was and what his nature was like, did I allow him to roam about the streets and has he attacked anyone?

The policeman was making a fuss of Charlie saying what a lovely dog.

I told him he was about three months old, and we'd not been able to take him out until after his twelve-week jabs.

The dog warden appeared annoyed. He got up to get close to Charlie, Charlie rolled over on his back waiting for a fuss from the dog warden.

Both men looked at each other and said, we have to take these allegations seriously and have to follow up on any reports of dangerous animals.

But they could clearly see he wasn't a threat to anyone.

I was almost tempted to say no shit Sherlock but bit the inside of my mouth instead.

The dog warden grunted and walked out.

The policeman followed giving Charlie another love and thanked me for my time.

I was so upset. Gave Charlie a dog treat and a big love, then went back to bed. I just wanted to hide under my blankets and avoid the world again. Slept for a few hours then got up to make a cup of tea.

What have I done wrong? Why are these things happening to us? Who would make such an allegation? Why am I so rubbish, why can't I just be left to get on with my life like everyone else?

I sat and cried again, until I heard super nanny coming home with the children. I went to quickly wash my face and put on a smile.

Bronwyn was looking a little flustered, what happened to the perfect nanny, oh sorry Doubla!

She then said that from tomorrow I need to start helping with the meals again, as I was looking better, she felt it would help with my recovery.

Cheeky cow! Who the hell does she think she is?

She then said could I take the twins while she prepared dinner.

I made a flippant comment that it was Thursday, so she must be cooking Spaghetti Bolognese tonight. She gave me a nanny glare. I actually felt quite good that I may have annoyed her.

I took the twins over the road, as I'd not really been out of the house much, to meet Christine. I felt I needed some help preparing our meals, there's so much pressure on me now if she's going to eat what I've cooked, and besides I've no food in the cupboards. It always surprises me that Bronwyn hardly ever goes supermarket shopping yet makes fantastic meals.

Christine commented on how much better I was looking. She seemed so pleased to see me and the twins. I have to be honest it did feel really good to be out again with my babies.

I told her about the dog warden and policeman, but she didn't really say anything, then I asked her if she had any ideas for good meals that were tasty and easy to make. I was starting to feel a bit overwhelmed as I've been struggling to think and do anything. Christine said that was a normal side effect to my medication, then she got up to go to the kitchen.

To my surprise she produced Beef Wellington, Lasagne, Beef Stroganoff, Spaghetti Bolognese, made with homemade pasta and garlic bread, Sweet and Sour Pork and Green Thai Chicken, boxed up in silver trays so I could just re-heat them in the oven.

Perfect! As Bobby has loved all the dishes that Bronwyn has been cooking. I can stick with the same meal schedule for the next six days, and to top it off Christine gave me some Fondant fancies.

I asked if Bronwyn had been baking for her too?

Christine tipped her head to one side and just smiled. And told me I will feel better soon, and my head won't feel quite as foggy.

She then suggested that she kept them in her fridge as she had the space.

Bobby was home on time this evening and we all sat at the table to enjoy Bronwyn's Spaghetti Bolognese.

Bobby wasn't raving over her meal like he has done.

It was a bit of a strange atmosphere. When he asked if I'd got the message about mum and dad calling. Bronwyn looked flustered and said she'd been so busy and forgotten to tell me.

I left the table and came to bed early wondering if I was imagining the change in the atmosphere tonight.

All I want to do is sleep. I'll call mum and dad tomorrow.

Thank you Christine for helping with our family meals and thank you Charlie for being such a lovely natured dog.

Thursday 1st May 2003

As I was leaving my appointment with Georgina today, I bumped into Christine in the reception. Quite a shock!!

I hardly recognised her she looked so smart and the gentleman she was speaking to, who looked quite important, seemed to be very deferential to her.

I waited until she had said her goodbyes and then she saw me. I was dying to ask her why she was there and what she thought of the place but before I could she said ah Clarissa what a pleasant surprise, let's go for a coffee, as if it was the most natural thing in the world!

I was so surprised that I fell into step with her.

Latinos for coffee with Christine, whoever would have imagined it, fortunately she looked quite unlike her usual mousey self so I am sure no one would recognise her.

I was not surprised when she said she had never been in Latinos while she was busy studying the menu for evening meals, after all it is quite up market. Why on earth would she ever go there.

Most annoying how every time I tried to find out why she was at the clinic she managed to side track me and then Luigi appeared at our table with the coffees and news that from tomorrow he will be closing for ten days to return to Italy. I suggested it was inconveniently short notice for a holiday and he said he was attending a family funeral. Christine jumped straight in with sympathy, and he seemed very taken with her. They chatted about the menu and by the time we left he had arranged to drop her off a selection of meals and cakes to try as he would have no need of them. He claimed to know exactly where our street is and that it was his pleasure. I have never seen such outright flirtation and felt I needed to apologise to Christine when he left us. She threw her head back and laughed at me, telling me not to be such a prude.

We then went on to discuss an art show that she had seen advertised. She asked me if I would like to go but sadly, I felt I should say no as Michael would not approve. Of course, I could not say that to her, so I just said I was busy.

Fortunately, she did not push me, but raised her eyebrows in that infuriating way that makes it clear she is sceptical.

I noticed she did not attempt to ask me why I had been at the clinic, and I would so have loved to discuss Georgina, I'm sure she would be so impressed with her.

Monday 5/5/2003 - Bronwyn's day off Bank Holiday Monday

The house feels so calm without Bronwyn, I can't put my finger on it, I heard her leave quite early this morning before anyone else was up. I'd forgotten how lovely it is to have our home to ourselves.

I'd got up quietly, so as not to disturb the children and to take Bobby a cup of coffee up to bed for a change from him bringing me a drink.

He was still sleeping so I left it on the bedside table. He looked so peaceful I didn't want to disturb him.

As I stood on the landing I suddenly had a gut feeling to snoop around Bronwyn's bedroom. It was her day off and I wasn't expecting her back until this evening, so I dared myself to go into her room. After all it is our home.

I opened the door feeling nervous and very naughty.

At first glance the room looked very tidy, then I noticed a framed photo of my children, Bobby and herself by the side of the bed. I felt sick to the stomach, what the hell is going on?

To the far side of the bedroom was the twins cots and a mini fridge. I can't remember ordering a mini fridge for the attic. I went over to open it. Inside it was the twins bottles, sweets, and chocolate bars.

It doesn't make sense she's so slim. I had no idea she had such a sweet tooth, and what's the problem with using our kitchen fridge?

On top of the fridge, I noticed a large bowl of what looked like dog biscuits.

I was so bemused by everything I hadn't noticed that Charlie had followed me. He came bounding into the bedroom, whizzed past me and went straight to the fridge to helped himself to the dog biscuits. How did he know where to go?

As I tried to grab him, I knocked the little side table over with such a clatter and a pile of papers that were next to the photo seemed to go everywhere.

I scrambled around trying to tidy up, hoping not to get caught by Bobby, I was still feeling angry about the photo.

As I was busy on my hands and knees I had a feeling

someone was watching me, when I turned round I nearly jumped out of my skin. It was Bobby. Just standing there wearing his dressing gown, hands in his pockets and shaking his head.

I froze, he looked angry but then his expression changed when he saw the photo, he picked it up looking completely shocked. He muttered, "What the hell!"

Bobby then asked me what I was holding. I'd not really looked at what I was picking up, I was just placing them back on the table. They were receipts, invoices, and my credit card.

He took the paperwork from me and studied it. Bobby and I looked at each other. He asked me what was going on, I said I'm asking you the same question.

We then heard the children downstairs.

Bobby said would I sort the children and animals out while he sorted out the mess.

I wasn't arguing. I was too cross and upset about the photo.

It was about half an hour before Bobby came into the kitchen, all showered and dressed.

He didn't say a word about my little incident. I was expecting a lecture from him about privacy in his posh doctors voice, but instead he said he had no idea about what is going on.

He was livid that his and the children's photo was in her room. He promised he would get to the bottom of it and assured me there was nothing going on with him and Bronwyn. We had a huge hug and he told me how much he loved me, and our family and he would do anything and everything to protect us.

I've known him long enough to believe him and feel a little better that he will sort it out.

Then he sent me to get ready as we were all going out to an adventure park and bird gardens to meet mum and dad this afternoon.

It was lovely to see my parents. Bobby and dad played with Robbie and Frank. Dad was having more fun than the boys, going down zip wires and climbing obstacles.

Mum and I walked around the bird gardens with the double pushchair. This is the first time all six of us have been out together. The sun was shining, and the birds were singing, and I had chance to have a good chat to mum about Bronwyn's room and the photo.

She looked quite upset but said she believed Bobby will sort this and she had no idea that I'd been feeling so low. Mum said she had been calling most days but was told I was unavailable.

It was reassuring to know they had arranged to stay at Hannah and John's so they could be close to me, and I was not to worry about anything. It was such a relief to hear that. I gave her a big hug and sobbed.

We had a lovely afternoon, and the children were so well behaved. Fresh air and exercise always seems to do the trick. I'd forgotten how much I love being a mum.

Back home for afternoon tea.

The children bathed and in bed by seven o'clock. Result!

Bobby and I sat down with a cup of tea and cuddled.

Bronwyn arrived back about nine o'clock. Bobby to my surprise was quite rude to her and asked to have a word. I left them both in the front room and went to bed.

Thank you Bobby being there for me and arranging a

lovely afternoon with mum and dad and the children.

Monday 5th May 2003

Michael drove himself to Sebs and they have gone off on a golfing trip again.

I commented I haven't seen Seb for several weeks and asked if he was avoiding me, Michael snapped that he preferred to keep Seb from coming here as he was so easily distracted. Most intriguing, what on earth was that all about.

I was still pondering when I had the idea to paint Seb a portrait as a birthday present. That is of course if I ever dare confess to Michael how I am spending my time.

I have found a rather good photo of both Michael and Seb together; It's from one of their golfing trips and the light is very good, they are very close, and the camera seems to have perfectly captured their bravado, I have decided to add Michael into the portrait as perhaps then he won't object so much.

I really do need to find a way to persuade him to allow me my hobby. I think it is quite clear I can remain a useful wife and still be an artist without it being an embarrassment to him. I just need to broach the subject when he is in the right frame of mind.

I realised I have not seen anything of that woman from next door for a while, well not since she finally took the hint about not coming up our drive. She has obviously decided to stay out of sight.

Her absence and Michael refusing to discuss the subject of the visit to the police station is making me a bit anxious, what if someone saw us there, what if Michael finds out about me going into their garden and the art things. He has even refused to elaborate on the file he has on them or return my notes.

I looked in his office for them, but the desk was locked and the keys missing.

I am wondering if I should ask Bronwyn what is happening. I do hate not knowing. If I discuss it with Bronwyn she may misunderstand and gossip. I can't question Christine because she can be terribly judgemental and always has a way of making me feel in the wrong. She is far too involved and under the influence of that woman. She has no idea how awful it is having her as a neighbour. Its disruptive and completely at odds with how things used to be in this street. I just wish they would up and move and life could be simple again.

Georgina was quite heartless in her assessment of events and still lays the blame squarely on my shoulders, most unkind of her, after all she is employed to counsel and support me.

Tuesday 6/5/2003

This morning, to my surprise, mum and dad were in the kitchen. The boys were dressed and eating breakfast while mum was feeding the twins.

There was no sign of Bronwyn, and nothing was really discussed about her, apart from she needed to be elsewhere and would not be coming back. I've no idea what went on. But I am glad she's gone.

Mum just smiled and said, "It's ok. We are here for you. Dad is taking the boys on the school run and I want you to take these headphones and then go for a fifteen-minute walk."

I wasn't sure what she was talking about. Mum then gave me a portable C.D. player.

Off I went around the block listening to positive affirmations.

- "I am safe and in control."
- "I am strong."
- "I trust myself."
- "I am capable."
- "I inhale peace and exhale worry."

I have to admit I did feel better for it. When I got back, mum had tea and toast ready.

She told me I have to do this every day.

She's also booked me in for an art class with a difference this evening and not to worry about anything as they will sort the children and Bobby out. I've Just to take one step at a time.

I then had a lovely day with mum, pottering around the house. We had a chat about my biological parents. I wonder if my real mother had postnatal depression. Is it a hereditary thing? I need to ask Bobby.

Christine brought one of our ready meals over for tea, and said I'll see you at seven o'clock.

I wasn't sure what she was on about. I just thought she must be doing the class with me.

When I arrived at Christine's she took me to the back of her house. Her garden is huge and at the bottom was a separate annex. She asked if I was ready for my first Art Therapy lesson.

The annex was her own personal art studio. It was amazing. Better equipped than college. About five or six easels all set up ready, pots of brushes, pencils, paints, oils.

She even had a daylight lamp.

I had no idea Christine loved art. I still wasn't sure about the therapy bit. She showed me around and then said. Off you go.

I enjoyed every second. I can't believe I was there for over two hours. The time just flew.

I'd remembered seeing a Monet painting in the National Gallery, I think it was called Bathers. I painted it to the best of my memory on to the canvas.

Christine was very complimentary and didn't realise I enjoyed painting. She said she loved my brush strokes and had an eye for detail.

I felt so proud of myself. It was so good to be painting again.

I felt like Robbie and Frank, wanting to take my artwork home to show my mum and dad. But I decided to keep it there in case I wanted to add more detail.

When I got back home, mum, dad and Bobby were sat in the front room. I thanked them all for giving me their support.

My face is aching from smiling. It's feels like such a long time ago since I last smiled. Very much looking forward to my next art lesson.

Thank you mum and dad for being here for me. Thank you Bobby for getting rid of Bronwyn and thank you Christine for allowing me into her studio (she's a dark horse with all her hidden talents).

Tuesday 6th May 2003

This morning at 5 am what a mystery!!

I had got up and was looking out of the landing window wondering if it was too early to go and paint at Christine's as the light was so clear, when I saw Bronwyn reverse her car out of the drive onto the street. She looked quite dishevelled and not her usual smart self at all.

I would almost be inclined to say she looked quite suspicious really.

She stood for a few seconds scanning, almost as if she was checking no one was around in the street and then leaving her boot up she disappeared back down the drive. For several minutes she rushed up and down filling her car boot with boxes and bags then jumped back in her car and sped off as if the devil was on her tail. It was all most odd.

I told Christine what I had seen but her only comment was good riddance to bad rubbish, which was really no information at all!!! and what on earth did that comment mean.

Bronwyn was, by all accounts, outstanding at her job.

I must confess I did wonder about her and the doctors relationship as she had seemed quite enamoured by him and the children. I had almost felt sorry for his wife, moving his bit on the side in under her nose. Perhaps he was trying to set her an example and jolly her up into a more acceptable wife.

Sometimes Christines refusal to inform me what's happening on my street and with the neighbours is so frustrating!!

Today she was very preoccupied with getting the studio ready for her art class. I do hope that I am not going to be disturbed by them after all I am very settled and busy with my own work.

When Michael came home from staying at Seb's, I told him what I had seen but he had no explanation, just a bitter comment about how he didn't know how anyone could live with that family and it would be in everyone's best interest if they packed up and left!

I took that opening to ask him what had happened to my notes that he had taken from me for our visit to the police station.

He narrowed his eyes at me in an angry glare, and it struck me, not for the first time how cold and piercing his eyes can be, so totally void of any warmth, he replied that they were now his notes and I should stick to my gardening, his tone was very flat and final and I found myself backing away from him.

Really sometimes he is quite menacing!

In the end I told Georgina about the incident with him because I couldn't quite shake the unsettled feeling he had stirred up, she listened quietly but when I paused, she began her questions.

I told her I am his wife and should not have questioned him really, after all he had my best interests at heart. She was quite interested in my reply, and it took me some time to get her back to not probing my relationship with Michael. I do enjoy her challenging me but at times she does ask far too many questions! It's almost as though she is trying to make me see Michael in a different light and it is quite disconcerting! After all he is just Michael, as long as he is happy with me, that's all that matters.

Saturday 31/5/2003

Another month has flown by.

I've decided to come off my medication. I'm almost becoming my old self again. I've been going for longer walks with my headphones plugged into positive affirmations and I've started taking Charlie with me. Although he's not always that easy to take. (I think I need to book him in for dog classes). He's a strong dog and wants to say hello to everyone. He almost pulled me in front of a car the other day, dragging me to say hello to another Labrador.

Mum and dad are staying with us now. I don't mind that they are in the attic room! I'm so lucky to have their support.

I decided to give Beth a call it was really good to catch up with her. I got a bit of a shock when she said Paul is going on loan to a Scottish club. I said that's amazing but then Beth burst into tears. She said she's as far up North as she would like to be and has no idea how to cope with a new baby without anyone to help.

I feel awful for being such a bad friend. I've been so wrapped up with my own problems just trying to get through the day. I haven't been there for her. I hope she can forgive me.

I then started telling her how I was coping and that perhaps Christine could help, and maybe Beth could come to the art classes with me. She said that would be lovely. I then invited them over for dinner next week after Paul's game.

When I nipped over to Christine's she was giggling to herself. I wasn't sure what had amused her then she showed me a raffle ticket that she was selling for the W.I. They'd obviously made a spelling mistake as it read - 'Spick and Spank. Cleaning more than just your ovens.' At least it put a smile on Christine's face.

I offered to buy a few tickets. Having your house cleaned

sounds like an amazing prize. Although the dinner at Latinos sounds wonderful too.

I told Christine about Beth and she said she was more than happy to help, and if we fancied doing some life models she can arrange that for the next session. It would be like old times again at art college.

Christine also mentioned she was very impressed with the sunflowers I painted last week. It was very much like the Van Gogh. And was most impressed that I'd used the brush handle to score into the thick wet paint just like the original painting. It was such a compliment. I'm loving painting again.

Back home to take Frank to a birthday party. Robbie was happy to go as he still loves running around at the soft play.

Mum came and we sat and had a coffee together while looking after the twins.

Bobby had a good morning playing golf with Dad, Seb and John.

We then had a takeaway with everyone. I love having all our friends and family round.

Thank you for a lovely day. And thank you everyone for helping me feel human again.

Saturday 31st May 2003

Christine is very busy persuading everyone she knows to buy tickets for the WI raffle. Honestly, I was really trying to paint without distraction, so bought a book full just so that I could get on in peace. I didn't realise until later that there were a hundred tickets in a book! Surely, I must win at least one of the prizes, like the hairdresser's voucher, or manicure or better yet the meal at Latinos!

It did make me think though that I have very much neglected the ladies lunch club and Gardening club.

I can't particularly say that I have missed them, I have been so busy painting. I am surprised that no one has been in touch to see where I am.

Now I am worried that they might just mention my absence to Michael. That would be a problem! He has been so preoccupied lately, shutting himself in his study and making long angry sounding phone calls. Seb has been nowhere to be seen which is a little worrying as it makes getting across to Christines difficult.

As if life isn't complicated enough, I am about to lose my cleaner. She complained Michael had been particularly rude to her on more than one occasion over the last few weeks, and she didn't feel she could continue cleaning for us.

I can hardly tell Michael she has left so I will just have to organise my time to fit the cleaning in until I can find someone else suitable.

Yesterday Georgina said she thinks I would benefit from her extending our sessions for a few more months. I must admit she does make me feel more in control of day-to-day life.

I have even stopped noticing how annoying the neighbours are, or perhaps they are just being more mindful of avoiding upsetting us!

If only Georgina would focus less on Michael. I suggested to her she had a very unhealthy interest in my husband and her response of simply raising her eyebrow did not reassure me!

On the whole my art is making the days pass so quickly I can hardly believe where the time goes. Perhaps when Michael is more approachable, I will tell him about the painting and ask if I can have my own studio.

The idea of admitting to him how I am passing my time is quite worrying but as Georgina points out I am a grown woman and accountable for my own actions...

Wednesday 4/6/2003

Frank is still going on about wanting a chicken for his birthday. Who put's the idea of a chicken as a birthday present into the mind of a soon to be four-year-old?

I've decided to get him a toy farm. I nipped into town after the school run with the twins. It was hard work. As I'm wondering around the toy shop, there was a massive crash behind me. To my horror, Tommy had grabbed a Lego model of an aeroplane (it must have taken someone hours to make). There were bits of Lego all over the tiled floor. As I moved to the other side Skylet leant forward and grabbed a jigsaw box which then knocked a load of other boxes off the shelves like dominoes. I wanted the floor to swallow me up. Why do these things always happen to me?

I'm guessing it was the store manager who came over. To my surprise he said, 'I have told them the shop isles are not designed for parents to bring in a double pushchair.'

I was expecting him to be really angry, but he was so lovely, told me not to worry and could he help me with anything.

I've come away with a very large farmyard, four tractors, ten hens, five pigs, two horses, and one farmer. I walked out of the shop with boxes underneath the pushchair and more boxes balancing on the rain canopy. Job done! Such a relief.

Dog walked, Budgie fed, Paul's hutch cleaned, back for nursery run and then school run.

Mum and dad had gone off for the day but came back to help with tea.

I've spent most of the day looking forward to seeing Beth and going to our art class. Beth arrived early to see everyone then we went over to Christine's.

There were a couple more ladies in the studio who Christine introduced us to. They were lovely one about our age the other looked a little older. There was also another lady in the far corner. But I couldn't really see her, she kept herself to herself and Christine seemed to ignore her.

Christine asked us how we were all feeling, we had to give her a score out of ten. Ten, positive, zero, feeling very low. Beth and I both gave a five.

She said it was a safe place for everyone to share emotions and to feel free to express whatever we were feeling through art.

Before Christine started to speak a six foot three, hunk of a man walked in. Beth and I looked at each other - OMG he was gorgeous!

She introduced us to her nephew Philip and then proceeded to tell us she had a treat. He sat quietly on a stool in front of us. Christine told us to draw what we felt rather than what we see.

He was an absolute pleasure to draw, he had the perfect chiselled jaw line, very symmetrical features and certainly had a cheeky sparkle about him, wearing a black and red lumbar jack shirt. The rough and rugged look.

Beth and I just smiled at each other. The last time I drew a life model was at Art college with Beth. The time flew by.

I got home feeling like I'd achieved something. And it was the perfect way to have quality time with Beth.

Thank you for a productive day, the shop manager being so nice to me and Christine for your male model surprise.

Wednesday 4ᵗʰ June 2003

Christine's art therapy group has started.

I thought it would be disruptive, but it was actually quite pleasant to have other like-minded people in the studio chatting about influences and techniques. It created an ambient backdrop to my work.

I was a little disappointed that the terrible woman from next door was part of the group, but I don't think she even realised I was in my own area of the studio.

How on earth she has time to paint and be away from all those brats is beyond me. She seemed to be very popular among the other students and had plenty to say about technique.

When she had gone, I went over to her easel and had a look at what she had painted. I thoroughly expected her to be all theory and no talent.

Oh, my goodness, she may be awful and a terrible parent, but she has got a very impressive hand. Christine caught me studying her canvas and came to stand beside me sharing my appreciation of the painting. She suggested our technique is very similar, I hardly think so, although it did remind me of another artist, I used to know who could create the most unusual, captivating pieces of work, and who I greatly admired.

I suppose, somewhat begrudgingly, that for all her failures in life art is not one of them. That said she is still not appropriate as a neighbour. The sooner she can be moved on the better.

Michael was extremely grumpy when he arrived home today. Shutting himself in his office with a pile of letters. There was a time I would have wondered what on earth he was up to, but now I'm just glad of him being out of the way.

I do so prefer the days when he is away from home. Life is so much simpler, and I can please myself what I do, well almost.

He did almost snarl at me that I needed to tidy myself up as the golf dinner was approaching and if I expected to attend, I needed to present myself more suitably. I wondered how Georgina would have responded to that!

As it was, I said nothing, just nodded and when he vanished went and checked the mirror. My reflection stared back at me from a face that I hardly recognised. What a difference longer hair has made. I look less like my mother (and her age!) and more like, well I don't know, but I'm not going back to starchy me!!!

I suppose I can blame Georgina and art for that!!!

Monday 9/6/2003 - Frank's birthday

With everything going on I forgot about our first-year anniversary in this house, 6th June, what a year we've had.

We've gutted it. Only a couple of rooms left to decorate. The Garden is now like a proper sports field. Football goals, trampoline, tennis rackets, swing ball. In fact, any ball! Climbing frame. It is a bit busy, but I love it. The boys can play outside all day. Mum always told me it's good for the body and mind to be in fresh air.

We've extended our family. Welcoming Skylet and Tommy and of course Paul, Clarabel and Charlie.

We have laughed and cried. Had really happy, joyful experiences and unfortunately horrible ones that I never want to go through again!

I do wish that woman next door would be nicer to me. What have we ever done to her. I feel like I'm constantly walking on eggshells. If the dog barks too loud, or the kids lose one of their balls into their garden. Talking of balls, I did see Michael cutting his grass around a football instead of throwing it back over the fence. He's as nasty as she is.

It's hard to be grateful for everything all the time.

But today is about Frank. I Still can't believe he's four. My little boy, who constantly wants hugs and still sucks his thumb and strokes a silky label, especially the label from my underwear. He often walks around with a pair of my knickers, sucking his thumb when he's tired.

I'll remind him of my knickers if he's giving me grief later on in life.

We all got up to sing happy birthday before the school run and he seemed quite happy with his new farmyard. But not as excited as I thought he'd be.

I had a day of running around. I honestly don't know what I do in a day.

After last year's bouncy castle experience. Bobby has refused to do that again. (I think he's a bit unfair as I like to keep the children equal). We've arranged next Saturday to meet his friends for a soft play day at The Time Machine. They can charge around to their hearts content then we will feed them chips, pizza's, lots of sweets and say goodbye to them. I have to agree that is the easier option.

So, I organised a grown-up family birthday tea for Mum and Dad, Helen and Peter, Christine, Hannah and John, Beth and Paul and even Seb.

After schlepping that farmyard home. Frank played with it for about ten minutes, until Hannah and John arrived.

They only went and bought him a real chicken for his birthday, with a double storey chicken coop and a bag of grain. We now have a bloody chicken!

Frank was over the moon. He sat and cuddled the chicken, which seemed quite happy.

He then took it outside to introduce it to Paul (the rabbit) while Charlie barked a couple of times at it as he wasn't sure. He then got a handful of grain and threw it all over the garden.

Paul and the chicken were both quite happy nibbling away.

Then Frank came running in and said Paul and Tandoori are now best friends.

He's called the chicken Tandoori! We all sat around the table laughing. I just love that little boy to bits.

John, dad and Peter got the coop set up properly. We had to persuade Frank that Tandoori wasn't allowed in the house. So, he gave her another big hug and happily went to bed exhausted.

As it was becoming dusky Tandoori went into his coop and Paul followed.

The pair were snuggled up.

Bobby looked at me and said, "Seren sometimes I think my life is a little bit surreal living with you".

Thank you for Frank having a lovely birthday and on the positive side we can enjoy fresh eggs.

Monday 9th June 2003

Georgina actually smiled today when I told her about my surprise at how well things were going sharing the art studio. She really is quite attractive when she allows herself to relax. It's such a shame I can't introduce her to Seb. It would be quite inappropriate now as she knows far too much about me and about my relationship with Michael.

She lost her smile when she asked how things were between me and the neighbours. I don't think she approves of them any more than I do, but still, she manages to make me feel as if I'm in the wrong.

I told her about Michael being furious and ringing Environmental Services complaining that they were causing a rat infestation and throwing rubbish into our garden.

I suppose by rubbish, he meant the football in the middle of the grass, that he refused to even touch and shouted at me when I thought to move it out of the path of the lawn mower.

Georgina was silent for a moment then asked me if I thought Michael was perhaps over reacting. Honestly, what was I supposed to say!

These days I so prefer not being at home when he is. Christines is such a sanctuary, art is my escape. I can't believe I actually said that to her, but it started a whole new avenue of questioning that in the end I had to say I didn't want to discuss any further.

I'm sure she is trying to wreck my marriage, though quite why I am not sure. I do know that I have started to see Michael differently over the past few months.

Perhaps I should stop seeing Georgina.

Tuesday 24/6/2003

It was a funny start to the day; we were all woken up by an horrendous noise.

The sound was like someone being murdered and it was coming from our back garden.

I sent Bobby out to check everything. But there was no sign of anything unusual just Paul and Tandoori roaming around the garden together.

I also asked Bobby to check if we had any eggs. I was hoping she would be laying some by now. Maybe Tandoori needs time to settle in.

Frank has been a delight, bless him getting up every morning to give the chicken a hug, then the chicken and Paul follow him down to the shed and await their breakfast.

I have noticed that the grass needs cutting. Paul is eating the chicken grain instead of the grass. They are a funny old pair.

Did all the usual running around, nothing too exciting.

The day just seemed to drag. I guess it's because I was so looking forward to my art class.

Beth and I were all set up at our easels, having a lovely chit chat with the two other ladies Lucy and Alex.

Philip, Christine's nephew, walked in with a dressing gown on. Sat on the stool and then allowed his dressing gown to seductively fall to the floor.

I thought he was gorgeous with his clothes on. I found myself staring at a Greek Adonis. He had muscles on muscles. He put one leg over the other in a man's crossed knee pose, leaned over, placed his elbow on his knee to then rest his chin on his hand. As he was trying to be professional giving all us ladies his smouldering look. He then slipped slightly off his perch and let everything hang loose.

Well, he didn't look quite as confident then. We all burst out laughing. Apart from the quiet woman in the corner, wearing a red head scarf who has never interacted with anyone.

I know we shouldn't have laughed. But the last thing we had come to see was a blokes tackle swinging around.

Christine never ceases to amaze me.

All I can say is Bobby has nothing to worry about in that department.

Luckily, Philip smiled, didn't seem offended at all and then joined in laughing.

We had one of the best art classes ever. Until I saw the woman in the corner get up and rush out. My stomach turned. I felt sick. It was only the cow next door. What was she doing there?

Christine could see I looked shocked. She came over and suggested that I focus on his silhouette and concentrate on the good things around us. She knows me so well.

I finally calmed down and enjoyed myself. It feels like such an achievement when you captured all the right lines of your model.

I thought I drew Philip very well. Even Beth said my sketch was really good.

When I got home I told Bobby about Clarissa, not the male model. Thought I'd leave that for another day.

He pointed out that Christine is a lovely lady and wants to help everyone.

He's right, I shouldn't judge. Maybe art is Clarissa's outlet as well. Especially being married to miserable Michael.

Thank you for a good laugh. My score out of ten was six, when I left it was off the scale! Everyone always feels better with laughter.

I've not laughed and enjoyed myself so much for a long time.

Tuesday 24th June 2003

Today has been absolutely dreadful.

I was woken up by what can only be described as farmyard noise, very like a cock crowing. Really on a street like this not what you would expect to hear.

It seems to have woken Michael and he was far from impressed as you can imagine, he is just so grumpy.

He was straight on the telephone to the RSPCA at 9 am, complaining that the terrible family were not fit as pet holders.

I thought he was never going to leave home to go to Sebs.

I am still having to secretly clean as I haven't found a replacement yet, but at least he hasn't noticed, and her wages are keeping me in art supplies. It was so frustrating that he hung around so that I couldn't get on and then out to Christine's. Honestly, life is so busy these days, but in a much more productive way.

The garden club and monthly lunch club are the only things I still attend and that's only because Michael is friends with the husbands of some of the ladies who also attend.

I'm not sure how I felt when I heard Seb had asked Mrs Smythe to organise the captains dinner at the golf club.

To be honest I had completely forgotten that should have been my job. Seb has obviously been avoiding me so that he didn't have to tell me. I am surprised at Michael not mentioning it.

Christine had her art group today. For me that was not a success!

I was happily working on my painting when I realised there was quite a stir among the ladies behind me. Glancing round to see why they were disturbing me; I was quite taken aback by the sight of a totally naked young man. I mean totally naked. I don't think I have ever seen anything so, so NAKED in many years. I felt quite faint and tried to go back to my own work but had to just look once more to check he had not made anyone else so upset. I am sure he saw me and smiled and winked at me. It was terrible and, in that moment, he was so very like someone else I once knew I was pinned to the spot and unable to look away until Christine very calmly asked me to join the group and perhaps do a painting of him.

I was so mortified I couldn't leave the room fast enough. I am thoroughly shocked. I know he was there as art but really, in a studio on my street and all those women staring at him. Of course, next door will have been in her element!

I simply cannot return to such a den of inequity.

Monday 21/7/2003

We've had a lovely long weekend away. Bobby's partner Dr Walton has a caravan near a seaside town called Saltburn. Yorkshire towns have such lovely names.

Christine looked after Tandoori and Paul. The odd couple. They are inseparable. Hannah and John offered to look after Clarabel for us.

It was lovely not having to wake up to that horrible noise in the morning. I've no idea what's going on in our neighbourhood.

Charlie, I feel like he's our fifth child, came with us and had a fabulous time playing with the children in the sea. It was magical.

I got a blow-up paddling pool for Skylet and Tommy, who were happy crawling around and watching the world go by.

The weather has been amazing, we took a picnic down to the beach every day and fish and chips and a bottle of wine for tea every night. Not for the children obviously. What a waste of wine that would be.

The simple things in life are brilliant. The children with their buckets and spades, building sandcastles. As Bobby lay in the sand while the boys covered him up. Robbie had a creative moment. For some reason Robbie seems to have a fascination about breasts. Bobby was lying there with a pair of massive sand boobs on his chest. I decided I wasn't going to interfere. I think the best thing to do is ignore it.

We decided to leave this morning and drive back before it got too hot. I can't believe how glorious it's been.

When we got back, the children were desperate to see Clarabel.

So, Bobby, bless him, offered to pick her up. Although I did think it was a bit odd that he didn't want to take the boys with him.

He was gone ages. It was late afternoon when I noticed Bobby on the drive with the boot open. I clocked his golf clubs and decided to confront him, but as I was coming out of the front door I saw Bobby performing what looked like CPR on the budgie.

He then looked around to see who was watching, how he missed me I had no idea. He then placed the bird back in the cage and drove off.

He came back home about an hour later. The boys ran to meet him at the door to greet Clarabel. I then heard them say, 'Why is Clarabel a different colour daddy?'

Bobby's answer was amazing! He told them Hannah and John had Clarabel sitting in the garden with them because the weather was so lovely.

He asked, 'Do you know what colour the sun is?'

The boys both shouted, 'Yellow.'

There was a long pause, and I couldn't believe the next thing Mr Scientific Medical man said.

'What do blue and yellow make when mixed together?'

Frank wasn't sure but Robbie knew. He shouted, 'Green.'

'Yes that's right. Clarabel is magic and the sun has changed her from blue to green because she's been sat in the sun.'

I've heard it all now!

The boys came rushing into the kitchen excited that we have a magical budgie. As Bobby carried the cage in. The magical budgie then gave a loud whistle.

The boys were even more excited that their new look magical budgie sounded different.

I glared at Bobby. But couldn't say a word in front of the boys. I had it worked out that he'd sneaked off to the golf club. I bet that's the reason why we left early. All this because of Seb's captains day. Trying to get as much practice as possible for the competition.

He just shrugged his shoulders and went to put the kettle on.

He told me he had left the budgie in the boot. While he tried out his new club.

In the boot, in this heat! I said Well you might as well put tin foil around the cage and cooked her! I was so cross and very upset.

The poor budgie must have died from the heat when left in the car. Why did he go to the golf club first? I thought he was a clever man.

He said he went to the local pet shop to buy a replacement, but they didn't have any blue budgies, but at least he managed to get one.

I had no answer!

Well, the boys seem ok for now. How do I explain this one in years to come.

RIP Clarabel mark one. Welcome Clarabel mark two.

Monday 21st July 2003

I was working in the front drive tidying the borders when their car pulled up.

Obviously, the Doctor didn't know I was there because his expletive was quite loud. Naturally, I wondered what had caused such an outburst so stood up to get a better look.

At first, I couldn't work out what he was doing then realised he had a lifeless bird in his hands trying to revive it.

The next thing he slammed the boot shut jumped in the car and sped off. Really, they are quite insane.

Thank heavens Michael didn't witness that incident, he would have had all his accusations confirmed.

I have not been back to Christine's since her naked model debacle. Instead, I have had a wander around a few of the local art galleries. I wonder if Christine was right, and I could sell my art via one of these galleries. It would be very nerve racking in case Michael found out or perhaps it would show him that I can still be respectable and an artist.

How lovely would it be to have him proud of me and be able to openly do what I love. I am so foolish it will never happen.

I blame Georgina for encouraging such ridiculous fantasies.

I saw Christine try to catch me on the way out of Latinos, but I pretended not to hear her and rushed off. Then found a note from her through the door saying I had won a prize in the raffle. Perfect really as it is for a house clean.

I will wait for Seb and Michael to go off for a few days and get them organised to come in and do a deep clean while Michael is out of the way.

I just hope they are more particular with the cleaning than they are about the spelling of their name on the raffle prize. Spick and Spank does not sound very appropriate, even though it made me smile (almost) when Christine found it so amusing. She is so incorrigible, not at all appropriate as a friend.

Saturday 2/8/2003

Bobby was up early to join Seb for his Captains Day at the golf club.

Honestly, the amount of organising. Tables to be co-ordinated with napkins, tablecloths, menus, seating plans. They've been preparing and talking about it for months. It has been like planning a wedding. And that's just the dinner tonight. Although I am very much looking forward to it and so pleased for Seb. This is his big day and I love black tie events.

But the day didn't start off too well.

We've received a letter from the Environmental Agency.

We have had complaints about our cockerel.

It's crowing has caused a 'statutory noise nuisance.' And

we need to get rid of it. But we have a hen not a cockerel, they cluck not crow.

I went straight over to Christine's. How can someone complain about our lovely Tandoori.

Christine didn't seem too surprised by the letter and asked how many eggs has Tandoori laid? What an odd question. Then when I thought about it she hasn't laid any.

It hit me. How stupid, that noise in the morning is our cockerel who hasn't learnt how to crow properly yet. How on earth am I going to explain this to Frank, he loves that chicken. Decided to let Bobby deal with it.

Going to have a bath and get ready for tonight.

***

I've just had a phone call. Bobby has told me the dinner is cancelled and to pour him a very large whiskey.

He'll explain when he gets home.

Saturday 2nd August 2003

Michael is gone, dead, it's not possible... It's so final...

I write the words and hear them resounding in my head over and over

Michael is gone, gone, never coming back

Writing it down does not help

I feel quite empty and lost

What will become of me

He is really not coming back

I should be crying or reacting, but I think the shock has numbed me...

Thursday 7/8/2003

I'm still in shock.

Bobby said, Michael should have been in their team but just before the competition, Michael and Seb had been heard having cross words about Bobby playing with them, and that's when John stepped in, to swap with Michael.

Seb and his team set off down the fairway and were almost at the last hole when a message came for Bobby to help Michael as he'd collapsed.

Bobby thought Michael was just being a prat wanting attention, so he played his shot as he was playing very well in the competition. Then took his time walking back to the 13th hole.

It wasn't until he saw Michael he realised the urgency. He tried his best to perform CPR, but it was useless, he was too late. If only he didn't play his shot he may have been able to save him.

Seb was a few minutes behind Bobby, probably thinking the same that Michael was just attention seeking.

As Bobby was carrying out CPR, Seb flung himself on top of Michael, hugging him close and whaling. Bobby said he's never seen another man so distressed; it was heart breaking.

Such a sad situation.

Bobby is off work feeling guilty. I've never seen him this way and Seb is in pieces.

I know we've had our differences with next door, but I would never wish anything like that on anyone. Poor Clarissa. What a shock. I could never imagine life without my Bobby and at least I have the children.

I saw her walk down her drive. She looked like a lost soul. I really wanted to give her a hug and take her some flowers but I'm not sure she would want to see me. Christine has advised me it's probably for the best and leave her alone.

It's funny how my own problems seem very insignificant at a time like this.

My biggest problem is having to give Tandoori away and break Frank's little heart. He's even stopped eating chicken nuggets because he doesn't want to eat any relatives of Tandoori.

We've had another letter from the Environment Agency and have to comply within ten working days otherwise they will be taking us to court. How do you explain this to a four-year-old?

It's a silly rule to me, why can't you keep cockerels in a residential area, He doesn't crow that often, only first thing in the morning and I'm sure most people are awake.

Luckily mum and dad are still here to help put life into prospective.

We all sat down for dinner, but Bobby didn't eat a thing. I'm not sure what to do. If I ring one of the partners, they may think he's incapable of doing his job. Especially after he's just gone back after his suspension.

But at least he's still with me.

Thank you for keeping my family safe despite the world around us.

Thursday 7th August 2003

Seb called to see me today, he let himself in when I didn't answer the door, I had no idea he had a key, he looked terrible and unlike his usual self and he reeked of stale alcohol. He has become a shadow of his former self since Michael died.

I thought he would have been here, and we could have

supported one another but he has been very distant and almost makes me feel as though he is avoiding me. I am so sorry for him but feel to numb and confused to offer him help.

Today he seemed very on edge as though he had something he wanted to say but couldn't quite bring himself to say whatever it was.

Fortunately, he didn't stay long and when he left, he got so far out of the door then turned back and apologised for all that has happened. Before I could respond he was gone.

I must ask him for the key back.

The funeral is all arranged. The undertaker rang and confirmed.

I tried to keep it up to Michael's standards but feel quite worn out with all the drama. I don't really know how I will get through the day never mind the rest of my life. I can't bear to even speak to Christine or even go over to paint. She does keep popping over and leaving meals on my doorstep, but I just want time alone.

I wonder if she felt this empty when her husband died. It's a good job she didn't rely on that Doctor to save her husband, after all he couldn't save a budgie so how was he supposed to save Michael.

Dr Mortimer called to see me, not like him at all. I felt obliged to let him in because he came from the front door to the back and could clearly see I was home. He offered me some pills. I have them but think I will just hang on to them. I'm not sure I need them.

Mrs Ivy rang and seemed to want to chat about some ridiculous gossip about another death and the person who *had died was in a gay relationship. I was totally at a loss as to why she thought I would be interested. Was I supposed to be sympathetic?*

Jo-Hannah Smythe called to see me earlier, with flowers but I pretended to be out. I'm sure she would just remind me I didn't apologise to next door, and I have no intention of doing so, so there is no point in speaking to her.

Wednesday 13/8/2003 - The funeral

Bobby was up early, he's still not himself. Hopefully after today he will feel a little better. I keep telling him it's not his fault, and even if he'd got there straight away, Michael probably still would have died. You are not a superhero. You can't change situations and make things right.

He put his black suit and tie on. His suit hung off him. I hadn't noticed how much weight he'd lost.

I took the boys to tennis. Bobby had gone to the funeral by the time I got back. He'd offered to pick Seb up.

I stood outside the house with Christine and the twins to show our respect for Michael.

Clarissa was all on her own in the car. I can't believe no one was with her. It was so sad.

As we watched the car slowly pull away, I think Christine must have been thinking the same as me. She then muttered something about she needs me, and dashed home to get her car.

I'd arranged for mum and dad to look after the children later so I could meet Bobby at the golf club. I am so worried about him.

Dad dropped me off so I could drive Bobby's car back just in case Bobby had had a few drinks.

I went through the side door as I really didn't want to upset Clarissa anymore by her seeing me at the wake. But a little bit of me hoped she did, so she knew I was here wanting to support her.

I nipped into the toilets and bumped into Janet Ivy, Nancy Warbottom, and Blanch White. All gathered around the sink like they were schoolgirls, but in reality just a cackle of bitchy wealthy women. You could have cut the atmosphere with a knife.

They were talking about Clarissa. They then looked me up and down as if I was something on the bottom of their shoe. I felt so sorry for Clarissa. I thought they were her friends.

I don't really know them, but Hannah has pointed them out to me. It's women like that who have put me off playing golf.

I quietly went into the toilet cubicle.

To my horror I could then hear them talking about my Bobby and me. How crass to be talking in that manner when I am within ear shot.

My Bobby isn't into men. How can he be? We are happily married.

OMG what if he's going to leave me to be with Seb?

I waited for them to leave. As I came out of the toilet I bumped into Christine. She smiled then looked at the other cubicle.

It was Clarissa coming out. She must have heard everything too.

I didn't say a word just touched Christine's arm and went looking for Bobby. He was at the bar with Seb.

Seb was holding onto Bobby's arm. I felt sick. I hadn't given it any thought before on how tactile Seb is with Bobby.

I bravely asked Bobby if he was ready to come home. He

actually looked relieved I was there and said goodbye to Seb.

Bobby went to bed. He'd obviously had too much to drink. I don't know what to think.

I gave the children and mum and dad a big hug and just got on with tea.

I need to sort my own mind out first before I talk to anyone.

Please let me be wrong. Please don't leave me Bobby, especially for Seb. I thought he was our friend.

And I've still got the chicken/cockerel to deal with.

Wednesday 13th August 2003 Day of the Funeral

I rode to the church by myself in the limousine behind Michael's coffin.

Seb said he wanted to make his own way. I was quite disappointed with his decision after all his support and kindness over the years I feel at quite a loss at the distance he has put between us.

As I got into the car, I saw Christine watching me. She was stood with that awful young woman and her small brats and a few other neighbours who would not be expected to attend the service.

At the church there were so many people, but I seemed to be completely alone. Seb acknowledged me with a bow of his head then Mr Cooper the undertaker said it was time to go in.

Seb hung back with the Doctor from next door, and again I found myself alone leading the way in behind the small wooden box. It was strange to think Michael was inside it under the multitude of flowers. He had seemed taller.

When I sat down in the front pew, I thought Seb would join me, he didn't.

I sat totally alone and as the Vicar began to retell the virtues of Michaels life I couldn't help it, no matter how hard I tried I began to cry, not so much for the loss of Michael but for the loneliness I feel.

It was a shock when Christine slid into the seat next to me and took hold of my hand. She didn't say a word or even look at me, just handed me a hanky, then sat reassuringly squeezing my hand.

The only person in the hundred or so, so called friends, who was there for me. The only person who had ever treated me with friendship. I know Michael would have disapproved but I was grateful and realise I am lucky to have her around.

She followed me out and saw me into the car with a reassuring pat on my arm. Her kindness was humbling.

I suppose I should have offered her a lift and invited her to the golf club, but I didn't really expect her to come, I know she had never really liked Michael.

At the golf club I found it so hard to be the polite hostess so headed for the ladies. Seb could deal with all their friends; I had had enough.

From the safety of the toilet cubicle, I heard Mrs Ivy chatting as she pushed open the door to enter the wash room.

She was talking about Seb and Michael, about them being an item since way back after they left school and met at a party, saying their relationship was common knowledge to all except me...

Mrs Warbottom suggested I surely knew when I had married Michael and didn't disapprove. Mrs White laughed and said perhaps that explained why I was such a frigid ice queen, and they all laughed.

There was a pause when the door opened, and somebody went into the next cubicle.

I don't know how Michael could be so self-righteous, Mrs Ivy said over the running tap.

Poor Seb, she continued, has had to put up with her icy ways and Michael. I bet he is glad he has met the Doctor, although he is married with children and certainly doesn't seem the type to be interested in a man.

I had covered my ears then. I wanted to cry and rant at them that I was listening, and it was lies all lies.

Seb was my friend and Michael's friend, nothing more. But I know that's not true, it explains Sebs discomfort and unhappiness since Michael's death.

The door opened and their voices faded away. I waited for the person in the next cubicle to wash her hands and leave before I opened my door. I couldn't go back in and face them all knowing what they were all saying. I thought the room was empty when I opened the cubicle door, but Christine was there, waiting.

She took me by the arm and said simply well now you know.

I don't know how she got me home. I just remember the large brandy, two of the tablets Dr Mortimer had left and her tucking a blanket round me.

I woke up alone with just the soft glow of a lamp dispersing the darkness and alone I fear is how I will stay. I do not think I can face anyone, certainly not our so-called superficial friends.

It's not just Michael who has died, I think I have too.

Tuesday 26/8/2003

Bobby was up super early, even earlier than Tandoori's weird crow. I was hoping it was to get himself organised for work. But I'd heard him on the phone to someone. Whispering as if keeping it a secret. I'm sure I heard him say don't worry Seb, I'm here for you.

He then came back upstairs. I pretended to be asleep, but he sat on the bed and gave a gentle nudge to wake me with cup of tea in hand.

As I opened one eye to look at him, he started telling me that he'd organised mum and dad to babysit tonight as we need to talk.

I bolted up and nearly had tea everywhere, but Bobby managed to move it out of the way. I smiled awkwardly, as I asked what about? He said he had a confession and will tell me everything tonight.

Confession!

He then gave me a kiss on the forehead and left. My stomach churned. I felt sick!

Why would he just walk out after making a comment like that. Then it dawned on me. It's so obvious. He's leaving me for Seb. He doesn't fancy me anymore, is it women full stop now? How can I live without him, how can I live knowing I wasn't enough of a woman to keep him.

I kept thinking I should cry, but I couldn't so I've got up and made myself some toast. I've got other things on my mind like poor Frank and the Tandoori issue. Christine has organised for Tandoori to go to her friends farm, so Frank can still visit. How am I going to deal with the chicken as well as my life falling apart?

Bloody hell, Bobby chooses his moments.

I'm going to make a real effort for tonight.

If he's going to leave me for a man at least it's not because I look a mess. I'll show him what he could be missing!

Come on Seren, get on with your life!

***

Well, it was definitely worth making the effort.

Bobby was so complimentary, and he took me to Latinos for something to eat.

Why do I put myself through it. He's not leaving me for Seb. I think my face said it all. Especially when he asked if I thought there was something going on with him and Seb. He burst out laughing and told me not to be so stupid, he loves me. And only me. Such a relief.

He did say he's trying to organise bereavement counselling for Seb. He's heartbroken about losing Michael.

Bobby then announced he wants to move. But not just down the road. He wants to move to the other side of the world. Australia.

He feels that he's never really settled into the practice, especially after getting suspended. Living next-door to Clarissa and Michael has also taken its toll. There's a position come up where he can work on secondment in Geelong, close to the Great Ocean Road.

It's a chance to start again and do something we've always talked about.

It won't be for about six months because of all the paperwork. But the practice said they are happy to help.

I'm so relieved and actually very excited.

Thank you for an amazing evening. Thank you for my husband not leaving me for Seb and thank you for a new start for the De Lacey Williams family.

Australia here we come!

Tuesday 26th August 2003

I have not felt like keeping my journal, or doing anything but today has been a turning point.

I was not going to keep my appointment with Georgina but felt I should when her secretary telephoned to remind me. I didn't feel I could find an excuse not to go.

I am glad I went.

Georgina was very calm and said so much more than she normally would, a complete change from leading me to expose my life to her, I told her, I am so glad I never introduced her to Seb and about the horror of the duplicitous life he had been sharing with Michael. She didn't say very much to that, just raised her eyebrows.

She did ask how I thought I might fill the void of losing Michael, I said I wasn't sure.

Paint she suggested, let your emotions out in your art.

Christine was in the reception area as I walked through to leave. I have asked her a few times what she does to be there and treated like staff rather than client. Each time she has just smiled and changed the subject.

Today she was so pleased to see me I felt quite overcome.

We went to Latinos and when I would have found a quiet table at the back, she insisted I had my usual front and centre seat where I could see all the comings and goings.

She was clearly on a mission to bring me back to the land of the living.

Apparently, it was time to start my life how I would like it to be. I suppose I should think myself lucky she did not actually tell me to pull myself together.

I remembered to thank her for her kindness, and she squeezed my hand, saying it was what friends were for. I told her it had been a long time since I had had a real friend. She was quiet for a full minute before she said, only I could change that.

On the way home I realised she was right. It is all down to me now because there is no one else.

Not that I can admit to, anyway, except Georgina who kindly said under the circumstances she would like to extend my appointments.

Tomorrow I will go back to the studio and paint.

Thursday 4/09/2003

Up early for Frank's first day at school. I can't believe where time has gone. My little boy is growing up so quickly.

Bobby got a gorgeous photo of Robbie and Frank in the front room before he left for work. I had a proud mummy moment.

Frank wanted to show Tandoori and Paul how grown up he looked now he was going to big boy school. I had to intervene and told him we had to get going, because we can't be late on the first day, I was very careful not to let the boys go outside. Christine's friend came to collect Tandoori last night. I know it's the right thing to do and I'm sure he'll have a lovely life on the farm. But it's quite sad. And Frank will be so upset even I have grown quite fond of our little feathered friend.

Robbie ran to his classroom as soon as we entered the

school grounds. He really seems to have matured over the summer and had a growth spurt. He was towering over some of his classmates.

Frank was a little nervous at first until he saw his friend Matilda from nursery. They sat together like a little old couple chit chatting away. It was so sweet.

The morning went really quickly, and I picked Frank up after lunch.

He came out buzzing, words were coming out at one hundred miles an hour, to tell me every detail of the morning then suddenly he went very quiet and started sucking his thumb. I let him sit on the front of the pushchair, with his little legs dangling down over the wheels. Skylet and Tommy were both reaching out to him for a hug, but Frank was struggling to keep his eyes open. It was bloody hard work walking home with the three of them in the pushchair!

As soon as we got home Frank disappeared. I thought he'd gone to his room to lie down and never thought anymore about it.

As I was sorting Tommy's nappy I heard a strange noise. It sounded like someone was shouting for 'Tandoori' with Frank.

I grabbed Tommy with his half-changed nappy that then leaked all over me. Honestly, boys just seem to get pee everywhere, left Skylet in the pushchair and dashed to the garden to find Frank. But then Skylet let out a loud cry. So, I went back in.

Skylet was halfway out of the pushchair and had got herself stuck. How she'd managed to get into that position I have no idea, then the phone rang. Holding both babies I managed to answer it, expecting Bobby to call to see how

Frank's first day went, but it was someone trying to sell me Sky sports. I told them if I got any sports packages then my husband would just sit and watch sport all day, if he just sat watching sport all day then he wouldn't do anything with the family, and if he wasn't doing anything with the family then I would divorce him. At that point, the young man said, 'So you don't want the Sports package then' and hung up on me. Honestly do they not know how my husband's brain works! I was a bit curt with the young man. It's not his fault, he's only doing his job, but they do need to get their timings right.

At this point I'd forgotten all about Frank, what a bad mother! Until he came back in telling me that the lovely ghost lady, Penny, had helped him look for Tandoori and they'd drawn a picture together.

Penny. Who the hell is Penny?

I asked him where his picture was. He said the ghost lady was looking after it, so she knew what Tandoori looked like.

I hope he's not going back to worrying about the ghost lady. Although he seemed quite calm and actually quite proud of the picture he painted.

Back on the school run. At least it's only going to be for the first term that I pick Frank up early.

Cup of tea and good old Thomas the Tank Engine.

I'm exhausted.

Thank you for a good first day back at school for the boys.

Thursday 4th September 2003

What a strange day!

I was in the greenhouse collecting my hidden art supplies when I heard a little voice calling for Tandoori.

Imagine my surprise when I stepped back into the garden

and found the blue-eyed brat resplendent in his school uniform but clearly distressed standing in the middle of my garden path.

I thought he was going to turn and flee when he saw me, but his sobbing became louder. I don't know why I did it, but I opened my arms, and he came running to me.

Apparently Tandoori is a chicken, so that explains the Cockerel crowing, clearly not a chicken at all and he is missing!

We searched the garden together but thankfully, to no avail. In the end to distract him I suggested he come into the green house and paint me a picture of the missing chicken so that I could keep an eye out for it.

I told him my name was Penny to my friends. He told me he was called Frank, Frankie to his friends. I said I hoped we could be friends and I was a little regretful when he warily said he thought I was a Ghost lady...

I rather hope I can lose that title but never mind for now.

He will clearly one day be a Picasso in his own right, the chicken he painted was a glorious multitude of colour, and I have pinned it on the kitchen wall. Michael would have had a fit and that made me smile.

When he left to slip easily back through the hedge, Frankie turned those beautiful blue eyes to me and very seriously said, Penny I like you, you are not scary...

It made my heart skip a beat; it has been so long since anyone called me Penny... and I realised I liked to hear that name, even if only from the mouth of a four-year-old.

Just something else to think about.

I wonder if I might start using Penny again. It's the kind of *name that doesn't sit as heavily on me as Clarissa. It's from a time in my life when for a while at least, I was happy and yes even loved...*

How my thoughts have wandered back to that time over the last few weeks. If I am still feeling a loss it's for the past and not Michael.

So much time has passed since that time but oh how I wonder about the what ifs from those days...

Foolish daydreams...

Tuesday 9/9/2003

Getting all four children out of the house is hard work at times. I always feel like I've climbed Mount Everest by the time I've dropped the boys off. And if I can get there on time I give myself a big pat on the back. My life is so sad at times.

Bobby has been on a course, so he's not even been around on an evening.

I popped round to Christine's for a coffee and had a strange conversation. She mentioned that the ice queen might be melting - maybe beginning to thaw.

I gave Christine a look and a half. And asked her if she was taking anything. I was a bit harsh and regretted my comment. That wasn't fair of me.

I went back to pick up Frank. Stopped off to buy Christine some flowers to apologise. I'm just exhausted and my patience isn't the best.

I went back to Christine's. She was lovely as always. Frank asked if he could do some artwork. Christine took him down to her studio and let him paint on the easel. He sat and drew another portrait of Tandoori. I have to admit he's got an eye for colour.

Absolutely shattered! Tea, bath and bed.

Tuesday 9th September 2003

Today I finished the portrait of Michael and Seb. If I say so myself, it is very good. I have caught them both at their best.

Studying the picture, I wonder that I never realised the bond between them. Perhaps it was easier not to.

After all, one does not expect their "holier than thou", hand-picked for respectability, husband to be involved with another man.

Oh, how I would have liked to make that announcement to my parents. Did they know when they ordered us to marry to turn me back into a respectable woman... had the whole of my life as a married woman purely been to shield Michael and Seb from gossip... So many questions...

If I feel any sadness over Michael's death at all, it is that I have lived his life, not been free to be myself. So many regrets...

I admit, I have been a bit angry but deep down I don't so much miss Michael, as much as I miss Sebs kindness. He was always a good ally and friend and often deflected Michael's unkindness and indifference.

Christine asked me if I have seen or heard from Seb, she suggested he was probably more of a friend than I had appreciated, and that perhaps I should try and make contact with him.

Georgina asked me what was stopping me, and I admit I am feeling guilty. She asked why and finally I was able to say out loud that in a way I was glad Michael had gone, glad that my life was no longer regimented and restricted.

When I stopped speaking and dared to make eye contact with her, her expression was unreadable. I had braced myself for shock or disapproval. It didn't come. She just gently moved the conversation on.

I think I do need to see Seb, after all it is not appropriate, he still has keys to my home which under the circumstances is quite unacceptable.

Perhaps I will call round unannounced, easier than a telephone call.

I have also written to Mrs. Warbottom and handed in my resignation from the garden and lunch club, after all I really do not want to associate with women of such clearly unkind and unsupportive, demeanours.

Friday 12/9/2003

Can't believe Frank has been at school for over a week. He seems to be doing ok, but he's still very upset about Tandoori.

Decided to go for a little walk with the twins and Charlie and make the most of the good weather.

Saw Clarissa, she looked so upset, I actually felt sorry for her, so I decided to offer an olive branch and say how sorry I was to hear about Michael.

Well, I won't bother again, she just bit my head off and made it out that it was my Bobby's fault that her husband died. What a cow! I hate that woman!

Rang Bobby and begged him to speed up the paperwork for our new life so we can move on. He actually agreed with me. Maybe he just wanted a peaceful afternoon.

Felt I needed to escape from our home. I shouldn't feel like this.

I have organised to see Beth, Paul and baby Natahlia. I've not seen them for ages. Paul has now been transferred to a team near Liverpool, a bit closer than Scotland, so I've booked a weekend away to stay with them and give Beth a hand. Although Beth is amazing, I don't think she needs any help, she seems to have taken to motherhood like second nature.

I've told Bobby he has to be around for the children as I just want to get as far away as possible from that vile woman. I never ever want to see her again! I couldn't imagine her being a mother. She seems to hate families.

Did the school run and met some friends at the soft play for a catch up.

Why do I let Clarissa bother me so much?

Friday 12th September 2003

Going to Sebs today, was not as easy as I thought. I was so terribly nervous.

I had wrapped the framed painting of him with Michael and carried it from the car to his door rehearsing my speech.

At first, I did not think he was going to answer then as I turned to walk away the door opened and my wits and words deserted me.

Seb looks like a dishevelled little old man and so unkempt I was truly shocked. At the sight of me his eyes filled with tears, and he began to apologise profusely.

I was so shocked by how he appeared I just thrust the

painting at him and muttered it was ok and turned and fled back to my car. I don't know how I drove home. I am so upset by how badly Seb has taken this whole thing.

I went over to Christine's to ask her advice, but she was out, and on the way back the stupid neighbour caught me walking up the drive, all eyes and gushing sympathy.

I told her, clearly it was all her fault, if her stupid husband had done his job properly Seb wouldn't be so broken, Michael would still be alive... and then I realised how my life would still be and while I don't think I was actually in the wrong in putting her in her place, I did stop shouting at her and fled inside. What a mess, what a dreadful mess.

Poor Seb, whatever will become of him. I suppose I have not helped by rushing off in such an unladylike state.

I will have to speak to Georgina.

Frankie must have been around at some point as there was another picture waiting for me in the green house when I wandered down to check my plants. This time it was a very brightly coloured flower. At least somebody knows how to make me smile...

Friday 26/9/2003

Frank learnt a Spanish word at school - he was very excited to use it. So excited that when the dustbin men turned up, Frank opened the front door to shout Hola! At that point Charlie darted out and chased the dustbin man out of the garden. I shouted at Frank, told Robbie to look after the twins while I had to chase the dog down the street with my dressing gown on.

The dustbin man wasn't very happy and threatened to kick

our dog if he went anywhere near him. I was very upset and could only apologise. Sometimes getting ready for school is very stressful!

Turned up to baby group that wasn't on. Why do all the other mothers seem to know more than me.

Went home. Mum called but I couldn't talk to her because Skylet has found she has a tooth and wanted to practice using it on Tommy. Bless him he screamed the house down.

Bobby rang because he'd forgotten to organise a leaving gift for one of the team so asked me to nip into town to find something appropriate for a 54-year-old woman.

Nip! Who nips anywhere when you have children. Oh, and to gift wrap it and get a card and drop it off for him!

What do you get an older woman who you know absolutely nothing about. I had a naughty thought of organising a stripper gram. Could you imagine Bobby's face. Best keep that to myself. I bought a vase instead. Well actually two vases because Tommy with his elastic arms reached out and smashed one.

I was mortified. The shop assistant was not impressed. Well, they should design shops for people to go in with pushchairs.

Dropped present off at the practice.

Late for the school pickup, Frank and Robbie were the last ones in the classrooms. Feeling like the worse mother ever.

Got home to find a Tupperware box full of scones, a bag of sweets and a Disney video, with a lovely note from Christine. Saying 'A cup of tea always seems to make the world a better place, but even better with something to go with it.'

That put a big smile on my face. How lovely and thoughtful.

Got Robbie and Frank to get their blankets from upstairs

and all snuggled in the front room with Charlie and watched the film.

Bobby came home early with fish and chips for tea and a bottle of Chardonnay. Children to bed and suddenly life didn't seem that bad.

Thank you Christine for always being there and your amazing scones and treats.

Thank you Bobby for fish and chips, sorting the children and my very large glass of wine.

Friday September 26th, 2003

It was such a relief today, to hear from Seb.

I have been wondering what on earth to do to make things right between us. His flowers and apology for his behaviour and heartfelt thanks for the portrait were much welcomed.

I have asked him to come for lunch on Sunday and he agreed without hesitation. He sounded so much more like himself, and we chatted about all sorts for nearly an hour.

That made me notice that I have rather neglected to keep up with the housework. I was busy scrubbing at some marks on the floor when Christine appeared with freshly made scones.

We had a lovely chat and I appreciate now how lovely it is to have real friendship with her.

She reminded me I have the raffle prize with Spick and Span (the leaflet says Spank, you would think they would check their spelling!). She made me ring them and I have made a booking for someone called Jo to come and "Bottom the place'. A strange expression, but Christine seemed familiar with the term.

Perhaps if Jo is any good I might ask her to come once a month, just until I get sorted out.

Christine agrees that when I have cleared out Michael's office it could make a nice studio. She added that I wasn't to rush as she enjoys having me around. How times have changed, I realised how lonely and regimented my life had been with Michael.

I am lucky to have Christines friendship as I often behaved in a way that should have put her off. When I said as much to her she threw her head back and laughed at me saying my miss hoity-toity act didn't fool her, she knew I wasn't all bad out of Michael's shadow.

I still feel quite ashamed but actually at times my behaviour has been quite justified.

Sunday 28/09/2003 - Robbie's birthday

Happy birthday Robbie. Where have the last seven years gone?

He's looking so grown up and handsome. I'm really proud of him. He's looking more like Bobby each day, which isn't a bad thing.

Bobby agreed for him to have a few mates round for a game of football and a BBQ afterwards.

I was amazed he let him. I did make sure that Bobby didn't drink too much the night before. Even I didn't want a repeat of last year.

We bought him an amazing goal set, with targets to practice hitting different parts of the goal. Mum and dad came round with a ball bag and six new footballs. Peter and Helen arrived mid-morning with cakes and sweets and a new skateboard. Hannah and John popped round and so did Seb.

Both granddads helped put the goal together. I think they wanted to try it.

Paul and Beth sent Robbie a signed football strip. Robbie was so excited.

We decided to open the wine at around eleven. Because we could!

I sent a message to Christine to join us.

At two o'clock Robbie's seven mates turned up. All in their kits ready to play. I'd bought Bobby a whistle so he could referee them.

They had a great time playing four 'v' four. I think Bobby enjoyed himself. He seemed to like being in charge as he wouldn't stop blowing his whistle.

We all had burgers, cake and sweets. The boys then decided to have a shooting competition.

Unfortunately, their accuracies were not that great, and we lost a few balls over the fence.

Seb offered to get them. I think he's the only one brave enough to see her.

I had a naughty thought. I really hoped the balls had damaged some of her prized plants. She deserved to be upset with all the nasty things she's done to me.

I need to keep these thoughts to myself. I think mum and Christine would be mortified at how much I despise that woman. She makes my stomach churn, even hearing her name mentioned makes me feel sick.

I've never felt this much hatred towards anyone before.

The day went well. Robbie had a brilliant birthday.

Thank you for perfect footballing weather and Robbie having fun.

Sunday 28th September 2003

Oh, just when I thought things were getting quieter next door, today must be a birthday. I noticed the performance of erecting goal posts in the garden as I drew back the curtains this morning.

For heaven's sake it's like a playing field, not a single plant to be seen. I am so glad now that I rescued the best of the plants before they could wreck them.

I put up with the continual thudding of the ball against the fence and delighted shouts of "Goal" until half past two, then decided enough was enough.

Honestly, it's a Sunday, where is her respect! It's bad enough I am spending another birthday forgotten and alone.

Michael would have been furious and for the first time I could understand why and didn't feel like I was just reacting as he expected me too.

My head was pounding so I decided to go for a walk. Anything to shut out the infernal din they were making.

As usual there were more cars parked on the street than in the local car park. I wondered if I should go back in and get the no parking tickets. Then I saw Sebs car tucked in out of the way.

Obviously, he was there. Part of the unruly goings on. I expect Christine was there as well, and the Smythes. Everyone who was anyone but not me.

I must have walked for a good hour and didn't see anyone I knew.

I feel very lonely and quite sorry for myself.

Friday 3/10/2003

Bobby has organised a day a week for the twins to go to nursery. I am so grateful.

I spotted Clarissa leave her house, so I decided to be brave and potter around the garden, I wanted to get organised for winter. Christine popped over to give me some advice on various plants. I also felt a bit safer that I wasn't on my own in case that cow had a go at me about nothing. It was a lovely feeling to have accomplished so much. Normally I can't get anything sorted because I'm on constant demand with the children, although I would not be without them. They are my world.

I got the grass cut, Paul's cage cleaned, bushes pruned, and toys put away.

As we were walking back to the house for a cup of tea we noticed Seb standing in Clarissa's back garden. It was very odd. He was just standing there. Staring through her patio doors with a rapt look on his face. He was absolutely oblivious to us saying hello to him.

Then we heard a scream, but it sounded like it was two people screaming. So, we ran round to see what was going on. Christine charged through Clarissa's front door. I followed.

OMG Clarissa was swooned on the floor with wire bondage and a half naked very bronzed and very toned gorgeous man. The dark horse. Who knew she was into kinky stuff.

Well, it just goes to show you have no idea what goes on behind closed doors.

Seb was still in the garden looking through the window. Well, I guess everyone has their own fetishes. Seb spotted us and then dashed into the house and politely introduced himself to the hunk and helped him up as Clarissa was still sprawled on the floor and tied up with the hoover cord.

I had to bite my bottom lip to stop myself from making any comments.

Christine helped untangled her and made sure she wasn't hurt.

Clarissa looked in shock. So did the gorgeous hunk who then explained he was a cleaner.

I wouldn't mind having him cleaning for me!

I was struggling not to laugh at her, I didn't want to look mean in front of Christine and Seb, so I offered to make everyone a cup of tea. Christine suggested a sweet tea to help with shock. I added extra sugar into Clarissa's, thought it might sweeten her up.

Who would have thought I'd ever go into her house, let alone make her a drink in her own kitchen.

We all sat in the garden, as Christine thought fresh air would be good for everyone.

The gorgeous hunk, Joe, explained this was his full-time job and never had this kind of cleaning experience before.

We eventually all saw the funny side and sat and laughed loudly. I was actually laughing at her, not with her. I still hate her.

Mind you, I quite fancy my house being bottomed.

I then left still giggling to myself, to pick up the twins and collect the boys from school.

Can't wait to tell Bobby about our sex starved neighbour.

Thank you for a day to remember.

Friday 3rd October 2003

Today has been a catalogue of shocks.

It began when I had to rearrange my times to meet with

Georgina. I didn't want to miss the appointment so agreed to go earlier. Christine said she would happily let in Jo the cleaner from Spick and Span.

Imagine my shock when I returned home to find a half-naked six foot something young man veraciously pushing my Dyson around in a very determined way.

I was so shocked I started to scream, and he screamed too as clearly, he hadn't expected me to be there. As the hoover went silent I turned to run, catching a glimpse of Seb outside the patio doors looking stunned.

I'm not sure what happened next, but I went sprawling in a tangle of wires and strong arms across the floor. My face against a very muscled very naked torso that smelt of something quite heady and distracting.

It was most disconcerting when Seb appeared to be helping the young man up and Christine, always the level-headed one appeared behind Seb demanding to know what on earth had happened.

I found myself in a chair in the garden with hot, sweet tea faced with half the neighbourhood and a very embarrassed Joe who was apologising profusely, his lovely brown eyes full of such sincerity I couldn't help but believe him. Although I did wish he would cover up some of his chest and not stand quite so close, I was quite short of breath, of course that would be the shock.

Christine was very quick to weigh up the situation and as usual placated everyone.

Joe explained Spick and Spank was a cleaning service with a difference, it was meant to be pleasing to have a half-

naked man do the housework.

Naturally, Seb agreed he could see the business sense behind the idea.

Suddenly the madness of the whole situation struck me, and I began to laugh like I have not laughed in years.

After a few seconds I realised we were all laughing even the terrible woman from next door. I met her eyes and offered the explanation for the scenario was I was having my house bottomed. That seemed to make us all laugh more. There was something in Seren's eyes, a sparkle that was so familiar it gave me a lovely warm feeling of recognition. Such a shame she's such a problem.

In fairness Joe did actually continue the cleaning for the full three hours, after he put his clothes on, and did a very good job.

So much so that fully clothed I would have him again and told him as much.

Seb took his number and I'm not sure if that was for cleaning or because they seemed to be getting on rather well.

When everyone apart from Seb had left, we began to sort through some of Michael's office paperwork. There is so much. Thankfully, Seb offered to take it to his house and go through it there in his office.

I also gave him an old, battered suitcase from the back of Michaels cupboard that weighed quite heavily and was locked. Not one of Michael's many keys appeared to fit it and I was unsure quite what to do with it.

Seb looked as though he had seen it before, so I assume it is hiding something personal to them.

To spare Seb any more awkwardness I haven't and won't ask about its contents. I feel I really don't care, and his friendship is too important to me.

Friday 31/10/2003 - Halloween

Last day at school - thank goodness. I'm so looking forward to the half term holiday. Not having to rush around in the morning. The boys are definitely needing a break, especially Frank. Bless him I can't believe he's done his first term at school and after these holidays he will be going full time, which will certainly make my life easier.

Bobby is also ready for a few days off. He's been working all hours.

I know I'm exhausted, but he seems to be really grumpy and hasn't come to bed with me for ages, just falling asleep downstairs. I have noticed our love life isn't what it was. I've put on my to do list to have sex with husband, but not being able to tick it off.

I hope he's not going off me.

The boys were very excited to get home and ready for Halloween.

I decided after that horrible letter last year, we would go trick or treating with friends on their street. That way she couldn't accuse me of anything.

The twins were dressed up in cute little pumpkin outfits. Frank dressed up as a goldfish. Robbie wore a plain mask and carried a mad man's axe, plastic obviously. Should I be concerned?

The boys wanted to show Christine their outfits. So, we popped to hers first.

I think Christine must have had company. She was giggling

at the doorway and had a mischievous look about her as she handed the children a big bowl of sweets. I wonder if she had a male visitor. I think she's a bit of a dark horse at times.

The children had a lovely evening, back home, bed and a very large glass of wine.

Well, I think I earned my treat.

Friday 31st October 2003

I had been painting in Christine's studio for most of the day when she popped her head in and asked me to join her for supper and a drink when I was done.

Well, there was nothing else to rush home for.

Christine is so very forward, at times quite inappropriate and wicked, she was teasing me terribly about hunky Joe and his sexy body... really I had tried not to notice!!!!

Today we were discussing relationships and somehow she elicited from me that Michael and I were inactive in the bedroom.

She asked how we had met and why on earth we had married. I couldn't tell her the awful truth about how we had ended up in such a sham of a marriage. I simply could not admit that to her.

Instead, I told the half-truth that my parents hoped he would have a stabilising effect on me, and I would be in a socially acceptable position.

She looked so sad and hugged me like I was a child, saying something under her breath about interfering parents who should never have children.

She is such a kind person but so blunt, I was half shocked when she stated there was no wonder Michael and I did not consummate the marriage as his preference was clearly for men and therefore, we would never have been compatible.

She asked me if I had ever been with a man. I was so flustered I couldn't answer. Really, she has no boundaries. I know she means well but for heaven's sake! I was so embarrassed but can clearly see the logic in her statement.

She went on to say that unless I had an alternative preference to men then I should remember I am only forty-four and could be a very attractive normal woman with normal needs. What on earth am I supposed to make of that!

It's terrible when she talks so openly, but for some reason it fascinates me how terribly to the point and shocking she can be. I've never known anyone quite like her!

She poured us both a sherry and I am afraid I drank mine much too quickly trying to take the edge off her startling conversation.

Pouring more sherry into my glass she announced she knew just the thing I could use to bring me back to the land of the living...

I couldn't believe it when she left the room and returned with a plastic male appendage in her hand which before I could gather my wits she dropped in my lap. "Now," she asked as if she was sharing a kitchen gadget, "do you know what to do with this?"

I was so alarmed I tried to pick it up, but the awful thing began to rotate and buzz. I was so horrified I jumped up and knocked over the small table beside me spilling everything and making a terrible mess.

I was so mortified, Christine burst into laughter and the awful thing lay beneath the upended spider plant and debris humming away as if it had a life of its own.

To make matters worse the doorbell rang insistently, and she dashed off to supply the trick or treaters with a dish full of sweets while I scrabbled around trying to clear up the mess.

She really is terrible. I was so shocked and embarrassed.

She came back from the door chuckling to herself about the damn thing being my trick or treat as she picked it up, shook off the dirt, and twisted it to shut it up, then stood it for all to see, in the middle of the mantel piece.

As if all that wasn't bad enough on my way to bed, I found it half pushed through the letter box with a note saying I had forgotten it and to enjoy.

Enjoy! I can barely touch the awful thing! Imagine if I hadn't seen it and it had still been there, half in half out of the letter box in the morning when the postman came.

She really is awful!

I've stood it in the bathroom by the toilet and sat a toilet roll over it to hide it as I really can't think what else to do with it!

Tuesday 4/11/2003 - Mischief night

Today started off really well. The sun was shining, the boys were playing nicely. The dog slept through and hadn't wee'd on the floor. Bobby and I got a full night's sleep. The twins were angels.

I think this has to be one of the first times I've ever felt so relaxed in our home.

As everyone seemed happy we decided to have a pottering around the house day. Sometimes I think life is so full on we forget what's around us and just need time to breathe.

The boys then went to play in the garden with Charlie. That dog is definitely confused. He hasn't realised he's a dog, he thinks he's one of the children. It really is sweet how he follows them around and they include him in all their games.

We were all enjoying our uneventful day. Bobby and I sat in the kitchen, feeding the twins, when we could hear Charlie howling. There was the most piercing noise coming from outside. Then the backdoor flung open and there was Frank and Robbie stood with their hands covering their ears shouting, "Mummy, mummy stop that noise."

Bobby and I gathered the twins and went outside to see what on earth was going on. Charlie was sat still howling. But it wasn't the howling that was making the piercing noise. It sounded like a cat was being murdered. It was most alarming. It seemed to be coming from the direction of Clarissa's bedroom window.

We got everyone inside and then the noise stopped for about half an hour. We let the boys and Charlie back outside. But then the noise started building up again, but this time it only lasted for about five minutes.

What was that woman doing upstairs in her bedroom?

Then a sick thought popped into my head. I asked Bobby to go round the front of the house to see if she'd got any visitors.

While I persuaded the boys to come in and watch a film. At least that way we can turn the volume up.

There were no cars on the street or in her drive.

What was she doing? Trying to make a point about something? At sixty years of age, she's still active? Oh, my goodness she's getting it more than me!

But I don't understand why she left her window open for the town to listen to her pleasures. She's definitely losing it.

I couldn't get the horrible image out of my head. Those sounds will haunt me forever.

Luckily, the boys had no idea about what was happening. I decided that if they asked any questions then Bobby could explain in doctors talk. He's very good at skirting around subjects. Maybe he should have been a politician.

Anyway, the boys were happy snuggled up on the sofa with their quilts and hot chocolates.

Thank you for DVD's and surround sound.

Tuesday 4th November 2003

I feel extremely self-satisfied, like a cat who had the cream.

I blame the wine I had with my lunch after visiting the art gallery this afternoon.

And Joe the cleaner who even with his clothes on is a delightful sight.

Yes, I definitely blame Joe.

And of course, Christine...

Joe had cleaned the bathroom and replaced the toilet roll.

I wondered what on earth he meant by novel toilet roll holder as he left grinning like a naughty boy... I realised of course that he had exposed Christines appendage.

I really don't know what came over me... the thought of him handling it and, well, I really can't write more... I think the memory will suffice!!!!

Wednesday 5/11/2003 - Bonfire Night

Bobby and I were out early this morning. I still cannot get

that noise and image of Clarissa out of my head! I needed to do something.

So, we went for a very long walk around Fewston reservoir. Double pushchair, dog and four children. Not a two-minute job going anywhere.

I love this time of year when the leaves are changing colour and there is a freshness in the air. The boys ran around with Charlie to let off steam and I could have quality time with Bobby as there was no mobile reception so he couldn't take any calls from work.

I'd made tuna sandwiches, so we sat in the car with our little picnic, crisps, Kit-Kats and a flask of hot chocolate. It was lovely.

When we got home Bobby organised the garden for our little bonfire as we still had quite a bit of rubbish from all the work we'd done on the house, and all the wood from the collapsed potting shed.

The boys were happy helping Bobby while I got the twins sorted.

We'd arranged for everyone to come to us for six o'clock. I'd made pumpkin soup for the adults and hot dogs for the boys.

Christine had made flapjacks. Beth and Paul came over with baby Natahlia, Seb brought his special bonfire mulled wine, and Hannah and John brought toffee apples.

It was lovely all being together and watching the fireworks.

When I went to put the twins and boys to bed, Bobby followed me. I thought he was being kind giving me a helping hand. But how wrong could I be.

He started getting amorous with me. Honestly talk about a time and a place. Was he getting turned on from listening to last night's performance by Clarissa?

I told him he couldn't ignore our guests and he needed to check on our fire outside not ours in the bedroom!

It wasn't a late night but as soon as everyone had gone Bobby dashed to bed.

I know it was on my to do list, but not with a garden full of friends and my imagination of that woman has put me off sex, it certainly is the best type of contraception you can get. Thank goodness Bobby fell asleep straight away.

Wednesday 5th November 2003

Oh my, I am exhausted. I can hardly write.

I would have just gone to sleep but the fireworks and the fact next door are, yet again, having a party, this time with a bonfire have made it impossible to.

At least Christines appendage will help me sleep later if I am still unable to get off.

What a disgusting thing it is but really it's most fascinating. Who on earth would have ever thought of such a device.

It really is inconsiderate; they have been out all day and now when we should be able to sleep, they are banging and laughing and lighting up my bedroom with a multitude of colourful flashes.

I am sure when I looked out of the window, I saw the Smythe's and Seb. I feel quite sad that he is there and not here visiting me, I imagine Christine is there too.

Perhaps I should go round and ask them to keep the noise down, they might ask me to join them.

I suppose I had better not, I wouldn't want to appear lonely.

Monday 10/11/2003

Half term holidays have flown by. It was a bit of a shock getting up early for school this morning.

Frank was excited that he could stay at school all day and have big boy school dinners and leave at the same time as Robbie. Robbie was more bothered about football practice. They are so different.

I arranged to meet Lucy, one of the mums in Frank's year for lunch at the play centre. She has a little boy a similar age to the twins. It was so lovely not having to rush back to pick up Frank.

As I arrived home I saw her next door. Confidently walking and smiling to herself.

Who does she think she is? How can she be so disgusting deliberately making everyone hear her sexual pleasures, acting like a porn star.

The dirty old woman. And the fact she did it in hearing distance from my children is despicable.

I gave her a look of disdain. Although I'm not sure she noticed me. She's probably thinking of some other kinky position to satisfy herself.

Pottered around the house, walked Charlie, then back to school, football practice, homework, tea and sorted the children, bath, story and bed.

Need to start thinking about Christmas. It doesn't organise itself.

I've come to bed. Bobby still isn't home, he's at another doctors meeting. I've never known anyone have so many meetings.

I'm so tired all the time. How do working mothers do it?

Thank you for Frank doing full days at school and thank

you for not having to go to work. I don't think I could cope.

Monday 10th November 2003

I had a very good meeting with Georgina today.

She was very positive and not so interfering. She wondered if we might reduce our sessions and I think we possibly could.

I met Seb for lunch, and he was very strange, if he asked me once if I was ok, he asked me a dozen times, and then still not satisfied he asked me if I was sleeping alright.

Well, that made me blush, as Christines appendage seems to have that effect on me, but Seb was then concerned I looked hot and began to fuss even more.

Thank heavens Joe arrived and stopped to say hello... although that made me feel quite hot until I saw the way he was all eyes for Seb.

Life is so funny.

On the way in I passed the woman next door and her brood, she stared at me all the way down the drive.

She is very odd.

Wednesday 24/12/2003 - Christmas Eve

I'm so excited. What an amazing early Christmas present.

We've got our moving date and Bobby's new employers are paying for everything! Removal, rent, new furniture. I cannot wait for our exciting new life to begin.

I want to sell our house, so I never have to come here again and see that vile woman next door. It does worry me what nasty thoughts are going through her head with her artificial red hair colouring. Old women usually go for a blue rinse.

Unfortunately, Bobby won't sell. He said it makes more

financial sense to rent it and he's told me that I need to focus on other things and not be obsessed with her.

He's no idea how I really feel. He's not around, so she doesn't affect him.

I've had a naughty thought. We could rent the house to a rough and extremely loud family, that would take no rubbish off her. That would upset Clarissa. I know I should be careful what I wish for, but I really do hope karma will teach her a lesson.

I will be sad saying goodbye to Christine, Seb, Hannah and John. But I think I'll wait until after the festive season before I tell them. I want to enjoy this moment with our children and make this the best Christmas we can.

This morning the boys finished off their chocolate advent calendar, then we all had breakfast. Bobby stayed with the twins while I took the boys to the butchers to collect the turkey and trimmings.

I decided to take the boys go-kart with me. After trying to carry everything last year. I wasn't getting caught out again.

Frank loved it sitting on the go-kart holding onto a very large turkey, sausages, pork pie, stuffing and bacon. While Robbie and I pulled him through the High Street back to the car. I think we made a few people smile. It's not every day you see a child hugging a turkey. Couldn't have done that with a chicken. He still talks about Tandoori. That would have been cruel. I am glad I've told him that Tandoori is living his best life on a farm. Frank seems quite happy about it now.

Back home to get everything ready for our little soirée and of course Father Christmas.

It was so funny when everyone arrived. There was a knock at the door and the deafening tuneless sound of Good King

Wenceslas with giggles and laughter. I gave the boys some chocolate coins to pay everyone. That really tickled Seb.

As I stood laughing at the doorway, I could see her next door. Being nosey.

I know it's wrong, but I don't feel sorry for her. She's brought it all on herself.

Had a fabulous evening and even managed to get the boys and twins to bed at a reasonable time.

It was nice to have a few drinks and as always I'm so grateful that mum and dad, Peter and Helen could be with us.

Family is so important to me.

Thank you for our family and friends being here for us, sharing special occasions and thank you for our moving date.

Merry Christmas.

Wednesday 24th December 2003

Since Michael died, I have spent so much time at the art gallery in town that Melissa, the owner, and I have become almost friends.

Tonight, she had invited me to a drinks gathering that I almost didn't accept. I was shocked to encounter Mr Harrison, my old art tutor. I think he was quite shocked too but wasted no time in demanding to know if Melissa was carrying any of my work as I was a brilliant student.

Most embarrassing for lots of reasons.

Melisa was intrigued that I had kept my painting secret when Mr Harrison was so obviously impressed by my ability and a big benefactor of her gallery.

Why I agreed to take her some of my work for perusal, I'm still not sure, but I have.

On the way home I could hear carol singers next door, I almost stopped to listen when that woman opened the door and they all started to laugh as she ushered them into the house. I thought just before she closed the door she had seen me; I was so sure she smiled but she shut the door firmly.

It made me realise how alone I am and how much I would like to be part of that noisy life.

Thursday 25/12/2003 - Christmas Day

7.00am Robbie and Frank jumped on our bed shouting 'has Father Christmas been?'

Bless them I think they had been awake since 5.00am as I could hear little whispers coming from Robbie's bedroom as I went to the loo. The boys did well to wait. I guess last year's threat must have stayed with them. I hope it doesn't affect them for life thinking all their presents will turn to ash if they open them too early.

Bobby and I followed the boys holding the twins. Followed by Charlie, mum, dad and Helen and Peter.

This year felt even more special as it was Skylet's and Tommy's first Christmas. I do feel really blessed having four healthy happy children.

Bobby sneaked into the front room first to check Father Christmas had done his job and set up the video camera.

I felt like the children with butterflies of excitement.

It was beautiful watching memories being made. Skylet and Tommy sat on the rug giggling getting covered in wrapping paper. Even Charlie had his own stocking and was quite happy chewing his big Christmas bone.

I had to tell Bobby which presents we had bought. I say we; he had no idea of any of them. I don't think he's any idea how Christmas works. Father Christmas is not real! The buying and wrapping do not happen with a wave of a wand.

I'm glad to say all the organising paid off. The boys loved their amazing wooden castle and all the accessories with it.

Bobby and Peter disappeared into the kitchen for most of the day planning and preparing Christmas dinner, with quite a few bottles of beer.

Seb and Christine arrived around lunchtime. Christine came to join us in the front room, and Seb went to offer his help in the kitchen with a bottle or two of champagne.

After about quarter of an hour, I thought it wise to check on the timings for dinner and offer my gravy making skills.

As I walked into the kitchen the men seemed very close together, like a secret business meeting, whispering. Then when they saw me all three stepped away from each other and just looked pitifully at me. It was most odd.

I felt so uncomfortable I went back into the front room.

Christine then made a really odd comment about how awful it must be for Clarissa to be on her own today.

I didn't respond but I could feel my cheeks flushing. How dare she mention that woman in my home, especially after all we have been through. Then dad announced that dinner was ready. Saved by the bell!

Christmas dinner was fabulous. I think you appreciate it more when someone else has cooked. The wine was flowing. We laughed, told jokes and had a wonderful time.

But then it just seemed to stop, and I noticed Seb and Bobby were huddled up together deep in conversation. Is Seb making a move on Bobby again, especially now he's single.

Seb noticed I was staring at them and just out of the blue

said, 'I saw Clarissa this morning. She's doing ok.'

It took me a few moments then I said 'why is everyone talking about that cow next door when she deserves to be on her own. She is horrible.'

The whole room went silent. Seb looked awkward, Bobby glared at me, and Christine reacted badly telling me to be kind! Be kind!

What about all the horrible nasty things she's done to me, to Bobby, to my family?

What does Christine know about family anyway. I've never seen her with this wonderful son she's supposed to have.

Bobby then started to say she needs help, and we should give it to her. Seb agreed saying he'd been to visit her this morning and felt sorry for her.

Am I wrong? Is everyone missing what we have been through? I just scoffed. They are happy to be sat at our table eating our food and then judge me!

I can't wait to leave them all. They can have her. What is so wonderful about that evil woman. She must be a witch who's put a spell on them.

She's ruined my Christmas Day. I've done all this work, tried to please everyone and all they talk about is giving her a chance.

I've come to bed out of the way before I say any more.

Well Clarissa you have won again. You have even managed to ruin my Christmas Day!

Thursday 25th December 2003

Seb came to see me this morning, my first Christmas without Michael, his first Christmas without Michael.

He seemed very uneasy being here. I suppose it's all the

memories of past Christmases. It was almost a relief when he
left to go next door for lunch.

The first couple of hours did not seem so bad but then
all the laughing and obvious enjoyment of the day emanating
from next door made the silence unbearable, so I went to
Christines to paint.

As I opened the door I almost stood on a homemade card
from Frankie and laughed out loud when I discovered several
packets of opened sweets with what must have been his
favourites missing.

That lightened my mood, so I took them to Christines and
enjoyed them with my painting.

Friday 26/12/2003 - Boxing Day

I was still feeling sorry for myself when I woke up this
morning to Bobby bringing me a cup of tea and said sorry.
He didn't mean to spoil dinner, he said Seb is having a hard
time and just needs someone to talk to and there are quite
a few things that we really don't know about Clarissa and
what's she's been through. What do I even care about what's
she's been through, look what's she's put me and my family
through. But I stayed silent.

I apologised and told Bobby I'm feeling exhausted
mentally and physically with everything going on, and I guess
I did react badly.

He then randomly asked me about my adoption certificate,
what's that got to do with anything? I reminded him we had
talked about all this when we met. He frowned and said he
was sorry he was just curious as Seb had been talking about
adoptions. At that moment, the boys appeared.

How odd he would ask me about that again, I wonder if it has anything to do with us emigrating.

We then had a quiet, lazy morning. Helen and Peter went home so it was lovely just spending time with mum and dad.

Frank and Robbie played really well together with their wooden castle. Robbie was sat inside it lining up all the soldiers and Frank had his tractors and farm animals surrounding it.

Tommy sat watching the world go by with that gorgeous smile and two front teeth. Skylet looking for the next thing to crawl to. Suddenly she was off towards Frank and Robby, leaned on the wooden castle and stood up. Robbie thought that was amazing, as she proudly stood there grinning to say look at me, but Franks reactions were a little different asking her to move as she's blocking his tractor route.

Tommy rolled over as if to say. I'll do it when I'm ready.

I'm so glad mum and dad were with me to watch this special moment.

I have to say since Bobby asked me about my adoption certificate, it has made me think how much my biological parents have missed out on life. As a mother I cannot imagine ever giving up my children. Yes they are hard work at times, but they give so much back. First smile, first word, first tooth and first steps. I just appreciate what I've got even more.

I decided to ask mum and dad about where my adoption papers were.

They both went quiet. And then said it's funny because Seb had asked them the same question.

How odd. Maybe he was adopted too?

We decided to go for a family walk and get some fresh air.

As we were leaving I noticed Seb walking into Clarissa's

with an old suitcase. He didn't seem to acknowledge us. Maybe he just didn't see us.

I hope he's not going to live with her. I don't want lovely Seb turning into miserable Michael. I know you shouldn't speak ill of the dead. But you never know what that nasty woman is capable of.

Back home for a hearty stew, all children settled. Feeling absolutely exhausted but needed to start a list to organise the move.

I'll tell Christine and everyone soon. But for now, I need to get my head around things.

Thank you for my wonderful children and being there for our daughters first steps.

Thank you mum and dad for being there for me and giving me much love and support.

Friday 26th December 2003

I was expecting Seb to be a bit happier today, but he arrived looking like death itself carrying Michaels old suitcase.

I tried very hard to jolly him up, but he was very uneasy and in the end, by teatime, I got quite cross and sarcastically apologised I was not as much fun as the people next door and perhaps he should go.

It was quite a shock when he finally blurted out that he had made a terrible discovery, that Michael was cruel and heartless (not a surprise to me!) and that what he had done was beyond his comprehension.

He was so distressed I told him I was so sorry he had had to see that side to Michael. That just seemed to cause him more agitation and I confess I was at a loss.

It seems the case holds some secret that I need to discover while I'm alone.

Heavens knows why Seb was being so dramatic. Fortunately, Christine arrived, and he made a concerted effort to pull himself together.

On his way out he hugged me very tightly and said I was and always would be very special to him.

Very strange indeed.

I have put the case back in Michaels office and will tackle it another day as I'm sure Seb was just overreacting to whatever sordid offence Michael was hiding from us.

Tuesday 30/12/2003

The day started off really well. Cup of tea in bed, Bobby off to work.

The boys were behaving themselves, happy playing in Frank's bedroom with their fabulous wooden castle. I have to say it has been one of my best buys, it's kept them happy for hours.

The twins seemed to be happy letting me dress them without the normal running around and pinning one down while holding onto the other to change their nappies.

Breakfast was peaceful, not the normal food fights we have.

Charlie was being no bother, Clarabel chirping away, and I just sat and had a moment to myself planning our new life in my head.

Everything just seemed perfect, until I heard a loud scream. Then I saw the castle crashing down in front of the kitchen window.

I almost jumped out of my skin. It shattered all over the back garden. What a mess!

I left the twins strapped in their highchairs and shot up stairs to the boys room.

Robbie was in tears; Frank was just staring out of the window.

I've no idea how they actually opened that window. Then I spotted the key box. (I'm sure that was in our bedroom wardrobe), and dressing gowns. They had got everyone's dressing gowns.

The little monkeys had taken the dressing gown belts off and tied them together. They had then tied one end to the castle and the other end through the metal bed headboard and made a pulley system. I thought that was brilliant and was really proud of them for a split second.

The boys had pulled the castle up onto the windowsill because they wanted to play with it in the garden. But it was too heavy, and they didn't have enough length to lower it all the way to the ground.

Then reality hit me. If the twins or me were outside when that dropped it could have killed us!

I shouted and gave them a lecture on how serious an accident they could have caused. Locked the window, removed the keys and told them not to move. I was so cross but also quite impressed with what they had done.

The boys were really upset that their new Christmas present was smashed to smithereens.

Back to the kitchen and I noticed Tommy still sat quite happy in his highchair, but Skylet had escaped. I have no idea how she managed to get out of her straps. Honestly, I've got a pair of Archimedes upstairs and a Houdini downstairs.

Then that horrendous sick feeling of panic as I noticed the back door was open. I grabbed Tommy, I wasn't going to lose him as well and ran outside.

There was no sign of Skylet in the garden and the gate was open. I had images of her being taken away by someone or knocked down by a truck.

All I want to do is protect my children.

I ran clutching onto Tommy in sheer panic, but then the strangest thing.

There was Clarissa in the middle of the road, just hugging Skylet and Skylet hugging her back. Skylet never lets anyone pick her up at the moment, she kicks and screams. The pair of them were giving each other the biggest hug ever. Not just a protective hug of picking her up so she didn't get run over, but a loving, nurturing hug. I got that lovely butterfly feeling in my tummy. I just stood and stared. I did not want to disturb this moment.

A sudden feeling of Deja vu.

I spotted her hair roots; they were a warm reddy colour glowing in the sunlight. Skylet seemed to have the same colour and there was a look that they both seemed to share.

She saw me and walked over still hugging Skylet.

There was something really lovely about that moment, a weird connection between us.

Then she spoke. And told me I was an irresponsible mother, and I should be reported.

Well, that didn't take long for her true colours to show. How stupid am I thinking she could ever be a nice person.

I took Skylet from her and muttered thank you. I am incredibly grateful that nothing happened to my baby. But does she have to be so awful to me.

Went back inside to deal with two very unhappy boys.

Unfortunately, it was far too early for a glass of wine.

Bobby was home much earlier than expected, thank goodness to help clean up the mess and deal with the boys.

Well on a practical point of view at least it's one last thing for me to pack for Australia.

Thank you Clarissa for saving Skylet and thank you for not letting any of us have our heads smashed in from a castle!

Tuesday 30th December 2003

I was on my way back from a short walk this morning, as I was about to cross the road to my drive I saw the girl child from next door balancing precariously on the edge of the curb.

Those eyes, so green, stopped my heart. I walked cautiously towards her, and she held up her arms smiling brightly, all dimples and rosy cheeks.

For a second I hugged her remembering so long ago another moment, the warm scent of clean baby and the trusting eyes.

So long ago.

But oh, for an instant I couldn't lock out that dreadful memory of excruciating loss as we looked at each other. It was as if she knew, and she hugged me tightly.

At that moment I realised that her awful mother was rushing towards us and the spell broke.

Thrusting her daughter at her, I quickly told her she was more than inadequate as a parent and hurried inside.

But oh, the feel of that child has brought back so many memories. I must get a grip.

Trying to distract myself I decided to open the suitcase. I think I rather wish I hadn't.

Any feelings I had for Michael have completely died...

The man was a cruel heartless monster.

I could have had contact with my child... and he kept that from me... he hid her from me... and now I don't know what on earth to do.

My heart is broken.

I sat for hours going through the suitcase of my daughter's life.

I can't even say her name, because I never had the chance to give her one, and in none of the letters can I see it. It's just like she was an incredible dream that turned into a nightmare.

I wonder what we would have called her.

I wonder why her father left me, he said he wouldn't, but he did and then she arrived into my broken world and barely had I chance to know each perfect part of her and mend in the perfect creation of our love, before they stole her away and damned me to a life of empty living.

A life, they said, that was socially acceptable and would make me a better person.

How wrong they all were.

So much wasted time I feel quite depressed.

Wednesday 31/12/2003 - New Year's Eve

Another year gone. And what a year we've had. Two more babies, one starting school, one budgie, a dog and a chicken. A weird Nanny. Bobby suspended and reinstated at work, the death of our neighbour, art classes. Beth's baby girl, and

Bobby's got a new job offer in a different country.

Christine offered to baby sit so we could go to Hannah and John's with mum and dad and Seb.

It was all very civilised. Hannah had cooked a big pan of chilli and had prepared a huge cheese board. We sat around the table just talking and socially drinking.

I asked Seb about his suitcase and if he was moving in with Clarissa. It was really odd as the colour from his face just seemed to drain away. He then excused himself and went to talk to my dad.

Dad and Seb seemed to be having a very serious conversation. Then Bobby went to join them.

It was all very strange, So I sat in the kitchen with Hannah and mum.

I have to say it was the quietest New Year's Eve I've had for a long time.

But it was lovely to be out. We put Big Ben on the T.V. and joined in with Auld Lang Syne. Still don't know the words.

Bobby and I were the first to leave, I didn't think it was fair on Christine to be too late back. Bobby asked me questions again about my real parents. I told him I didn't want to talk about them unless it has something to do with emigrating. He said he was just curious. That made me cross, so I told him I have no idea who they are or where I come from. I don't think he understands how much it hurts knowing your parents didn't want you. So, we walked back in silence.

Honestly, what is this obsession with my biological parents. Especially as it's past midnight and officially my birthday and they gave me up.

Where's my birthday kiss, cuddle and wishes!

Happy 2004! And Happy birthday to me!

Wednesday 31st December 2003

The last few days have been terrible.

I have been back through the letters and contents of the case so many times I think I know them off by heart.

Seb arrived this afternoon with flowers and when I saw him standing at the door I burst into tears, he hugged me so tightly and I think he was quite emotional too.

I had been wondering how I would ever face him, now he knew my shameful secret and what Michael had done to keep it hidden from us all. I was sure he wouldn't want anything else to do with me. The fact he had come was such a relief.

He said he had not been able to get the contents of the case out of his mind and had come up with a plan.

Perhaps there was still a way we could find my daughter and her new parents, and he wanted to make amends for Michael's appalling behaviour in not allowing me to know about the letters offering me the chance to stay in touch and watch my child grow so that if the time ever came, we could have met.

The letters had come from her adoptive parents, they had signed them, and he said that was a good starting place.

Reluctantly I agreed to give him back the case and trust him to help me. It is such a relief to have him as a friend. I just hope it's not too late to put things right.

I should be celebrating the new year and her birthday, instead I have sketched dark pictures based on memories of those sad months.

The face of two men super imposed into one, one full of life and laughter the other evil and grotesque. I wonder what

Georgina would think of it, I don't think I will show it to her, but I will keep it to remind me how I feel today.

Then I sketched how I thought my daughter might look, strangely that was not as easy as the first sketch of the two men who had passed through my life and ruined it and me.

I know so little about her, so much time has passed.

I wonder if she thinks of me... or her father... did he ever know about her... what if he did and she is with him, or he found her, and she thinks he loves her, and I didn't care... My head is spinning with all sorts of scenarios.

I feel so lost, I am going to bed without seeing in the New Year.

Thursday 1/1/2004 New Year's Day - Happy birthday Seren!

Woke up not feeling as rough as I should with Robbie and Frank bouncing on our bed super excited to open my presents.

Bobby had brought up a cup of tea, then put Skylet and Tommy in the middle of us. Charlie was wagging his tail, with his chin resting on the top of the duvet cover, hoping to climb in too.

Bobby had bought me a lovely ladies watch and a box of chocolates from the children, well obviously for them to eat. And a set of towels from Charlie.

Who knew dogs could go shopping! They were perfect as we have a shortage of towels because he keeps pulling them off the washing line and eating them.

Mum and dad were downstairs waiting for me in the kitchen with an old wooden box on the table, they just smiled and wished me happy birthday, then pushed the box towards me, saying it wasn't from them.

The box was covered in beautiful sketches, like the Last Judgment by Michelangelo. When I opened it there was a pair of angel wings on the inside of the lid.

Inside were documents, letters and photos of me. Some of the letters were still in envelopes with return to sender stamped over them, while others were photocopies of letters in mums handwriting, a tiny handmade white baby dress with the initials PCC embroidered at the bottom, a beautiful but grubby white bunny with a pink ribbon that looked very old and very worn, and a pressed flower wrapped in tissue paper.

I recognised the flower from our garden, well Clarissa's garden, growing through the fence. Christine had pointed it out as Queen Anne's Lace. Odd I thought it was a weed.

And there in black and white was my adoption certificate.

Mum explained that the adoption agent said my mother wanted me to have these things but was under instruction to wait until I was thirty. But thought there was no point waiting another year as they felt this was now the right time for me to know everything especially as there seemed to be lots of questions being asked.

In their instructions they said my real mother hoped I'd forgive her one day and to say she loved me. She had requested correspondence from them to be sent to her, but they had to keep it a secret.

They would send letters weekly, then monthly but never got a reply. They stopped after a few years when letters were being returned by the post office.

Mum wanted to know if I still had my necklace that they had given to me as a little girl.

I'd forgotten about it. I'd put it away in a drawer a long time ago. I knew it was from her, but I never felt right wearing it and I thought it looked odd.

I don't understand. Why did my biological mother leave me gifts and yet she didn't want me?

Mum and dad said there could have been all sorts of reasons. And I should never judge but if it wasn't for my mother giving me to them, I would never have brought so much love and joy to their lives. All they wanted to do was love and protect me.

The three of us hugged and cried.

Mum and dad then took me out for a birthday brunch. Bobby stayed with the children. He said we needed time together.

I got home feeling quite strange, an odd emptiness until I saw my children and hugged them all tightly. Bobby had made a birthday tea and the boys had helped make sandwiches and baked buns and cakes with Christine.

After tea I took some time out and sat with the box. I read through the letters and cried.

Mum and dad had written down dates, times, every detail of my life from the day they got me. My first tooth, the first time I sat up, I stood, walked, first word and beautiful photos of me.

Who am I? The last year has been an emotional and physical roller coaster. I have so many unanswered questions. My head is spinning.

I need to think about what I want. If I go looking for her, she may reject me, and I don't want my parents to go through any pain.

It doesn't make any sense, why wait until I'm thirty? She

abandoned me.

I can't turn back the clock and there's no point wishing things were different. If they were, then I'd never be here now with my husband and my four beautiful children. Maybe it was all meant to be. Maybe this was the plan for my life.

I couldn't wish for better parents and the life I've had. I love them dearly as they love me. I need to be thankful about what I have.

Turning twenty-nine today, I feel different. When did this all happen?

The one thing I truly know is I am loved and have been given a chance in life, that may not have happened if I was with my biological parents.

Thank you for a birthday experience that I will never forget.

Thursday 1st January 2004

The last few days and nights have been so difficult.

Seb called to check on me again. He told me not to lose hope, it is early days. But my heart just feels so heavy.

He is such a good man.

When he left I opened a bottle of Michaels very expensive wine and toasted my child wherever she was in the world, then took delight in emptying the remaining contents of the bottle down the sink. There was great satisfaction in knowing how angry he would be that I had plundered his prized wine collection.

Tomorrow I will give the lot to the local food bank.

This is the new me.

A better person, just in case the day comes when I can meet her. I so don't want to disappoint her.

Monday 5/1/2004

I'd booked the twins into nursery for some extra days while I get everything packed. Can't believe we will be leaving here in just under a month.

We haven't told Robbie and Frank yet, so they've gone back to school all excited to see their friends after the Christmas break. I think I'll let them have this week and then we can arrange a leaving party for them. I just need to get my head around everything else first.

I managed to get more boxes, tissue paper and industrial tape from town and then spent the day packing the spare bedroom and dining room.

How odd, after my conversation with mum and dad about the necklace. There it was sitting in the dresser drawer amongst my dinner service. The silver was tarnished. I hadn't realised how unusual the shape was, as if it's only half a pendant and there's a missing piece.

I sat looking at it for a while. There's been so much going on in my head after opening the box. So many unanswered questions. It's been making me feel ill.

So, I've decided I need to take control of my life and what I have going on around me, appreciate what I have now, and leave the past behind. I really do need to let go of the past and move forward.

It was also time to tell Christine that we are emigrating. I can't keep avoiding her and it wouldn't be fair if she heard from anyone else.

Picked the children up, had a ready meal from Marks and Spencer's then waited for Bobby so I could nip over the road to see Christine.

My stomach was doing somersaults as I walked to her

house, armed with a bottle of red and the tarnished necklace.

She was surprised to see me but still gave me a big hug.

I wasn't sure how to start the conversation. But handing a bottle of red over always seems to do the trick.

We went to sit in her front room. There resting on the mantel piece was a beautiful painting, I stood admiring it for a while. The detail looked familiar, angel wings just like the artwork on my box and how odd it was signed with the initials PCC.

Christine asked if I was alright. This prompted me to tell her about my conversation with my parents and the box that was left to me by my biological mother.

She did look very sad when I told her that I've decided to move on and forget about finding my biological parents. I was really surprised by her reactions. When she said, 'don't give up on her.' I then felt a little annoyed as she had given up on me.

So, I thought this was the best time to lay all my cards on the table and tell her about Australia.

I then gave her my necklace as this was very much part of me and I explained that I needed to move on in so many ways especially after all we had been through with that cow next door. She scowled and then started to cry.

I felt awful. We then silently finished off the red wine and had another big hug. She said she understood, and Australia is an amazing place to live. She would give me her son Henry's details, as he has an art shop in Apollo Bay, and she would be sure he would help if we needed anything and of course that gave her more excuses to visit the country to see us and her son.

I feel quite empty now I've come back home. I will really

miss Christine and lots of my friends. But I know it's all for the best.

I have to put my family first.

Monday 5th January 2004

I thought this year was getting off to a bad start but actually at my appointment with Georgina she pointed out that I have a clean slate and can be anyone I want to be.

I didn't tell her I was trying to be a better person.

Of course, as usual, I find I must agree with her logic and to that end I have signed my pictures in my maiden name and taken them to the gallery, I kept one back that I have gifted to Christine because without her encouragement I may never have got this far. She was genuinely happy when I told her about the gallery assessing my work and my decision to go back to my maiden name, to be me again.

Who knows perhaps one day my daughter may see my name on one of the pictures... oh but I'm dreaming... but it has given me something to aim for, almost the future I had hoped for before it all went wrong all those years ago.

Seb has reassured me he is making the necessary enquiries in his bid to help me but reminded I must be realistic that I may never establish lost contact.

I am not going to be negative. I have been given a chance to alter my life so I am taking it, I hope to be a better person and come out of the shadow Michael cast so that if I meet her, she may actually be proud of me and like me... that is just so important now.

The builders are starting next week, to convert the office

into my very own light and airy art studio, that's very exciting...
When I told Christine she hugged me and reminded me that
my space in her studio will always be there for me. I actually
laughed and reminded her she is not rid of me yet.

My how a year has changed life so completely.

I hope to eventually erase every trace of Michael from my
life, except of course Seb.

I have not seen Frankie since the sweets on the doorstep
at Christmas. I do hope he is not ill. The whole family seem
to have gone very quiet. I did glimpse her in the town looking
very sternly in my direction but with no children in tow and I
could hardly ask her about Frankie.

I suppose the best I can hope for from them is that she
remains silent, and we get on with our own lives on our side
of the fence. After all there is absolutely no way we can be
friends or neighbourly in the way Christine is. They really are
not the type of people who fit into this street.

Christine says very little about them, she has told me to
concentrate on me and my life and of course as usual she is
right.

This year is the year to reinvent who I should have been.

Thursday 15/1/2004

I think my boys must be oblivious at times. We've been
tripping over large boxes everywhere and neither of them
have asked any questions. Apart from Frank who wanted to
use one of the boxes to make a magical boat house that he
could live in, with Penny, at the bottom of the garden and wait
for Tandoori to come and visit.

He'll have a long wait and I've still no idea who Penny is.

Mum and dad were looking a bit tired. They have been amazing helping me. So, I suggested that they had some time to themselves.

As usual Christine was busy today, she has been amazing too, looking after the children and cooking for us. I really am going to miss her.

It feels strange being on my own in this big house, I'm not sure I like the quietness. Even Charlie seems to be sulking around.

I keep looking at my box. There's something quite perfect and yet very sad about it. Part of me thinks I should just get rid, then the other part of me thinks I should keep it for our children, obviously when they are old enough, it's only right that they should know where I have come from so they will know some of their own history.

Then I started to think about the picture at Christine's, it looked freshly painted and very familiar. Odd the technique was very similar to mine. I must ask Christine where she got it from. Perhaps it's just a famous painting and someone from Christine's art class has copied it.

I need to empty my mind and focus. There's far too much going on at the moment.

Bobby and I decided to tell the boys this evening. I wasn't sure how they would react, and if it would even sink in with Frank. It was Robbie I was more concerned about.

Robbie went quiet. While Frank jumped up and down excited to be going on an aeroplane.

We then told them they could have a big party and invite all their friends. Which made Frank even happier. Then said is it ok for Penny to come. Penny? I asked him who is this Penny?

He said 'you know mummy. It's ghost lady.'

I looked at Bobby and he rolled his eyes. Hopefully, this will all go away when we move.

Then Robbie asked if he could still play football. Bobby told him he could, but it's called soccer. But there are so many more sports to try like surfing. Robbie grinned, nodded his head and said 'nice.'

Thank you mum and dad, Christine and Bobby. Thank you for all the help and strength you have given me.

Thursday 15th January 2004

I had some good news from the gallery today.

They are going to hold an exhibition of my work.

I was so excited I rang Seb and invited him for lunch to celebrate and get his opinion on the more tiresome business and financial implications of the show. He is such a clever man I would be lost without him.

He was so pleased for me and didn't seem at all shocked when I told him I was painting under my maiden name, he agreed that it was a sensible idea to protect my privacy.

During our conversation I had distractedly been playing with my pendent that I had designed so many years ago, and never been able to wear in case Michael found I still had it.

Seb was very curious about its design, so I explained that my baby daughter had the other half.

He clearly had his business hat on and suggested I should add jewellery making to my artistic talents.

I rather like the idea, although will never make another pendent like this one.

Christine was equally ecstatic about the news from the

gallery, but very distracted. Apparently, she is helping next door by watching the children on Saturday morning while they prepare for yet another party.

Honestly, it's all they seem to do... so Christine was busy cooking extras for the do while she could.

I must say I was quite disappointed she had put that family before me. I had hoped she would ask me over to celebrate and talk some more about the plans and art.

Saturday 31/1/2004

Everything packed up, it's been hard work. But will all be worth it.

Bobby worked his last day yesterday. He had his leaving do, so he's not been much use to me all day. Good job I've employed Joe (with his clothes on) to come and help.

The boys had there last day at school. I found that really emotional and the nursery presented me with a big book listing all the activities Skylet and Tommy had done with photographs, hand and footprints, who their friends were and every new experience. I will treasure that forever.

Then I'm looking at the house thinking are we completely mad having a leaving party today!

Christine, mum and dad, Hannah and John, Helen and Peter have all been brilliant! Emotionally and physically getting me sorted. I feel so blessed to have these people in my life.

At midday all of Franks friends arrived, then at two o'clock most of Franks friends left and then all of Robbie's friends arrived.

This time I did not care about how many cars are parked

outside. She's not going to upset me anymore.

The boys had a great time, running around every room, playing hide and seek while us adults just cracked open the wine.

Bobby had arranged for pizza deliveries throughout the day and then for the evening he'd organised Latinos specials for the adult party. (Adult party that sounds like we've just thrown keys into the middle) I know what I mean. And of course we had Christine's amazing cooking, plenty of food and drink for everyone.

There was just one point in the evening, after watching Seb and Joe flirting together. Seb went to talk to Christine. She was on her own in the corner. They were both looking at her chest. It was really odd.

I wonder if Seb swings both ways.

Bobby then stopped the music and gave a beautiful heartfelt speech to all our friends. I really do love him.

When everyone had left, Bobby asked me about my necklace.

What is it about that bloody necklace? So, I told him I'd given it to Christine. He just said. 'I thought so. She was wearing it tonight. That was a lovely gift you gave her.'

I felt really good about doing the right thing.

Great night seemed to be had by all.

Bobby and I commented on our party success and toasted each other. Looking forward to a fresh exciting life.

With that he kissed me on my forehead and fell asleep.

Thank you for all the wonderful people in our life. I wouldn't be the person I am without having amazing friends and family.

Saturday 31st January 2004

All day there has been coming and goings next door.

Loud children and the sound of absolute chaos.

The street is full of cars, some of them so badly parked it is quite unsightly.

My head is pounding. Honestly there is no wonder Michael got so agitated by them, it is just like when they moved in but without the police and fire brigade. I can't even sit and read it's so disruptive.

It would not have seemed so bad if they had been polite enough to invite me so that at least I could decline and make my thoughts known.

Christine rang and asked if I was ok. I told her in no uncertain terms how I felt, and she had the audacity to laugh and call me grumpy, twittering something about this would be the last party. I said I very much doubted it.

She actually had the nerve to tut, so I said I had to go and hung up on her.

Honestly, I don't know what on earth this street is coming to. The chaos this street is in is entirely down to that terrible family. How I wish they had never arrived.

Sunday 1/2/2004 - Bobby's birthday

I'm so glad I went onto drinking tea last night. And to be fair to Bobby he wasn't hanging either. But at least we still know how to party hard! It must have been about three this morning when we got to bed.

The children were super tired. It was far too late for them, but it's fine, they will have plenty of time to sleep on the plane.

Bobby opened a few birthday cards; we had agreed not to buy any presents until we got to our new house. There was no point in packing anything extra.

But I did organise a huge birthday cake. He couldn't have nothing on his birthday, and we could share that out with everyone who was helping.

Joe, Christine and Seb came round for one last time and helped bag up all the rubbish.

We all gave Paul a cuddle and said goodbye to him. Seb produced a very nice travel cage to take him back to his house. He told Robbie and Frank that he'd made an assault course in his big garden, and he will be very well looked after. Anytime we came back to visit they were always welcome to see him.

Who knew Seb was so much into rabbits.

Mum and dad took the children out for brunch while Bobby and I said goodbye to everyone and a massive thank you for all their help and just being part of our lives. It was really sad. I couldn't stop crying. Then everyone left and Bobby and I took one last tour of our home.

It was a beautiful home. We had spent a lot of time and effort to put love and life into this old house, to make it ours. It was just a shame we had an horrendous problem that took away the sparkle.

We locked the door and drove down silently to Hannah and John's to meet mum and dad with the children and Bobby's parents.

Clarabel was already in her new home by the big window in Hannah and John's kitchen. I feel really sad leaving our pets. They have so become part of our lives.

Then I heard John call Hannah Jo-Hannah.

After all this time I had no idea that Hannah is actually Jo-Hannah. That explains what the cow next door was on about. How funny.

We are all staying over. Early to bed, early to rise for the start of our journey.

Thank you for everything.

Sunday 1st February 2004

I am feeling very numb and confused.

Seb and Christine arrived with Joe this evening. Joe was, as usual, his amusing flirtatious self, though not I hasten to add with me or Christine.

The air between Christine and Seb was very heavy and Joe obviously picked up on it and took his leave. Before I could find the words to ask them what was wrong, Christine said that Seb had told her about my necklace and could she see it.

I was shocked, I had shared that confidence with Seb for his ears and not to be shared with anyone else, even Christine.

He stood looking uneasy and unhappy, and Christine had adopted her no-nonsense attitude. It was all very uncomfortable.

I took the necklace off and laid it on the table about to ask what on earth was going on. The question lodged in my throat when Christine laid the identical necklace to my half on the polished wood between us.

Seb caught my arm and guided me into the chair, my head was so confused, how on earth had Christine got this necklace. You need to listen she said sitting opposite me and taking my hand.

I could hardly believe the ridiculous words that came out of her mouth about how she came to be the owner of the necklace made for my daughter. My perfect beautiful daughter.

Was it some kind of game that terrible woman had induced them to play, trying to make me like her?

I seemed to be saying I don't understand a terrible number of times.

Seb had poured me a brandy and even the fiery liquid didn't take the edge off this appalling joke they seemed to be having.

It was all lies I was terribly sure. Some kind of wicked plot to take revenge on me.

I asked them both to leave and they refused so I have taken myself up to bed.

Let them sit there all night and think on what they have done.

It is all just too ridiculous to be true.

Monday 2/2/2004

Today has been so emotional, mixed between leaving lovely friends and family, our home and the excitement of a new chapter for our lives in Australia. I can't believe we are actually going.

Hannah and John had made us all a big breakfast. It was early but very lovely sitting and chatting. I believe it won't be the last time we do this with them, everyone has told us they will definitely come and visit, but for now an end of an era. Nothing will ever happen the same again.

A moment in time to cherish.

We returned to the house for one last time, checking we'd

not left anything. We needed to leave by seven this morning.

To my surprise Seb and Christine were waiting to wave us off.

We have fabulous memories, seeing our family grow, the new arrivals of Skylet, Tommy, Paul, Clarabel (1 and 2), Charlie and Tandoori.

Frank starting school, Robbie playing football and making new best friends. Hannah and John, Seb, Beth and Paul and of course Christine. I really am going to miss her; she has been my rock. I did have a little cry when Christine gave me a big hug. We've all been on such a journey, with lots of stories to tell.

Our home although it's a beautiful family home, has always had a big dark cloud bobbing over it, never knowing what malicious lies will be thrown at us, no more walking down our drive feeling uncomfortable in our own home.

No more looking over the fence in fear of what she is planning next.

Today I felt like that huge cloud has been lifted. She cannot hurt me or my family anymore.

Well Clarissa you've finally got your wish. You won, you and your dead husband have made our life hell. It's because of you we are leaving. Hopefully, you will be happy now.

Bobby is still very defensive about her. He's told me to be kind, again. How can you be kind to someone who hates you for no reason. To this day I do not know what I ever did to that woman.

At least I have my Bobby. We've been through so much, I feel we have grown so much closer, a deeper love I never thought existed.

She has no one.

Mum and dad, Peter and Helen have promised to come over for a few months at a time. I will miss them all dearly.

Our car was rammed. Robbie was very quiet. He was sad about leaving his friends. Frank was still excited to be going on an aeroplane but was getting a bit restless, something about needing to say goodbye to Penny. I've still no idea who Penny is. But thank goodness his imaginary friend isn't coming with us. I just accept that Frank is Frank in his own little world.

The twins, well I don't think they really have a clue where we are going, or they even care.

Charlie sat in the boot. We couldn't leave our fifth child. We've got a passport sorted for him.

I really do hope the new tenants enjoy our home. I'd not met them, but Bobby said they are a colourful family. I think that's his posh way to say they are very loud. He also said he couldn't see them taking any rubbish off anyone.

I understand they have won the lottery and are moving from Birkenhead with their six children and three dogs. Oooh Clarissa be careful what you wish for.

I've made the decision that this is the last time I mention her. No more thinking about that woman, she's out of my life now and so are any thoughts of ever meeting my biological parents. It's been an emotional roller coaster to get this far, but I know it's the right decision.

The next time I write in my journal it will be at the other side of the world.

Thank you for this amazing opportunity to start a new life.

You never know what's around the corner.

Monday 2nd February 2004

I hardly slept, my head was so full of the ludicrous suggestion from Seb and Christine.

During the early hours where night began to spill into day, I realised that it could well be the truth and not some ghastly prank.

I could see so many of Hanks characteristics in that terrible woman and Frank. The eyes and stubborn set of the chin.

Oh, and how they have unluckily inherited my red hair.

The painting skills of course should have been a giveaway.

Had I been so standoffish because some part of me recognised her.

I headed out into the freezing morning light, not sure quite what I planned to do. It wasn't just that if she was my daughter then her children were my grandchildren. Beautiful blue-eyed Frankie was actually part of me and the lovely green eyed little girl.

I wanted to somehow put this right with her but had no idea how.

I didn't mean to squeeze through the overgrown hedge but found myself once again in their garden, I had been in the garden so many times for such foolish selfish reasons, but as I stood at the bottom of their garden looking up at the house, the very empty house, I realised I was too late there was no one there.

I have lost my chance to put things right.

I have lost not just my child this time but my grandchildren too.

I have no way to repair all the damage I have done.

Sinking to my knees I began to cry.

What a terrible mess I have made of my life.

I stayed there for a long time until I heard Christine calling me.

As I pushed my way back to the other side of the fence Christine met me on her way down my path. She took me in her arms and rocked me like a child, whispering reassurances about it not being too late, I just needed to give things time and she and Seb would help.

Don't give up she said, and she's right, I won't.

I will find a way to put this right.